Praise for Na...
Two Time RITA ...
JODI ...

"Jodi Thomas will ren...

—*Romantic Times*

"Ms. Thomas *never* disappoints . . . she comes up with characters worthy of the title 'friend' and plots that sparkle with originality."

—*Heartland Critiques*

FOREVER IN TEXAS

"A winner from an author who knows how to make the West tough but tender. Jodi Thomas's earthy characters, feisty dialogue and sweet love story will steal your heart."

—*Romantic Times*

"A great Western romance filled with suspense and plenty of action. It is the two tremendous lead characters . . . who will have the audience forever reading *Forever in Texas.*"

—*Affaire de Coeur*

TO TAME A TEXAN'S HEART

Winner of the Romance Writers of America Best Historical Series Romance Award of 1994

"Earthy, vibrant, funny and poignant . . . a wonderful, colorful love story."

—*Romantic Times*

"Breathtaking . . . heart-stopping romance and rip-roaring action."

—*Affaire de Coeur*

"Interesting characters, a bit of mystery, humor and danger . . . enjoyable and hard to put down."

—*Rendezvous*

THE TEXAN AND THE LADY

"The woman who made Texans tender ... Jodi Thomas shows us hard-living men with grit and guts, and the determined young women who soften their hearts."

—Pamela Morsi, bestselling author of *Something Shady* and *Simple Jess*

PRAIRIE SONG

"A thoroughly entertaining romance."

—*Gothic Journal*

THE TENDER TEXAN

Winner of the Romance Writers of America Best Historical Series Romance Award of 1991

"Excellent ... Have the tissues ready; this tender story will tug at your heart. Memorable reading."

—*Rendezvous*

"This marvelous, sensitive, emotional romance is destined to be cherished by readers ... a spellbinding story ... filled with the special magic that makes a book a treasure."

—*Romantic Times*

Texas Love Song

Jodi Thomas

JOVE BOOKS, NEW YORK

TEXAS LOVE SONG

A Jove Book / published by arrangement with
the author

PRINTING HISTORY
Jove edition / October 1996

The Putnam Berkley World Wide Web site address is
http://www.berkley.com/berkley

ISBN: 0-515-11953-9

A JOVE BOOK®
Jove Books are published by The Berkley Publishing Group,
200 Madison Avenue, New York, New York 10016.
JOVE and the "J" design are trademarks
belonging to Jove Publications, Inc.

PRINTED IN THE UNITED STATES OF AMERICA

10 9 8 7 6 5 4 3

*I dedicate this book to
Jimmy and Dorothy Teague.*

*Thank you for listening to
my stories since childhood.*

Texas Love Song

One

THUNDER RUMBLED THROUGH the low hill country of Texas, rattling against the walls of the isolated stagecoach station like the fists of a rebuffed intruder. A winter storm, promising hail and snow before it finished, howled into the frosty night. As icy rain began a second violent assault on the roof, travelers huddled inside the log building. Dust-layered cowhands who'd brought a herd in just before dark ate their first meal of the day at a long table running the length of the north wall. German farmers spoke in a low foreign tone as they waited for even a slight letup in the weather so they could get back to their land. Weary travelers, passing through this sparsely settled country, were suddenly stuck in a place that would never have been a destination of choice.

Sloan Alexander also waited. He was trapped with them all, but part of no group. Unlike the other wayfarers, Sloan wasn't going *to* anywhere, only away from everywhere he'd ever been. He had no home and no one waiting for him. His wealth was barely enough to buy him a ticket west, and his only dreams were nightmares.

"Want another?" The station manager lifted a half-empty bottle toward Sloan's glass.

Sloan tipped his hat slightly in a nod and leaned into the counter, his slim body seeming as solid as the mahogany. He laid worn buckskin gauntlets beside his drink. The gloves were the only part he'd kept of his last uniform. A reminder of his days fighting on the frontier.

The manager didn't meet Sloan's eyes as whiskey filled the glass to the brim. The spidery-thin man wearing a dirty butcher's apron looked tired, Sloan thought. As out of sorts as most of his guests, he was obviously ready for the storm to stop and everyone to leave.

Scanning the crowd, Sloan carefully sized up each of the men for trouble. The back of the large room was filled with mostly locals who'd been Confederate soldiers. They were busy reliving their days of glory and drinking enough to forget their losses. With each passing hour their voices grew louder. The farmers sat along the wide stairs leading to the second floor. For the most part they were unarmed and more concerned with their families than in causing any trouble. Two Union officers drank at a table by the door and openly flirted with the stage station manager's daughter. The soldiers were making a grand effort to appear relaxed, but a Yankee this far into the South, even three years after the war, would be a fool if he relaxed too much.

A woman, dressed in black traveling clothes, sat alone at a table near the kitchen, looking out of place in this menagerie of humanity. Distant from the others, even though the manager's wife and daughter stopped by her table with each passing, she seemed to watch the crowd as a bystander watches a play. Sloan briefly wished it were another time, another place, and he were the sort of man such a lady would allow to just come over and talk to her.

He could almost see himself walking up and lifting his glass slightly in salute. She would smile and fan her hand toward the empty seat. Sloan shook his head and took another drink. It would never happen, so why was he wasting his time daydreaming of such a thing?

He had been little more than a boy when the war broke out and he left Kansas City. Sloan had never even kissed a girl when he'd killed his first man in battle. During the war there was never time to talk to women, and the kind he'd met hadn't been proper ladies like the one sitting alone. After the war ended, he had to finish his duty on the frontier before he could try to look for the pieces of his life to pick up and start over. Now, he felt too old to even try to learn the subtleties of flirting. He had nothing to offer, not even in conversation.

Leave the flirting to young station girls and Yankee officers. They had dreams of the future; all he had were enemies from the past haunting his nights.

"That's him!" one of the rebels from the end of the bar shouted in a half-drunken slur. "That's the man I was telling you about. We made him haul out of the stage and ride up with the driver as soon as we knew who he was. It'll take more than three years to clear the smell of a traitor away."

Sloan felt his muscles harden to granite as he swore beneath his breath. He'd let his guard down a moment too long. The folly of staring at the woman might cost him dearly now.

The band of rebels moved toward him, their courage heightened by their number and abundant whiskey. These were not fresh young boys going to war, but hardened, broken men who'd returned home full of hate and despair.

A large redheaded man toward the front of the crowd pushed several travelers aside and headed directly toward Sloan. He was close enough for Sloan to smell his whiskeyed breath when he finally stopped and swelled like a toad. "My friend here tells me you're one of them Galvanized Yankees." The man's voice rose with each word until the final two spat from his mouth in an eruption of hate.

Sloan knew he should run or deny the accusation, but he'd been running for years and this seemed as good a place as any to stop. Maybe he'd chosen Texas because there he knew he'd face his fears one nightmare at a time.

"You a southern boy?" The redhead poked at Sloan's ribs with huge, dirty fingers.

"I'm a southern man," Sloan corrected.

"And you wore blue during the war after you'd already sworn allegiance to the Confederacy?" The local was staring at Sloan as if he'd seen his first true freak. "Forgot your loyalties to the South and helped the damn Yankees?"

Several of the others wearing parts of tattered gray uniforms moved closer and mumbled words Sloan had heard before, like *traitor*, and *yellow-belly*, and *turncoat*.

Glancing at the two Union officers by the door, Sloan saw the hate in their eyes as well. A Confederate soldier who changed sides was hated by southerners for what he'd done after he joined the Union and hated by northerners for what he'd done before he changed. Old Pete in the prison had tried to warn him when the soldiers came in to recruit their Galvanized Yankees from among the southern prisoners of war. Pete said that a man don't change seats in the middle of a poker game unless he's playing the devil for his soul.

A gang in prison who'd called themselves Satan's Seven had shown their hatred of the idea from the beginning. They'd voiced a final oath when the Galvanized Yankees left camp that the seven would find them, no matter how long it took, and kill every last traitor.

Sloan had had his reasons for changing sides, but these men before him now would never allow him to answer.

He'd known this confrontation would come since the day he'd left the Northern Territory and headed to Texas. Sloan straightened the buckskin fingers of his gloves lying on the bar, and shook his head. If he'd had any sense, he would have changed his name and identity and gone to California like most of the other Galvanized soldiers. Not even Satan's Seven could find him then. There was nothing for him in Texas. There was nothing for him anywhere, north or south. No one would ever take the time to hear of the filth in prison and how staying alive in Union blue was better than rotting among the thousands with dysentery and fever.

Thunder rattled the walls and hail rifled the roof. Suddenly, men came at him from all directions like hungry wolves on a winter-thin rabbit. Gray-sleeved arms grabbed from both sides. Sloan fought to free himself, but was pinned against the bar, his arms pulled behind him before he could deliver his first swing.

"We don't want your kind in Texas," someone behind him mumbled. "My guess is no one wants traitors around. You're worse than the damn Yankees. You traded sides."

Sloan strained at the human chains, but he couldn't free either arm.

The redheaded man took the first blow. Sloan didn't try to dodge. He felt the man's knuckles plow into his ribs, shattering bone.

The station manager's daughter screamed and ran beneath the protective arm of one of the officers. The families nesting on the stairs moved away, wanting neither to interfere nor witness.

As the rain pounded outside, Sloan took another blow, and another and another, until he could no longer stand erect to face his attackers. His left eye swelled and closed in pain and he tasted his own blood along his lip, but Sloan didn't make a sound. Just as all happiness had long passed from him, so had all sorrow. The only feeling that told him he was still alive was pain.

The Rebs took turns, laughing at the impact of each blow on his body, needing to release the anger they felt.

Just before the welcomed blackness of unconsciousness reached him, Sloan felt the hands holding him slip slightly.

Forcing his head up, Sloan saw his attackers back away one by one, lowering their heads like guilty children. He tried to reason. The manager of the station would never interfere, not with this. The Yankees would have stopped the fight earlier, if they'd planned to help. Only a fool would hold a gun on the Rebs to force them to stop a beating in such a crowded room. Yet the men were backing away as if he were diseased and they didn't want to be too close.

"Turn loose of him," one man behind Sloan grumbled to the other, "and come to attention, Brady."

"Why?" a second voice asked in almost a child's cry of disappointment.

Sloan looked around, trying to focus on who demanded such respect. He saw only the woman wearing mourning black moving nearer. Her hair was combed back in perfect order and a white lace handkerchief slipped from beneath her cuffed sleeve. She wasn't the kind of woman to draw closer during a fight.

"That's Major Harrison's widow," the first man whispered and let go of his captive. "There weren't a braver man who fought under Lee."

Sloan slumped to the floor while all the ragged Confederates around him strained to attention. Pulling himself up on an elbow, Sloan wiped the blood from his lip with his own worn coat sleeve. When he looked up, the woman was standing above him like a statue. She had hair the color of her dress and eyes as blue as a winter twilight. Her skin told Sloan she was young, but her sorrow seemed ages old.

Without a word, she knelt and touched his chin with two fingers. Her pale face was lined with worry. Her eyes filled with a heartache caused by far more than witnessing a beating.

The redhead removed his tattered hat and began twisting it in his huge scraped-knuckled hands. "Meaning no disrespect, Mrs. Harrison, but a lady like you shouldn't oughta have to see the likes of this man. It ain't fitting. Me and the boys shoulda taken this to the barn and not gone and done such a thing in fronta you."

Sloan thought any woman in her right mind would have shrunk from these men with only pieces of uniforms left. They were bone mean and hard. But this woman, this widow, walked past them as if they were no more than trees or neighbors she'd known all her life and had no need to fear.

The woman brushed the hair from Sloan's face as though she hadn't heard the man's warning. "You're bleeding," she whispered. "That cut right at your hairline needs attention."

"Don't touch the likes of him." The redhead's frustration flavored his words. "He ain't nothing but scum."

Sloan couldn't take his gaze off the pale woman with midnight hair. Though she looked like an angel, he had to still be alive or he couldn't hear the Rebs mumbling around him.

The widow pulled the spotless handkerchief from her cuff and touched his lip. "Are you hurt bad, soldier?"

There was no disgust in her voice, only concern. She'd called him soldier as though she'd called every man that for so many years it came natural.

Sloan bit back the pain and shook his head.

"Can you stand?" She offered her help.

"Mrs. Harrison," a clipped northern voice interrupted before Sloan could answer. "I'm Lieutenant Murry from the fort." The young Union officer looked nervous, but clearly saw this as his duty. "We've all heard how brave your late husband was and there's not a man in this room, northern or southern, who doesn't respect you for what you did when your man died." He glanced at the Rebs. "But I think you should stay out of this discussion between these Texans."

The widow's face darkened in anger for the first time. "I am also a Texan, sir." She straightened her back slightly as if she'd stand against any or all in the room. "Do you plan to stop me, Lieutenant Murry?"

The lieutenant backed away, raising his hands as if she'd turned a gun on him. "No, ma'am."

"Do any of you plan to interfere?"

To Sloan's amazement everyone took a step backward. The redhead looked worried. "No, ma'am," he mumbled. "There ain't a man in this room who'd stop you if you wanted to kill this traitor right now. We'd be happy to drag the body out for you."

"And if I wanted to help him?"

Her suggestion seemed to startle them.

She turned once more to Sloan without waiting for any answer from the Rebs. "Can you stand, soldier?"

"I don't need your help," Sloan mumbled. He didn't want to depend on anyone. He'd seen people turn too fast from friend to enemy. "I'm fine," he lied.

She gave her full attention to him. "I asked if you can stand, soldier."

Somehow, her calling him "soldier" demanded his best effort.

Sloan nodded and gripped his ribs as she helped him to

his feet. Pulling away, he bit back an oath. He didn't want anyone's help, not even an angel's, yet he sensed if he didn't do what this woman asked, no matter how insane it seemed, every man in the room would take a turn at killing him.

"Help me get him upstairs, Annie," she ordered the manager's daughter. "Miss Alyce Wren will doctor him."

The station boss wiped his hands on his dirty apron, then nodded for his daughter to follow the lady's order. The young girl circled Sloan's arm across her shoulder. She was probably no more than fifteen, but he couldn't help but notice she was strong and fully rounded. The two buttons open at her collar told the world she wanted everyone to notice the fact that she was now a woman and no longer a girl.

The widow, slimmer and taller, steadied Sloan from the opposite side. All the families camped out on the steps hurried to make way for the trio.

Fighting the darkness that threatened to blanket his brain, Sloan leaned against the woman in black, depending on her strength and not the girl's. He could almost feel everyone in the room holding their breaths, hoping he'd die before he escaped, silently begging the widow to turn him loose so they could deliver more blows. Maybe they were hoping she'd make it to the top of the stairs, then drop him.

But she gripped his shirt with her fist and held tightly as they moved. No man stepped in her way. Whatever power she had over these people was great. He could see respect, and maybe a little fear in all their eyes.

Sloan thought briefly that she was the angel of death dressed all in black, and she'd finally come for him. He'd waited many nights on the battlefield for her, even prayed for her to come in prison when the stench of rotting flesh thickened the air and the prisoners' cries of pain became a sorrowful song that never ended.

As he stumbled, she held tightly to him, giving him strength when he had none left.

"Where . . . ?" he whispered, wondering why he cared.

"I'm taking you to Miss Alyce Wren's room to get you patched up," she answered, "and if you die before I get you up these stairs, I'll shoot you. Miss Alyce may not be a real doctor, but she's the closest thing we got to one in these parts. She'll not take kindly if I deliver a dead man."

Sloan tried to laugh, but pounding pain in his chest muted all thought. "And if I don't go with you?" he asked as they reached the landing.

"You have no choice," she answered, helping him up another step. "If you stay downstairs, you're a dead man. Of course, if you live and go with me when the storm is over, Mr. Alexander, you may be just as dead in a week. Since it seems to make little difference to you, we might as well let Miss Alyce work a little of her charm."

"I don't need . . ." He gritted his teeth, fighting back the pain in his side. "How'd you know my name?"

"I know more about you than you may guess," she answered as they reached the second floor. "And you may not need my help as dearly as I need yours." She nodded for Annie to open the door. "I don't care what side you fought on. The war is long over. Right here, right now, you may be my one hope of survival," she whispered so only he could hear. "I need you alive and able to at least hold a rifle."

Sloan doubted she needed anyone's help, as he bit back a moan and gripped his side.

Annie opened the door and backed away as if she'd done what was asked of her and now had her own plans to execute. "I got to get back to that soldier I was talking to," she mumbled as if her excuse made sense. "He rode two hours just to see me tonight."

The woman in black smiled at the girl, then helped Sloan through the doorway.

Standing in the center of the room, surrounded by light, was the oldest woman Sloan could remember seeing. She wore a dress of dark green that made her hair seem even whiter. Her crippled, twisted hands were blue-lined and bone-thin as they extended toward him in welcome. Both wrists were layered in gold bracelets. He thought for a moment that this woman must make her own world, for she certainly belonged in none he'd ever seen.

She stared at Sloan for a long moment, then her aged face rippled in a smile of what Sloan thought looked like liquid insanity.

The woman the men downstairs had addressed as Mrs. Harrison helped him to a chair.

"Miss Alyce, I found the one I've been watching for." The widow lowered him slowly onto the chair. "If we can keep him alive, he's the man to help us."

The old woman laced her fingers together and stared hard at Sloan, then at the widow.

Her watery old eyes moved back to him. Her gaze traveled from his hair to his boots and back as if sizing up every inch of him. Sloan wouldn't have been surprised if she'd opened his mouth and counted his teeth. He'd seen men buy horses with less scrutiny.

Her gaze came to rest on his hand gripping his side, Mrs. Harrison's fingers atop his as she steadied him back against the cushions. "Oh, yes, this one will do." The old woman almost giggled. "You're right, my McCallie, he's just what I was hoping you'd find."

Two

MCCALL HARRISON MOVED her fingers over the bandage Miss Alyce Wren had tied around the stranger's rib cage. She wasn't sure if he'd passed out from pain, or if he was so tired he'd fallen asleep. His sandy hair, not blond or brown, curtained his sleeping eyes. He looked almost peaceful now, not all hard and cold as he had when he'd watched her downstairs. She'd known he was staring at her, but he'd been only one of several she'd watched since dusk. He had a kind of pride about him, though his clothes told her he wasn't a rich man. She liked the way he stood, as if no place were ever totally safe and he must always be on his guard. Also, he looked at people directly as only an honest man can do.

"Will he be able to travel soon, Miss Alyce?" McCall asked softly, fear creeping into her voice.

The old woman nodded as she folded her herb bags and sewing kit away. "He'll hurt, but he'll live if my stitches keep the dirt out of that hairline cut." She watched him closely as though trying to guess his fate. "And if one of the cracked ribs don't break and decide to puncture a lung. Not even those drifters downstairs can kill one of their own that easy. My guess is, he didn't fight his way through the past four or five years to die now at this crossroad in the middle of nowhere."

She rocked back in her chair and continued talking more to herself than McCall. "No matter what the men said downstairs, this one's a knight. I can tell just by the way a man moves. It's something they can't hide from a knowing eye like myself even with dirty, tattered clothes. My father was a knight. I know one when I see one."

McCall looked up at the woman her grandfather always called "the lovely Alyce Wren." Over the years McCall had gone from thinking Miss Alyce was crazy, to feeling sorry for her, to loving her even though the real world never touched her too closely. She was the one person who knew McCall, who understood her, who loved her without condition.

Gripping the stranger's gloves she'd retrieved from the bar, McCall asked, "Could you see his soul's face?" All her life McCall had heard Miss Alyce say she could see what no one else could. She could see the face of a man's soul. The gift hadn't come without its curse, for Alyce Wren once told McCall that her ability had kept her from marrying. When she saw what men really looked like, it cut the number of possibilities down considerably.

"I saw the true face of him, child. Young as he is, he's been walking in death's shadow so long he don't remember the sun, but these wounds won't kill him. I'd be willing to bet there's nothing in this world he cares about. He's lost a war, probably any home he ever had, and anyone he ever loved, judging from the look in those eyes. If he's one of them men who changed sides, he'll be taking other beatings if he doesn't get out of the South. He's a searcher without a map and all he'll find wandering is trouble."

"But his inside face." McCall had to know. She wouldn't

enlist the aid of a man who didn't measure up with Alyce Wren.

"His inside face is scarred with all the hurt he's suffered, but there's good in this man. A knight's kind of good."

"I can tell he's still got his pride." McCall brushed her fingers once more over the bandage. She could feel the slow rise and fall of Sloan Alexander's chest. "I knew it the moment the blows started flying and he refused to make a sound. I got the feeling he'd be one who'd die without a word. That's the kind I need along with me this time. I don't need a hero."

"So you think he'll help you because of his pride?" The old woman moved to the tiny stove and poured herself a cup of tea. The warm, sweet smell of raspberry tea filled the little room as she continued, "All that his pride will do is keep him from telling anyone about this crazy scheme of yours. Pride don't always make a man a fool."

McCall sat back in her chair. "You're right, pride alone would never make him do what I need done. I'm guessing money wouldn't help much, either, though from the look of him, he could use a little. I've decided to offer him the one thing he's still willing to risk his life for."

Sloan could hear the women talking, but he didn't open his eyes. The lady's words were smooth, polished with education and breeding, while the old woman's voice was slower, yet no less polished, as if she came to the language as a second tongue. They spoke in a comfortable rhythm of longtime friends.

Finally, the conversation stopped, and he slept, never bothering to open his eyes. He knew the proud widow was still near; he could feel her fingers rest gently across his heart from time to time. She was checking, he realized, making sure he was still alive. Part of him wondered what kind of past she must have had to test so easily for his life's breath. Part of him wanted her to keep her hand across his chest, for the weight of her fingers touched him far deeper than she realized.

Her nearness kept the nightmares away, and for the first time in longer than he could remember, he slept without dreaming.

Dawn slowly filtered into the room and Sloan opened his eyes to a clear morning. As the beams brightened from the window, he focused on layers of wood, polished to a shine, and fine lace washed so many times over the years it seemed spiderweb thin. A few fine dishes were neatly displayed on one shelf, and a silver service set for tea rested in front of the small stove. He smiled, remembering the old woman who'd met him at the door. She was the only person he'd ever seen who looked like she'd fit in such a room. The room, like her, seemed to have become almost timeless with age.

Slowly, Sloan turned his head. Years of waiting for an attack had created a sixth sense, something beyond touch or sight or hearing . . . a feeling. He knew someone was there before he saw her sitting beside him.

He'd expected the old woman, but the young widow looked back at him from blue eyes full of curiosity and an intelligence he'd rarely seen. Proper, as before, she showed no sign of having slept. Her hair was still in place and not an unwanted wrinkle bothered her clothing.

"Good morning, Mr. Alexander." She leaned forward. "How do you feel, soldier?"

Sloan raised an eyebrow, wondering if she'd been there all night, guessing she had. "Fine," he lied. "But I'm no longer a soldier," he paused, then added, "in any army." Bits and pieces of conversation came back to him, and he wasn't sure what this lady might want of him. "Thanks for helping me out last night, but it wasn't necessary. I've been in worse scrapes and always managed to get out."

The woman smiled. "Of course. You would have licked them all if I hadn't stopped the fight. You must have had far more to drink than I suspected."

Sloan tried to smile but his swollen lip protested. "It wasn't a fight," he mumbled, touching his mouth with his fingertips. "It was a beating. Eventually, they would have tired."

McCall frowned, realizing the stranger cared little about his own welfare. She stood and paced the few steps to the fireplace. "If I hadn't stopped them, you'd be in no shape to help me."

"Help you?" he whispered.

She turned toward him, a beautiful warrior making a direct assault. "I'm McCall Harrison and I need your help desperately, Mr. Alexander. I've been meeting every stage for the past week, hoping someone like you would come along."

He plowed his fingers through his hair, trying to clear his brain enough to think. "How'd you happen to know my name? And I wasn't aware I was applying for a job." If she was in some kind of trouble, the man on the floor last night—him—seemed to be the least likely pick. "Maybe you should try one of those officers downstairs. Or maybe one of those Rebs with plenty of fight left in him. I'm not looking for any more battles—not even on behalf of a lady."

"I don't need a champion; I only need someone I can trust to keep quiet." She handed him his gauntlets. "Those are Union cavalry issue. Can you drive a wagon as well as ride?"

"Of course I can drive a team, but what makes you think you can trust me to keep quiet about what you're planning?" He sat up, tucked the gloves in his belt, and looked for his shirt. "I've given up causes as well as fighting, and like I said, I'm not looking for a job."

"You'll help me because I can offer you the one thing you need." Reaching behind her chair, she handed him his shirt. As he raised his arms to pull on the shirt, McCall lightly brushed his bandage once more as though checking before she continued, "I saw something last night that told me they can't beat one trait out of you."

Slowly, very slowly, Sloan buttoned the shirt. "What's that, Mrs. Harrison?" He had the crazy longing to have her touch him once more, but she stepped a few feet away.

"Pride," she whispered, but it was as though she'd shouted "Gold" in a room full of forty-niners. "You may not care if you live or die, but you were still too proud to yell out during the beating I saw you take. So, if you'll help me, I'll give you the one thing I think your pride demands."

"And just what might that be?" Sloan's laughter sounded hollow even to himself. There was nothing he wanted anymore.

"I'll give you a reason to die with honor." Again, she whispered the words.

Sloan met her gaze then and a new fear crept across his tired mind. She understood him. Somehow, this woman in black knew the last hope, after four years of war and endless days on the frontier, that he allowed himself to have. He'd seen bodies rotting in the fields with not enough men left alive to bury them properly. He'd watched pickers move across the dying, pulling the valuables from soldiers not yet cold. A hundred nights when he'd been in prison, weak and sick, he'd thought he'd felt someone rolling him into a mass grave with stiff corpses all around him.

McCall moved closer and touched his arm. He could

feel the warmth of her body along his side. He wondered if she had any idea how rare such a warmth was to him?

"What I have to do will probably get us both killed, but I swear that if I live and you should die, I'll bring you back to my land and bury you with honor."

"And if I should live through this quest?" He started to smile, but saw that she was too serious to lighten the mood.

"If you live, and we make it back, you can never tell anyone what you did. But, all the rest of your life, you'll remember."

The warmth of her hand on his arm almost halted Sloan's breathing. Part of him didn't care what she asked. He'd try anything to be closer to such a woman for a few days. Even if he suspected she was as mad as she was beautiful.

"Name the quest." He straightened to attention. "I've nothing to lose from listening."

For the first time, she smiled. "Come with me."

They walked to the back of the room, and McCall opened a small door that looked like it might lead to an attic storage. Tiny bells jingled, sounding an alarm as they passed. "All we have to do," she whispered, "is take these children home."

Sloan stepped around her into a room packed with children of all sizes. The old woman who'd doctored him sat in the midst of them at a little table, cutting bread slices and passing them to each child.

He froze, speechless.

"We've found eleven in all, but by the time we have wagons and supplies ready there may be more." McCall knelt and hugged a little girl who looked about four. "I don't know how long it will take to find their parents, but we could hunt for food along the way if we need more, or I have enough money to buy supplies if we near one of the outposts along the fort line. Alyce Wren and I guess it will take a week, maybe two."

"McCall," Sloan knelt, too stunned to use her proper title. Now he was convinced the woman was crazy. "Mc-Call, these are Indian children!" He spoke slowly, as if trying hard to get the point across.

"I know," she answered. "I noticed. They are Cheyenne. Their leader was Black Kettle. From what I understand, they were camped along the Washita River for the winter when soldiers destroyed their village."

"And where are their parents now?"

"What's left of the tribe crossed the hundredth parallel three weeks ago after their village was attacked. So, I guess that makes them somewhere in the Great Plains and on the warpath."

"But how did the children get here?"

"An old medicine man hid them during the fighting, moving south each night. By the time he felt safe enough to travel in light, he was too far from the tribe to catch up and too old to hunt. A friend of Miss Alyce's found the old man and brought him here for her to treat. Before he died, he told her where the children were hiding. She needed me to get them here and smuggle them into the station." Mc-Call looked at him over the head of the little girl. "And I need you to help get them home."

Sloan tried to keep his voice from rising. "You can't be serious! If we take these children into the middle of an Indian war, any soldiers who find us will at best hang us and take the children back to Indian territory. At worst, they'll kill the children. Any Indian across the line is considered hostile, and some don't make exceptions for age."

He had to make her understand the danger. He'd spent two years fighting on the western frontier and knew the risk she'd face. "Should, by some wild chance, we make it through the fort's patrols and onto the plains, any war party greeting us will be taking our scalps." How could this woman think of such a crazy thing as transporting these children into country not safe for the frontier army, except in large numbers?

"I didn't say it would be easy. We're breaking the law, and we'll probably be killed before we can get back. But I'm going if I have to drive the wagon all day and scout the trail all night. And Miss Alyce has agreed to come with me. She thinks it a fine quest."

Sloan glanced at the wrinkled woman obviously older than any settlement in Texas. "Of course," he shrugged. Miss Alyce didn't seem strong enough to make it down the stairs for meals, much less across open country in a wagon filled with children.

He turned McCall toward him with a light grip on her shoulders. "This is impossible. You can't consider such a thing. The Great Plains isn't the town down the road, it's hundreds of miles of land. If the soldiers and Indians don't kill you, the storms and snakes will. There are herds of buffalo out there so huge a man couldn't cross them in a day if he could walk on their backs. And they move, thundering across the land, trampling everything in their path."

She looked at him calmly, as if refusing to be frightened or swayed by the truth.

"The weather can turn cold so fast you'll freeze before you can find shelter. No one in his right mind would travel alone through such a place."

The lady in black watched him with pleading eyes and a lifted chin that said she'd only ask once more. "I'm going. Will you go with us? I don't need a hero, I only need a driver."

Sloan studied her, then the faces of the children. Some stared at him, openly curious, some fought not to show fear. He guessed they'd been through hell to be this far south and alone. They were going whether he went along to help or not. He wasn't sure he could live with himself if he sent them out alone, and he wasn't sure he would live long if he went with them.

He took a deep breath, as if it might be his last, and answered, "I'll go."

She'd read him correctly. If he succeeded, he could never tell anyone, and if he died, McCall Harrison was right, he'd die with honor.

Three

SLOAN STRETCHED OUT across the hay in the barn loft and tried to make his bruised body relax. He'd spent hours talking and planning with McCall Harrison. Finally, after several arguments, he'd agreed that they would take two wagons, even though it meant traveling slower and much fatter with supplies than he'd have liked. They'd also take two extra horses. Once the children were delivered, Mc-Call planned to abandon one of the wagons and bring Alyce Wren home on the other. Sloan agreed to ride as far as the first fort with them, then he thought he would turn west toward Santa Fe. Somewhere farther west he'd lose himself and his past, if he had to go all the way to California.

McCall could have put most generals to shame with her detailed planning. Her only weakness lay in her insistence on comfort for the children and her inability to tell Alyce Wren no. These were Cheyenne offspring. They were used to hardships, but Sloan couldn't convince her. So, he would be heading north as soon as the storm cleared with twice the wagons and supplies they'd need and enough blankets to keep half the children in Texas warm for the winter. To top it off, Alyce Wren had decided she wasn't leaving her favorite rocker.

Closing his eyes, Sloan pictured how McCall's face had looked in anger. She had the kind of beauty that stuck with a man a long time, he thought. The kind of woman he'd probably never be so close to again.

A board creaked somewhere within the darkness of the barn. Icy wind blew between the cracks in the walls and rumbled in the distance like faraway cannon fire. Several animals below shifted at once. Sloan felt his muscles tighten.

"Relax," he mumbled to himself. "The war's over." How many times had he told himself that and still he couldn't believe the words. Awake or asleep, the war still haunted his thoughts. The memory of the curse Satan's Seven had whispered always seemed to follow him like a shadow. If he changed sides, they promised to find him, even if it took a lifetime.

As he closed his eyes once more and forced his body to uncoil, the thin blade of a knife pressed against his throat . . . cold, hard, and deadly.

Sloan didn't open his eyes as every instinct came fully awake.

The blade pressed harder, threatening to break the skin.

Sloan waited for his chance to respond. If he swallowed, the knife would be bloody.

"Don't move, mister," a young voice whispered, "or I'll cut your Adam's apple out and feed it to you."

Slowly opening his eyes, Sloan stared at a boy above him. The attacker was one of the older Indian children he'd seen earlier. In the darkness, Sloan could hear that his voice was filled with fear, but his hand was steady. His dark hair hung to his shoulders and his eyes were wide and black.

Sloan raised his hands above his head.

"That's right, mister," the boy whispered. "Now if you listen, you might just get out of here with most of your blood and some of your hair."

Sloan fought down a smile. The kid couldn't be more than seven or eight.

"The others sent me, 'cause I've hunted and killed things before, and I can speak your language better than most born to it. They want me to tell you to get on one of the horses and ride out tonight. We don't want or need you around."

"Or what?" Sloan shifted slightly, moving a fraction of an inch away from the knife at his throat.

"Or I'll kill you in your sleep. I swear," the boy answered with the chilling confidence of certainty.

"Why?" Sloan moved another fraction away. "I've done nothing to harm you. I've only offered my help."

"We decided we don't want you along. Miss Alyce Wren can doctor us and Mrs. McCall can drive the other wagon. We see you as nothing but extra baggage carrying trouble."

Sloan guessed that his attacker and one or two of the older boys already considered themselves men enough to protect the others. "And if I refuse?" Sloan whispered as he shifted slightly.

The boy thought a moment. "Then I guess I'll have to kill you now. There's no use waiting until you're asleep."

Sloan knew he could move suddenly and take the knife away from the child without so much as a scratch, but he'd rip the boy's pride apart. "Could we talk about this?" The boy hesitated and Sloan continued, "You could keep the knife ready to kill me at any time, but hear me out. After all, it's only a few minutes of your time and it seems to be the rest of mine."

The boy leaned back and nodded. "We'll talk, but don't

make any sudden moves, mister. I sharpened this knife on the bones of a deer."

Sloan slowly rose to sit cross-legged beside his attacker. "First, any warrior, even one about to die, deserves to know his killer. What's your name, brave one?"

The boy smiled, his dark eyes shining with pride at the compliment. "I'm called Winter."

"Winter is a fine name." Sloan offered his hand. "I'm called Sloan Alexander."

A warm brown hand slowly touched Sloan's palm. "We will not be friends, Sloan Alexander," the boy said as he shook hands.

"Then you will be my respected enemy, Winter. I understand a man can measure his worth by the strength of his enemies."

Winter nodded and sat a little taller.

"I know you and the others don't need me to go with the women to take you home." Sloan tried to guess why the children would want him to leave. "Many of you are old enough to fight and protect all the women and children."

The boy nodded agreement.

"But when we reach the camps of your people, who will take the women back?"

The boy lowered his knife. "We didn't think of that. Someone will have to. It would put our people in too much danger to ask them to wait while we backtracked."

Sloan smiled, thinking this bright little boy would make a great man someday, if he lived long enough in this crazy world. "Then, you wouldn't mind if I ride along with you just so I can bring the women back? I'll try to stay out of the way."

Winter shook his head. "All right. I'll let you live, mister. But you'd better never make me sorry."

"Thank you," Sloan answered. "I'll keep that in mind."

"Also," the boy added, "you have to swear not to tell anyone that I know English. Once folks find that out it's a real bother."

"You have my word, Winter."

As silently as the boy had appeared, he disappeared. Sloan leaned back on his blanket. There would be plenty of time to ask Winter how he'd learned to speak English so smoothly . . . or if he was of mixed blood. The boy brought up several questions, but of one thing Sloan was sure. Winter had been willing to kill him if needed.

A light snow continued to fall the next day and the next. Sloan spent most of his time in the barn making sure every inch of the wagons was ready to travel. The station manager's daughter made excuses to visit often, but soon grew bored with Sloan's coldness. She was trouble looking for a place to root and grow, and he wasn't offering to help.

On the third afternoon the sky cleared and a weak sun melted away the dusting of white within a few hours. Sloan pulled a workbench out into the sun and turned his face to the warmth. He carefully folded one leather strap over another, braiding a flat strip like he'd been taught while in the cavalry. In the three days he'd been at the stage station he'd managed to stay out the manager's way and out of sight of all travelers. Only Alyce Wren seemed to make it her business to keep up with him. The coldness that had worked so easily on the girl only seemed to encourage the old woman to stay longer. Sloan was starting to wonder if the old lady thought she'd hired him, or adopted him.

"I'd make one strap thicker." Her voice came over his shoulder. Sloan didn't turn around or stand from where he straddled the bench.

Miss Alyce Wren waddled closer, in a rustle of heavy satin and fur. "The vaqueros on our ranches in my youth always braided an irregular strap in with two of the same size to strengthen the rope." She moved around the bench so that she could face him. "Now, those were cattlemen—kings compared to the drifters who think they herd today."

Sloan didn't answer. He hardly ever answered, but she didn't notice. She loved to tell him of a time long ago when Texas was a part of Mexico and she was the belle of parties on both sides of the Rio Grande.

Miss Alyce Wren turned her face to the sun for a few minutes before looking back at Sloan. "I crossed the plains with my father more than once. I'm guessing we'll hit trouble about a day past the last fort. Before that, we'll be safe. The wind increases as we move onto the plains, and the Indians will be able to hear us coming. I remember that the land smells so thickly of soil and sun. A body can see a hundred miles across the tall grass and hear twice as far. You were right about the danger. It doesn't even have to snow; the cold wind is so strong it can freeze a horse in minutes, never mind a man. But the silent beauty of it took my breath away, and I'd like to see it again before I die."

"You could stay here. I'll return to tell you about it," Sloan encouraged as he glanced up to meet her gray eyes. "So could Mrs. Harrison. I could go alone."

"No." She shook her head slowly. "I have to go this time. My McCallie would never let you go alone. If she did, she'd just find another cause to fight without your help. She dances to danger's melody and doesn't plan to stop. For three years I've watched her. Now, maybe I can help."

"I'll watch out for her." Sloan halted braiding. The old woman was starting to spook him worse than the sound of a rattler in the center of a herd. She was such a mixture of southern lady and homeless fortune-teller. He guessed she'd been raised with wealth, but if she'd lived through the past fifty years in Texas, it would take far more than a cold wind or threat of danger to frighten her.

"You'll need McCall more than she'll need you." Alyce Wren's face seemed to melt with sorrow. "You'll go with her this time and, if you live, walk away with pride, but she'll go on to fight another cause, then another."

"What's she trying to prove?"

Alyce Wren wiggled her mouth, attempting to find words, then suddenly threw her hands in the air as if no language would tell her thoughts. With a mumbled sound, she turned and hurried toward the back door of the station.

Sloan shrugged and finished the braid. He didn't need an answer. He'd figured it out for himself from the bits and pieces others had said. According to the station manager's daughter, McCall Harrison had loved her husband so much she went to war with him, staying well behind the lines. But one dawn, he led his men into a bloody fight with the Yankees in Indian territory. The Rebs were winning for a few hours, but the battle turned. By dark, most of the men were dead, or dying. McCall drove her wagon to the edge of the battle and waded through the bodies until she found her gut-shot husband. He was too big for her to carry alone, so she held him all night while he died slowly in her arms. At dawn the Yankees helped her load his body into her wagon. She arrived home several days later, still wearing her blood-soaked dress and half dead herself from hunger and exhaustion.

Propping his foot on the bench, Sloan closed his eyes and tried to imagine loving or being loved by someone so much. He leaned his arm atop his knee and stared out toward the house. Maybe McCall's story was just that, a story. Folks like to color the truth from time to time. She was probably just a widow left half mad by a war no one seemed to understand. But he'd seen the respect the men had shown her the night he'd been beaten, and he had to wonder if parts of her tale weren't true.

McCall watched Sloan from the shadows of the barn. His lean body was war-thin, yet strong like the rawhide he worked in his hands. The bruises he'd suffered in the beating three days ago were still there, but he hadn't complained. His hair was such a remarkable brown, it looked sun-kissed at first glance and hung a few inches too long over his collar. Her husband would have ordered him to get it cut before the next formation.

Blinking away her tears, McCall realized there were no more formations. It seemed she'd lived all her life in a military camp. The few times they'd returned to the ranch, Holden Harrison had kept military hours for meals and lights out. He'd expected everyone around him, including his wife, to be ready to stand at attention.

Watching this stranger now, McCall saw little of the army left in him. Except in the hardness of his jaw and the depth of his brown eyes. She didn't want to admit to herself that he made her uneasy . . . like a scent that drifts across the land warning of a storm. There was a stillness about him that frightened her. Holden, her husband, had always been predictable in his actions, but this stranger didn't seem to live by the same code. He hadn't fought for his own life against the attack three nights ago. He'd agreed to help her without asking a price. And sometimes he looked at her with those haunting dark eyes as if he didn't believe what he saw. He looked at her with the hunger of one who'd never known being full. But a hunger for what?

McCall moved from the shadows into the long afternoon strands of light. She knew he saw her coming, but he didn't glance in her direction or stand as a gentleman would have done when she approached.

"Think it's going to snow tonight?" she asked softly, as if talking to herself.

"Might," Sloan answered, his fingers moving along the leather.

McCall circled him. The man was starting to bother her more than she wanted to admit. She'd thought he'd be perfect to drive the wagon, but now she wasn't so sure. In the past few days he hadn't spoken a complete sentence to her. She was beginning to think even if she could turn him upside down and shake him, she couldn't get more than a dime's worth of conversation out of him. Most men talked of home or the past; he only spoke when asked a direct question. "Do you think you're up to riding out with me to my ranch? I need to pick up a few things before we leave tomorrow. It isn't far."

"Sure." He stood and laid down the rope. "I'll hitch the wagon."

"No." McCall reached toward him, then drew her hand back, not sure how such a man might react to a light touch. "Saddle a couple of horses. We'll make faster time."

To her surprise, he turned and smiled. A brief smile that only lasted a moment before he moved to the stalls.

"Yes, ma'am," he yelled over his shoulder.

By the time McCall went inside to get her hat and gloves, he was waiting with the horses. She didn't say a word when he handed her the reins to one of the mounts without offering to cup his hands and give her a boost, as every man she'd ever known would have done.

She lifted the leg of her split skirt and pulled herself into the saddle. From three generations of Texans, she'd never considered herself spoiled, and certainly not pampered, but she did expect common courtesy . . . of which this man seemed lacking. She hadn't seen any sign that he knew how to treat a lady. The major would have had one of his men walk a month of night guard for treating his wife so. But the major had been dead for three years, and she was no longer his wife, only his widow.

McCall kicked the horse into action, angry both at Sloan for his rudeness and at herself for caring one way or the other. Getting the children to safety should be the only thing on her mind. What did it matter if the man she'd asked to help was a gentleman or not? He'd go his way soon and she'd find another cause to fight.

She could hear Sloan's horse thundering to catch her and knew he'd have trouble doing so. McCall had ridden before she had walked. Sometimes, during the war, Holden had sent her with messages because he said there were no men who could outride her. She'd heard the major brag once that a bullet couldn't catch his wife on a good horse.

They crossed the road and galloped past open fields she'd known all her life. She glanced back when she changed direction and watched Sloan. He rode well, but then she'd expected a man who kept his gauntlets from the cavalry to be able to handle a horse.

They rode along rows of winter-crisp fields. Everything smelled cool and clean after the storm. For the first time in longer than she could remember, the war seemed long past.

McCall slowed as she rode onto the ranch her grandfather had named Phantom Ridge. Away, she always thought of herself as confident and independent, but here, surrounded by ghosts, she changed. Her father and grandfather had dominated the early years of her life, until they passed on that responsibility to Holden when she married. Holden and her father were at West Point together, and many times in her marriage, she wondered if they hadn't been twins. Holden had been the first gentleman to court her, or rather the first man her father and grandfather allowed close enough to court. He'd done all the right things to impress a seventeen-year-old girl, and he'd looked so grand in his major's uniform. He hadn't held her hand when he asked her to marry him. She'd fallen in love within hours of meeting him. He was good, and fair, and solid as a rock. McCall dreamed of adventure at the major's side, but she had gotten war.

Holden Harrison had been a man no other could measure up to, in McCall's eyes, and she'd sworn the day she buried him to wear black until she also died.

Looking at the ranch house now, with its long porch and wide balcony, McCall knew, as she had the day she brought Holden back to bury beside her father and mother, that she'd never live in the house again. It was her father's house, and maybe a little bit Holden's, but it was no longer hers. Someday maybe others would run cattle over the rolling hills and finish the second floor her grandfather had built to hold many children. She never would. She'd make her home at the station with Miss Alyce, when she had time to think of home at all.

Sloan didn't say a word as they passed the small, neat cemetery and rounded the house. She glanced at him as he reined up at her side. The slight rise of his eyebrow told her he had a few questions. But he seemed the kind of man who'd wait for the answers.

"No one's around," she answered as if he'd asked. "I closed the ranch after my husband died. An old couple stayed on to see after the place. but they left a few months ago."

Sloan still didn't comment.

McCall waited. She didn't want to go back into the house for the guns she needed for the trip. Alyce Wren once said her father's house was built on woe, but McCall never understood why. Now as she looked at it, she thought she saw what Miss Alyce meant. The paint was starting to peel and the roof was in need of fixing. Yet the old house stood like an aging veteran, tall and proud.

Sloan watched her closely as he lowered himself to the ground and tied the reins of both horses to a tarnished ring hanging from a post in need of paint. His ribs ached from the ride, but he wasn't about to touch his side to let her know he was in pain.

When he turned, she reached out her arms for him to help her down.

On instinct, he circled her waist with his gloved hands and lifted her from the saddle. Her hands were warm on his shoulders, and her hair smelled of roses as he slowly lowered her beside him. He bit back the pain in his side from the blows he'd taken against his ribs. He decided he'd get the old woman to wrap them tighter.

"Thank you," she said impersonally as she moved away.

Sloan nodded, suddenly embarrassed at himself. What he'd done was a common act men did for women all the time. His reaction must mark him a fool to her for she could have no idea how rare such an action was for him.

McCall climbed the steps. "You're welcome to come in, or wait out here if you like. I'll only be a minute."

Sloan followed her into the house. He'd never been inside a home like this. It reminded him of the officers' quarters on a few old forts he'd seen back east, only this was larger. In fact, most of the hotels he'd stayed in were smaller. The rooms all seemed to open off a wide foyer, which had a staircase at the far end. All the furniture was draped and rugs had been rolled to one side.

McCall moved toward the stairs. She paused on the first step and glanced over her shoulder at him. Staring up at her, Sloan thought she belonged in this house. She was as proper and straight as it seemed. He wanted to ask her why she lived at the station, but it was none of his business. He was just someone she'd asked to help drive a wagon, nothing more. She wasn't offering friendship and he wasn't about to pry.

McCall turned and disappeared upstairs, leaving Sloan to wander around. With all the curtains drawn, the shadowed furniture seemed asleep beneath cream-colored sheets. The pictures were covered and looked as if they were bowing their heads in sorrow.

Pulling off a glove, Sloan ran his finger along the mantel, wiping off a layer of dust. He strolled past a parlor, then what must have once been a large dining room. The air seemed colder inside than he'd remembered it being outside. If houses could be lonely, this one surely was. The very walls seemed to mourn the silence of endless days without voices to echo.

As he moved through the rooms, more from impatience than curiosity, a tiny square of tin caught his eye. It seemed to blink at him from the corner of a room lined with bookshelves. Sloan bent, putting his hand between the leg of a table and the wall. Slowly he pulled out the twisted piece of metal.

Moving to the window, he straightened the two-inch-square tintype. Since the war, most pictures were photographs, but before and during the war men carried only tintypes of their loved ones. McCall, a few years younger and much happier than he'd probably ever see her, looked back at him from the glinting metal.

Over the years Sloan had glanced at a hundred squares made the same. Wives, sweethearts, mothers. But none had ever drawn him as this one did. Her face had a warmth not even the shadowy light could cool.

Footsteps sounded from the stairs. Sloan turned, slipping the picture into his pocket. He wasn't stealing, he silently told himself. The picture had been bent and discarded. Someone had tossed it away as worthless, but the square had missed the trash bin and hidden in waiting until now.

He wrapped his fingers around the metal in his pocket. It wasn't worthless anymore; it was his now. He'd never tell her he had it. But somehow he knew he'd carry the small square with him the rest of his life . . . as short as that might be.

Glancing up, he saw her hurrying toward him as if she didn't want to stay in this place a moment longer than necessary.

She tossed him a rifle and fully loaded shoulder belt. "Ready to ride?" Her face seemed as stiffly starched as the high-necked blouse she wore. At least the blouse was white and not black like the skirt, jacket, coat, and boots she always wore.

"Ready," he answered as he followed her from the house.

Neither looked back as he helped her into her saddle this time and she thanked him with a nod.

They rode slower back to the station, side by side, but both deep in their own thoughts.

It was not until almost midnight, when the wagon was loaded and ready for a dawn departure, that Sloan reached in his pocket and pulled out McCall's reflection. Carefully, as though the tin were fragile, he wrapped it in a bandanna and tucked it deep into his saddlebags.

Four

"AS SOON AS we're out of sight of the station, I'll climb up front and ride shotgun," Winter whispered from the back of the wagon as Sloan drove the team in line behind the horses McCall managed.

"I'd appreciate that," Sloan said over his shoulder. The sun wasn't up yet, but he noticed all the children were wide-awake. They seemed to feel it was their duty to listen for any sound that might mean trouble. Only Winter broke the silence. He talked in a low tone to the others in a language Sloan couldn't understand.

Sloan focused on the lead wagon. McCall was as good at driving a team as she'd been at horseback riding. Alyce Wren sat beside her, and for once the old woman looked like she hadn't slept in her clothes. She was dressed in shades of brown and had managed to pull her hair into a bun. She carried a faded parasol as though she were on an afternoon outing. She looked as out of sorts as ever. Sloan wondered if McCall had spent the past three days trying to talk her out of making the journey.

They moved through the few buildings too sparsely populated to be called a town. Winter knelt just behind the bench. "You worried about this trip, mister?"

"No," Sloan answered. "I figure trouble will find us in its own good time. There's not much I can do about it until I finally see it coming head-on."

"Me too," Winter echoed. "I'm not worried."

Sloan looked over his shoulder. "Why don't you climb on up with me? We're far enough along that it's unlikely we'll see anyone."

Winter jumped over the bench and took his seat. "I won't bother you none. I know how to ride shotgun. When my father was alive, I used to ride in the wagon with him all the time. He told me he'd teach me to drive a team when I was old enough."

Sloan raised an eyebrow in question.

Winter shrugged. "I guess I forgot to tell you that my mother is one of The People. She's Black Kettle's sister. But my father, he was a trapper named Adam McQuillen, who wandered into Black Kettle's camp one winter, half frozen and starving. When my mother's family took care of him, he decided to stay. My mother named me after the season that brought him to her."

Sloan looked at the boy carefully. The blood of two peoples blended in his features.

"My father used to tell me I needed to walk in both worlds, but after he died, I decided I wanted to stay with my mother. It's not as easy to walk with his people as it is with hers. In the settlements, I was just an Indian, but in Black Kettle's camp I am Winter, Adam and Elk Woman's son."

"Do you have any idea where she is?" Sloan asked. If Winter could remember something about his people camping across the one hundredth parallel, it could help Sloan locate the tribe. Maybe she'd said something when they'd parted.

Winter shook his head. "When we heard the horses coming that morning, she told me to run toward the river and not to stop until I hit the water. The river had a thin cover of ice on it, but I didn't let that stop me. I crossed the water and hid in the brush until it was dark, then I just started running with the current."

He looked up with huge eyes brimming with tears he refused to let fall. "I can still hear my mother's people screaming and the sound of so much gunfire rattling together like someone was rapping on the clouds. Sometimes at night, when I'm asleep, I think I can still feel the ice cutting my cheeks as I swam as fast as I could to get away. We thought we were safe, camped along the Washita. Black Kettle told us the army wouldn't bother us there."

Sloan had heard of the battle on the Washita, but he'd guessed it was more an open attack than an equal fight. Custer was looking for glory at any price. But Sloan didn't blame anyone anymore in the Indian wars. He'd seen both sides do unthinkable things. If one side started hating the other, it became a circle no one walked away from. Sloan had witnessed it in the War Between the States and now with the Indians.

He also knew what it was like to have his dreams haunted, and he'd never wish that on anyone. The months he'd been in the Union prison camp still shadowed his nights to the point that he no longer remembered dreams, only nightmares.

"The old medicine man called Willow Hawk found me a day later," Winter continued. "He already had four children with him, but one died before we traveled two more days." Winter's words were matter-of-fact now. "He kept moving south along the river, reminding us we had to get away and that he'd find someone to take us back when it was safer. He said he'd seen a few women escape and ride north to where several of the men had gone hunting.

They'll go to the plains, where no one can get within rifle shot without being seen. Miss Alyce told us she rode up there in a wagon once. She says the earth just opens up in a crack that could hide a herd of buffalo. Our people will be safe."

Sloan glanced at Winter, but didn't interrupt the boy by telling him that soon there would be nowhere for his people to be safe, maybe not even the reservation.

Winter smiled to himself. "Miss Alyce says she can take us to them. My mother will be worried if we don't hurry. My father used to say it was her favorite pastime."

Sloan wished he could say they'd find her, but he knew the chances were slim that she was one of the few women who'd escaped. Even if she was alive, there were hundreds of miles of land to cover, looking for a people who were doing their best to hide. A thousand Indians could disappear forever in the canyons.

"Since we've got some time," Sloan glanced down at the boy, so full of sadness he looked like it might ooze from him like sap, "I thought you might be old enough to teach to drive a team. I'm most likely not as good a driver as your pa was, but I could show you how to hold the reins. There will be times in the next few weeks when it would come in handy to have another driver."

The boy nodded, as if he understood the reason for Sloan's sudden change of subject and appreciated the effort.

Winter spent the day watching for trouble and taking the reins from time to time. He talked little, as did the other children. McCall stopped for a few minutes at noon and passed out biscuits and ham left over from breakfast. The road was little more than a trail, but now and then they saw signs of other people having traveled the same path—a cold campfire, a discarded wagon wheel, a trail leading off toward a dugout in the distance.

At sunset McCall pulled the wagons into a wooded area where they could camp without being noticed. Hundred-year-old cottonwoods framed a wide, shallow creek bed. Sloan tended the horses while McCall built a fire and Alyce Wren started supper. The children didn't run and play as he'd thought they might. Instead, they moved around, circling the campsite as though checking the perimeters for safety.

One little girl of about six picked up small rocks and stuffed them into a pouch. When the pouch was full, she continued to search. Another child the same size followed her, stepping only in the imprint of each of her footsteps. A third sat on the grass with a branch and wiped away the prints of anyone who passed within three feet of him.

As Sloan walked past them, he realized he'd seen soldiers do much the same thing after a battle. Yet these were children. He could tell them the camp was secure, but he wondered how many years it would be, if ever, before they would feel safe.

It was almost full dark when Sloan brought the last two horses from the stream. He tied them to graze near the tall grass at the water's edge and started back to camp. The night was crisp, but not as cold as it had been the past week.

He almost passed McCall without seeing her in the darkness.

She leaned against an aging cottonwood, so still she could have been a statue. The pale outline of her blouse reflected creamy in the moonlight.

"Mrs. Harrison?"

"Yes." She moved slightly, stretching her back against

the bark. Without the black waist-length jacket she appeared softer, more human.

He stepped closer, knowing he'd startled her. "Are you all right?"

McCall smiled up at him. "I'm wonderful. I just wanted to be alone for a few minutes and enjoy the stillness.

"I thought I'd give my ears a rest from Miss Alyce's stories. She's sitting in her rocker now, telling them to the children, though most of them can't understand a word." McCall suddenly sounded excited, as though she'd been thinking of something and had to share it with someone.

He didn't answer, but watched her closely. In the past three days he'd never seen her look so content.

"We made it without a hitch today, didn't we? I was afraid if we had trouble we'd cross it the first day. Someone would realize what we planned and stop us before we could try. But we made it."

Sloan leaned against the tree, so close beside her that his shoulder brushed hers. He wanted to enjoy her mood. "We made good time today. I can tell by how much my backside hurts." He'd never seen her like this, tired but content, proud of herself.

McCall laughed. "I know how you feel. Alyce Wren became so tired she almost fell from the wagon a few times. I finally had the children crowd up so she could spread out on a pile of blankets in the back. I didn't figure you'd want me to keep stopping to pick her up, and I couldn't find any rope to tie her to the bench."

The picture of Alyce Wren nodding off as they moved along made Sloan smile. The old woman drove him crazy with her grumbling advice, but he would never wish her harm. He wouldn't mind saying "I told you to stay home" to her a few times, though. In the hour since they'd stopped, she'd managed to complain about everything, including the hardness of the ground.

Suddenly, McCall's shoulder began to quiver against his, and he turned slightly to find her fighting to keep from breaking into a full laugh.

"She'd shake the whole wagon when she jerked awake," McCall added. "Toward the afternoon, I didn't know whether to encourage her to talk more, or to allow her to sleep. Her talking drove me crazy; her sleeping almost killed her."

McCall's hysteria was contagious, and Sloan couldn't keep from laughing. Something about being too tired to move made it impossible to remain calm.

She bit back her own chuckles and slapped at his shoulder. "Don't laugh. It isn't funny. She could have been hurt."

Sloan could only nod, for he knew if he opened his mouth to speak, a full roar would come out.

She slapped at his shoulder again, trying to make him stop. When he didn't, she buried her face against his shirt while her shoulders shook with a sudden release of laughter.

When Sloan could finally take a long breath, McCall was still leaning against him, her cheek next to his heart and his hand resting on the small of her back.

Without thinking, he did what he'd thought of doing from the moment he'd seen her smiling back at him from the tintype. He leaned and kissed her.

The kiss only lasted a moment before he felt her body stiffen. She jerked away as though he'd branded her with fire and not his lips.

"Don't!" She moved another step away, almost falling over tree roots.

"McCall?" He couldn't bring himself to apologize, though he knew that he probably should.

"Don't," she put her hand up as if to block his advance, "don't ever touch me again."

"I . . ." What could he say? That he hadn't meant to kiss her? That he was sorry? That she tasted better than he'd thought she might? He'd never learned to be so honest, or so much a liar.

"Never. Never do that again. Do you understand?" The cold formality was back in her voice.

"But . . . ?"

"I was married to a man I loved greatly; when the major died, I died inside. I never want to feel a man's arms around me again. I never want to feel anything ever again."

He wasn't sure if her words were ordering her, or him. In the watery light of the moon, Sloan could see the pain in her blue eyes. She was telling him there was no room in her life for him or any man, now or ever. Even a light kiss was too much for her to bear. "I understand, Mrs. Harrison," he answered in a low tone, wishing he really did.

McCall straightened, pulling herself to full attention. "There's no need for us to use proper names. My father named me McCall after my mother's family. You may call me McCall if you like. I need your help, Sloan, nothing more. I was out of line to become so familiar with you just now. From this point on, I think it would be better if we kept a proper distance."

Sloan wished it were darker and she couldn't see him. He'd never made such advances toward a woman; when he finally had, she'd put him in his place.

"We'd best go back to the camp and try to get some sleep." Her voice shook slightly, and she placed a hand around her throat, as if she could steady it. "We'll just pretend this never happened."

Sloan nodded but didn't follow her as she moved toward the camp. He leaned back against the tree and took a deep breath, wondering what had driven him to do such a foolhardy thing as kiss her. She was a major's wife, a proud southern woman with more money and respect than he'd ever—

"You call that staying out of the way, mister?" Winter's voice shook Sloan from his own thoughts.

Sloan knocked the back of his head against the bark, welcoming the pain. He and McCall hadn't been alone.

"I seen skunks with more social skills than you, mister. Just because a lady speaks to you don't mean she wants you to grab her."

"I didn't grab her." Sloan was about to decide the boy and the old woman were twins, accidentally born seventy years apart. Alyce Wren had taken every opportunity to advise him on how he should act, and now Winter seemed determined to do the same thing.

"Told you I'd be keeping an eye on you. So far you seem to be having a little trouble 'staying out of the way' like you said you would."

Sloan rubbed the throbbing between his eyes with his thumb and index finger. How could he explain to the boy what had happened when he couldn't explain it to himself?

Winter leaned closer. "If I was you, mister, I'd give up sleeping for a while. It might be better for your health."

Reaching for the boy, Sloan closed his outstretched hand into an empty fist. What would he have done with the child if he'd caught Winter? McCall would probably frown on him strangling one of the children they were risking their lives to save. Besides, he really liked the kid. Winter's in-

telligence seemed far beyond his years and almost
matched his need to meddle in something that was none of
his concern.

Sloan walked slowly back to the camp. If he slept
tonight, he wasn't sure whether or not Winter might truly
try to carry out his threat. If he didn't sleep, he'd be the one
they'd have to tie to the bench tomorrow to keep from
falling out. Either way, Sloan figured he was in for more
pain before this trip was over.

Five

MCCALL WATCHED AS Sloan circled the campsite, his path widening into the night with each revolution. She could feel his gaze on her from the shadows. He hadn't said a word more then necessary to her in three days. She wasn't sure if he was embarrassed or angry. The man was as hard to read as a week-old trail.

Each evening he took the first watch, promising to wake her after midnight, and each night she slept until dawn without waking. But tonight was their fourth evening out, and she knew he must get some sleep or he'd be little help to her when trouble came.

All the others were cuddled beneath their blankets. Alyce Wren and the three smallest children were bedded down in one wagon, pulled as close as they dared to the fire. The older children circled the dying campfire. McCall had made herself a space in the other wagon, but tonight she was determined to talk to Sloan before turning in.

His advance that first night had bothered her because she hadn't seen it coming. She felt she'd been one of the boys so long that having a man react to her as a woman seemed strange. After the war, she'd hidden away to mourn until Alyce Wren pulled her back into life by telling her how badly she was needed. McCall took on each of Miss Alyce's assignments like a crusader, but this mission was more dangerous than any had been. Since Alyce Wren knew everyone in Texas, she was never short of knowing someone who needed a helping hand, but she'd found the Indian children by pure chance. Somehow the old woman must feel McCall was in over her head this time. So Alyce had insisted on coming along.

McCall picked up an extra blanket and moved from the campfire's flickering light into the almost moonless black beyond. She needed to talk to someone, anyone, besides the old woman for a few minutes. McCall was starting to hear Alyce's voice when she was sound asleep.

Her boots made a swishing sound in the winter-dry brush as McCall walked into the night. She moved carefully through the darkness, knowing Sloan would find her long before she'd find him. He'd had an hour in the darkness, so he could probably see her clearly. All she had was a feeling that he was near.

After traveling only a few steps, she heard movement to her right and knew he was making himself known so as not to frighten her. McCall waited, hoping the movement she heard was Sloan and not some animal venturing too close to the camp.

"They call this a rustler's moon," Sloan whispered. "Bright enough to steal cattle, but not so bright that a gunman could draw a bead on a man."

McCall studied the blackness, but he was far into the shadows and she couldn't make out his outline.

"I'm no rustler. I only came to bring you an extra blanket," she whispered. "There's a chill in the air tonight."

"There's a chill in the air every night," he countered.

"I need to talk to you," she said, trying to keep any anger

from her voice. He made no effort to take the blanket she held out toward him.

"I figured that," he answered. "I've been watching you pace by the fire, waiting for everyone to go to sleep. What's the plan now, General?"

"Don't call me that," McCall ordered and took a step in what she hoped was his direction.

"Why not? You've been pushing this troop every mile. Planning down to the hour. Riding ahead each morning to mark our course and studying the maps till dark. Sherman didn't plan his march across Georgia so completely."

McCall spread her fingers before her and took another step. "I just don't want to waste any time. As soon as I get these children delivered, I have other things that must be done."

"Never rest, heh, General?"

"I said, don't call me that!" McCall snapped.

"Not only organized, but testy," Sloan answered with almost a laugh. "Or is being in a good mood just not on your list of things that have to be done? I haven't seen you smile in four days."

She guessed now the reason he hadn't talked to her was more from anger than embarrassment. He'd taken her cool politeness as hostility toward him. "I'm not in a bad mood and I'm not always angry." This conversation wasn't going at all like she'd hoped.

"Neither am I," he returned a lie for a lie.

"Good, then we can talk." She had to talk, just talk with someone, or she'd go mad by tomorrow.

McCall extended her hand further and touched his knee. He didn't move, but she felt his muscles stiffen. Lightly, she brushed his leg, then let her fingers rest on the rock he sat on, a huge boulder as long as a bench and twice as high.

"We've been safe so far," she said as she moved beside

him and jumped to sit on the rock. "But how long will we be if you don't get any sleep?"

"I'm sleeping some," he answered. His words were tight, as though her nearness bothered him, or irritated him, she wasn't sure which. "I think we're all safer if I stay away from the fire. That way if trouble should ride in at night, they won't see me until it's too late. Winter knows enough about driving the team that he can take a turn when the going is easy, and I sleep some during the day."

"But it's cold out here."

"I've slept in colder places than Texas. Out here, away from all the snoring and moving of the children, I can hear better."

"You still need to wake me after midnight and let me take a watch. It's only fair."

"Is that an order?"

McCall could never remember a man bothering her so. If ever there was a man in need of ordering, it was Sloan Alexander, but she seemed the only one aware of the fact at the moment. "No, it is not, only a request."

She remembered the last order she'd given him about never, never touching her. "Sloan, can't we relax around one another? Does there have to be a battlefield between us? We have to work together, to depend on one another. Can't we just talk like regular people?"

"I thought that's what we were doing." He paused a moment. "At least working together."

"But not relaxing," she added. "Not just talking."

"It's not easy." He took a long breath. "I haven't spent much time in the company of women. Also, how much time do we get each day between the kids and Miss Alyce? The old woman told me tonight that I made a jackrabbit seem like a great conversationalist. I don't know when I'd have a chance to say anything anyway."

"I know." McCall moved slightly, brushing his leg with hers in the darkness. "She doesn't need anyone to do more than nod every few hours."

A silence grew between them for a moment, then Sloan added, "I wish you were as easy to talk to, General."

"Couldn't you just treat me like one of the guys? If you'll relax, maybe we'd find it easier. When I traveled with my husband—" She stopped suddenly, not wanting to remember Holden. How could she explain how she'd changed from a wedding dress to riding clothes? She could never tell this stranger that she'd spent her wedding night on the ground in a campsite surrounded by four hundred men. Or that Holden would sometimes go days without saying a word to her that wasn't meant for all his men as well.

Sloan didn't say anything, and she knew he was waiting for her to finish.

She couldn't tell him of her life. How could she explain that most of the time she'd felt like she was in the army? Just one of the men, no more valued, no more in the major's confidence than any other. Holden's men always treated her with respect, but Holden often forgot she was by his side, even at night.

"I don't think I can," Sloan finally broke the silence.

"Can what?" she asked, forgetting her request.

"I don't think I could treat you like one of the fellows," he answered.

McCall reached across the darkness and brushed her hand over his arm. "We've trouble ahead, Sloan; could we at least be friends? I may not be as strong a general as you seem to think I am. This time I'm going to need someone to cover my back, because trouble may come from all directions."

"Friends," he whispered, allowing the wall they'd built

between them to crack slightly. "If you'll consider that I may not be as bad as you think I am. I didn't think I was attacking you the other night."

"I know." She pulled her hand away. "I may have over-reacted a little. But what I said was true; there's nothing left inside me for any man to care about in the way a man cares about a woman."

"It was only a kiss," he defended.

"For me it was far more than I could accept." She could never tell him how personal his act seemed to her. The major had only kissed her on the cheek a few times during their marriage, and never on the mouth. He would have thought it too personal. Holden's lovemaking, though never unpleasant, had always seemed almost detached from their real lives.

"Just out of curiosity," Sloan moved slightly, turning so he faced her shadow, "how many beaux did you have before the major?"

"None," she answered.

"And after?"

"None." She knew she was admitting that no man other than her husband had tried to kiss her. Maybe it would help Sloan understand why there could never be anyone else in her life. "How about you? How many ladies have you courted?" She wasn't brave enough to say bedded, but they both knew what the question implied.

Sloan laughed but didn't say a word.

"A thousand?" she guessed. Somehow the darkness made it easy to ask. She'd spent many evenings sitting around the campfires, talking with soldiers, but could never remember getting so personal. "A hundred?"

Sloan pushed himself off the rock. "I don't think we should be talking about this, General."

"Why not? You asked me." McCall was suddenly enjoying herself more than she had in months. "If we're going to be friends, we need to talk about things. My husband used to say one soldier needs to know the other well enough to read his mind. Especially going into battle."

"We're not soldiers," Sloan corrected.

"But we may go into battle," she countered. "So how many others have you kissed?"

"A man doesn't talk about the number of women in his past." Sloan moved away, thankful for the darkness.

"Not even to a friend?"

"No," he answered.

"All right, then answer one thing." McCall pulled her knees to her chin. "Were most of them willing, or startled victims like me?"

Sloan moved restlessly in the shadows. "I don't remember."

"You don't lie very well." She smiled to herself, knowing she was making him nervous. "I admire that in a man."

"And I'd be much obliged if we'd drop the subject of my romantic adventures."

McCall jumped off the rock. "All right. I guess admiration and being obliged are as good a footing as any to start a friendship."

She offered her hand. "Shake?"

He took her fingers in his hand. "Truce?"

"Truce," she answered. "If you'll wake me tonight so I can take a watch."

"I'll wake you," he promised as she pulled her hand away.

They walked back to camp without saying another word. When McCall reached the clearing, she noticed Winter kneeling on his bedroll. He looked at Sloan and smiled as he put his knife back in the sheath he kept strapped to his leg.

McCall glanced at Sloan, who nodded first to Winter, then to her, before disappearing back into the blackness.

She tucked the boy in, then curled into her space in the wagon. The night was getting colder, but she preferred the comfort of the wagon to the warmth of the fire. Just before she fell asleep, she smiled, remembering Sloan's and her talk. There would be no time to get to know him much better, but she'd enjoyed the banter.

While she slept, Sloan moved back against the shadow of the rock. From his vantage point he could see the campfire and the clearing beyond. He knew he'd sleep a little better knowing he didn't have to worry about Winter trying to slit his throat. He also knew he would let McCall sleep through the night.

He wrapped the blanket she'd left on the rock around his shoulders and thought about how he'd like to wake her with a gentle touch. She might be dead inside, but she was sure making him feel very much alive.

Two days past Fort Griffin, Sloan spotted the first soldiers on patrol when he rode out to scout. He stayed well behind them, but followed long enough to know the direction they were taking so he could avoid their path.

When he returned to the wagons, he told McCall about the patrol, and to his surprise, she moved into action as though she'd long had a plan she'd been waiting to implement.

Miss Alyce Wren was moved back to the wagon with Winter. McCall asked Sloan to ride far ahead to give warning. Then she turned in the direction the patrol had gone.

Sloan didn't see the sense of it. Except that he knew the patrol was looking for the same folks they were. Following them onto the plains might be the fastest way to find the Cheyenne or to get themselves killed.

But by dawn he knew they'd made a mistake. He was bringing the horses into line when McCall stepped to his side.

"Someone's watching us," she whispered, away from the children's hearing.

"Who?" Sloan looked around but saw no one.

"I don't know who, but Miss Alyce can feel them." McCall answered, still only an inch from his side. "Before first light, she told the children to disappear into the wagons. I thought I'd better warn you now, in case they are within hearing distance by the time you get the horses harnessed."

"I don't see anyone," Sloan tried to reassure McCall. "Alyce Wren just feels them? What kind of alarm is that? Yesterday the old woman told Winter she could see him as a man. He would dance in moonbeams with a woman with sunshine hair. What kind of thing is that to tell the boy? The day before that she told me she could hear my soul pacing even while I was eating supper. You might want to look for a more reliable source."

McCall looked at him as though he were the crazy one. "Miss Alyce is never wrong about her feelings. It's in her blood on her mother's side as far back as the Dark Ages. She can feel things all the way to her bones the way most folks feel with their fingers. It's a gift she's had since childhood. She showed up at my ranch the night before my father died and waited in the barn in case I needed her. Once he was dead, she came in the house without a word and did all the preparations before a burial. If she feels company, we've got company."

Before Sloan had time to argue, riders broke the horizon.

He watched as a small patrol of eight men rode directly toward them. They wore dusty blue uniforms, and from the looks of them, it had been some time since they'd seen a fort.

Without moving, Sloan watched the captain pull ahead of the others. He didn't slow his horse until he was within twenty feet of them, kicking up dirt as he pulled his reins.

McCall slipped her fingers around Sloan's arm in a way that looked like a familiar wifely gesture. But he could feel her tense beside him.

"Mornin'!" the captain shouted in a friendly voice as he climbed down from his horse. "How are you folks this frosty sunrise?"

"Morning," Sloan answered, watching the man carefully. He'd learned years ago never to trust a man who offered his friendship too quickly.

The captain removed his hat and nodded first at Sloan, then McCall. "We saw your camp and thought you might have some coffee left. We've been riding all night trying to make it back to the fort, and our coffee rations ran out days ago."

McCall smiled in an almost shy way. "Of course." She moved toward the coffeepot. "We have plenty since the others died."

The captain stopped so fast he looked as though he'd frozen instantly. "Others?" the words echoed from him.

Sloan shook his head, not believing McCall was trying to pull such a lame trick.

"There were seven of us heading north to a ranch just before you reach Indian territory. A fever hit us the third day out, killing all but my husband and me. And one of the children, of course, who is in the wagon burning with the sickness now."

To Sloan's surprise, the captain believed her lie. He backed away as if afraid to breathe the air near them any longer. "You folks are a long way from any fort." He seemed to be debating telling them to turn around, but that would mean they would be headed the same direction as the patrol. "I . . . I hope you find that ranch you're looking for."

"Don't worry, Captain." McCall smiled so sweetly she looked more like a girl than a woman. "You're in no danger. My husband and I aren't sick. And we'll gladly share the coffee for any news about what's to the north."

He didn't seem to want to believe her now. "I'd best be riding. All I can tell you folks is there's trouble north. I'd keep my guns oiled and ready." He tipped his hat at Sloan. "This is no land to be bringing a woman into, but I guess you got your reasons."

"I do," Sloan answered.

McCall slipped her hand back on Sloan's arm and waved as the captain climbed into his saddle.

Sloan watched in disbelief as the soldiers rode away. When they were well out of hearing range, he turned to McCall. "I can't believe they fell for such a story. Didn't he even think about how strange it looked for the two of us to be traveling in two wagons?"

Her face bore none of the satisfaction he expected. Instead, her eyes were dark and rimmed with tears. "It wasn't all a lie," she whispered. "Another reason I came to find you was to tell you one of the children is sick. Miss Alyce is holding her in the wagon now so she wouldn't cry out while the soldiers were here."

Six

BY NOON THREE of the children were ill with fever. Sloan rode ahead until he found an embankment that curved into itself, allowing them to pull the wagons close and have protection from the wind on three sides. He sent the older children to find as much wood as they could. Then he cut tall grass and spread it beneath the wagons for bedding.

Pulling out all the boxes of supplies, he braced them against the far side of the wheels to help keep any wind off and hold the fire's heat. Winter helped him use a horse to carry the water barrel almost a mile to the nearest stream to be refilled. When they returned, the other children had collected so much firewood it almost made a wall in front of the vee'd wagons.

While the others made camp, Sloan saddled one of the extra horses and circled from as far out as a fire might be seen to make sure they were safe. After half an hour, he knew he'd chosen the location wisely. The wagons disappeared into the terrain, and the ragged edges of cliffs beyond made any smoke blend with the gray-colored rocks.

At nightfall, when he headed back, he had a strange sense of coming home as he neared the campsite. Everyone was huddled into the space between the wagons with the fire in the center. McCall had untied the wagon tarps and roped them above with rawhide strips so that they formed an awning between the wagons, with plenty of holes for smoke to pass.

After he unsaddled his horse, Sloan rubbed the bay down before joining the others by the fire. To his surprise, rabbits were cooking on spits and Miss Alyce was stirring a pot of stew.

"What's this?" he asked as he stepped into the space that almost had the atmosphere of a teepee now. The smell of food and the warmth of the fire were thick in the air.

McCall looked up from where she sat feeding a child. "Supper."

Sloan grinned. She was starting to be as tight with words as he was. "I know," he said. "Rabbit. But how? I didn't hear a shot."

McCall pointed with her spoon toward the little girl across from her. "Morning Dove can kill rabbits with rocks."

Sloan looked at the child, who offered him a stick of meat with pride.

"Thank you," he said, wishing he knew her words. "I'm very grateful."

He leaned over and smelled Alyce's stew. An odor akin to rotting livers assaulted his nose. For a moment, he thought he might have found the reason Miss Alyce Wren remained a "miss." Cooking didn't seem to be one of her talents. Looking up at the old woman, he said, "I think I'll just have the rabbit." He moved away from the odor before he breathed again.

Miss Alyce laughed. "The potion's not for you, young fellow. It's to put on the children." She lifted the pot and moved to the opening of the shelter. "I'll cool this off in the moonlight. I'm in no mood to have folks turning up their noses at my potions. These potions have pushed away many a fever in my father's time and mine."

Sloan sat down beside McCall. He could hear Alyce still mumbling in the darkness beyond the fire, so he whispered to McCall, "How sick are the children?"

"We've three with fevers and two more who don't look so well. Alyce says she's not sure what it is, but she thinks we'd best stay here a day or two. Camped, we can keep them warm and doctored. On the road, that would be hard to do. If we got caught out in bad weather, it could mean pneumonia for any already running a fever."

"I agree." Sloan took a bite of his supper. "We're protected on three sides here; so except for the water supply, this is a great place. The sky to the north looks darker every hour. Even without the fever I'd suggest staying here for a while."

He glanced at McCall. Dark circles had formed beneath her blue eyes, and her shoulders weren't the military straightness he'd always seen. "Is there anything I can do? You look exhausted."

She shook her head. "No, we just have to wait out the fever. Miss Alyce brought dried herbs with her in case of trouble such as this." She looked at him with eyes that made him wish he could think of more answers. "We seem so alone out here. So very alone."

Sloan slowly reached and covered her hand with his. "Pray we are," he whispered. "For all our sakes."

Their glances met in the firelight, and he thought he saw a touch of fear in McCall's eyes. Fear from a woman who seemed made of granite? Maybe the fever was not something she thought she knew how to fight. Maybe the endless hours were catching up with her.

Without a word, McCall pulled her hand away. He

didn't try to hold on, though he felt a need to touch her just a moment longer than she seemed willing to allow. If she were crumbling, she wanted to do so alone.

Looking into the fire, Sloan decided he'd be wise to change the subject. "How'd Miss Alyce learn so much about doctoring?"

McCall resumed feeding the child. "Her father was a doctor in Mexico. Folks say he was so rich he owned land on both sides of the Rio. When Texas fought for independence, he sided with the revolution and lost almost everything, including all his family except Alyce Wren."

Sloan leaned closer as McCall continued, "My grandfather said Alyce's father had a little box of a wagon and traveled around doctoring when needed. He delivered me, then fought for three days without sleep to save my mother. When he couldn't save her, my grandfather said he cried like a child. After that he took Alyce Wren with him and started wandering across Texas, looking for answers. He learned some of the Indian ways of doctoring. But in the end, he grew sadder and sadder because there were so many people he couldn't save. My father said once that Alyce's father had too soft a heart to live on this earth. Alyce thinks he was a knight who finally got tired of fighting invisible dragons."

Sloan didn't move. He wasn't sure if he needed to hear more of the story, or if he just liked the idea that they were talking.

McCall finished feeding the child and held the little one tightly in her arms. "Alyce thought her father was a great man and never left his side. She acted as his nurse, cook, and driver for years. By the time he died she was an old maid and penniless. My grandfather never forgot the way her father had cried. When they built the stage station a few years later, he paid for the second floor with the understanding that Miss Alyce could live in a room there as long as she liked. At first she only spent the winters. In the summers no one really knew where she went in that little wagon of hers. As the years passed, her stays became longer and longer. Since the war, I don't think she's left the station except on day trips. She's always claimed she didn't have the 'gift' like her father did, but sometimes people still ask her advice. There's not a house within a hundred miles that she's not welcome in, or a man under fifty she doesn't order around as if he were a boy."

"An interesting lady." Sloan accepted a cup of coffee from one of the children. The warmth through the tin cup felt good on his hands . . . almost like a handshake. "Do you think your grandfather loved her?"

McCall's head jerked up. Obviously the thought had never entered her mind. "Why would you say such a thing? My grandfather never said a word about loving her."

"He took care of her. Even after he died, sounds like he made sure she'd always have a place in the station to call home."

McCall tried to remember back to her childhood. There had been little talk of love in their home, mostly just duty and honor, and bravery. But as McCall thumbed through the memories of her life, Miss Alyce's face, aging with time, kept flipping up. She'd been there for every crisis. When someone was ill. She'd also been there for every joy. Never close enough to be family, but never out of the picture.

"Is that what you think love, is, taking care of someone?" McCall watched this man called Sloan and wondered what kind of life he came from. Somewhere there must have been a mother, a family, a home. But he'd never mentioned any time in his life but the war.

"Maybe." Sloan shifted uncomfortably. He usually

didn't spend much time talking about love, but he wanted to talk to this woman. He needed to talk about anything. He'd been silent too much of his life. "I noticed at first men speak about love with words of passion, but as they get older they communicate in words of caring. You know, like they want to spend the rest of their lives taking care of someone."

"Have you ever felt that way?"

Sloan shook his head and threw the coffee grounds in his cup into the fire. "No. I seem to have enough trouble taking care of myself.

"Maybe I no longer believe in love. Maybe I never did. Not even love for a cause. There's nothing worth fighting for, nothing worth living or dying for, when you get right down to it."

McCall stood and carried the child in her arms to the bedroll beneath the wagon. She didn't look at him as she moved. He wondered if he'd disappointed her with his talk. She seemed to be searching for just what he didn't believe in. Something to live or die for.

Miss Alyce rattled back from the shadows, swinging her herb pot. "It's ready," she announced, as if she thought the children might line up for the smelly stuff.

Winter circled the fire away from Alyce and sat down beside Sloan. He didn't say a word, but looked as though he'd been elected to the spot.

Sloan nodded at the boy. "Can you get the water tomorrow? I need to scout around and make sure we're alone."

"Sure," Winter answered.

"We're alone," Alyce said as she frowned at Sloan. "I'd feel it in my bones if anyone was watching. So you get some sleep tonight, young fellow."

Sloan looked up and was amazed to find she was talking to him, not Winter. He opened his mouth to comment, but thought better, wishing he could see the Alyce of long ago. Fifty, even thirty years ago, she might have been a striking woman with less weight on her and fewer wrinkles. If Mc-Call's grandfather had loved her he'd kept quiet about it, but Sloan guessed Alyce knew. From the way McCall talked about her family, Alyce wouldn't have fit in, but that might not have stopped the love from growing.

"I'll still keep watch, though you feel safe," he mumbled as he grabbed an extra blanket and stepped from the flimsy shelter. It was warm between the two wagons, but he felt crowded. Walking thirty feet away, he sat down on a grassy spot where he'd left his gear and relaxed against his saddle. With the blanket beneath him and his coat slung over him, he was warm enough.

The day had been endless. He'd thought a few times of talking to McCall about turning back and waiting until spring. This was crazy, to head across open land in December. He'd heard men talk about how the weather this far north could change so fast a man would freeze before he could find enough wood to build a fire.

Sloan pulled his hat low and folded his arms across his chest. Stretching his legs out, he crossed his boots at the ankle and tried to sleep.

But Satan's Seven rode through his dreams as they did every night. When he'd been in the Yankee prison, a pack of seven men ruled the camp from the inside. The guards were only soldiers who'd drawn the short straw and had to patrol the perimeters. Satan's Seven set the rules inside. They were a rough group of cutthroats who would stop at nothing to ensure their power. Sloan managed to avoid them most of the time, but when the recruiters came looking for men to join the Union army and serve on the frontier, he crossed the Seven.

The Union recruiter spent days talking to the prisoners,

convincing them that all they'd be doing was fighting Indians—they'd hold no weapon against a fellow southerner.
Satan's Seven saw it differently. They swore to find any
man who joined and cut out his heart while it still pounded.
To prove their point, they murdered the first man who said
he'd join with the Yankees. After that the recruiter took his
converts from camp immediately. Sloan knew if Satan's
Seven were still alive, they were looking for him. Even
now.

Once in a while he would hear of a man being found
staked spread-eagle as the Seven would do, with his
heart cut completely out of his chest. Sloan wondered
and worried. He had changed in four years, shaved his
beard, gained a little weight, but they'd know him if they
saw him, just as he would know them. He had heard a
rumor once that three of the Seven were from Texas.
Maybe he'd come this direction because he was tired of
looking over his shoulder and wanted to finally face the
nightmares.

"Sloan?" McCall's voice interrupted his thoughts.

He leaned up, shoved his hat back, and watched her
walk through the darkness toward him.

"McCall," he answered in a low voice. "It's a little late
for a stroll."

She knelt beside him, so close he could feel her warm
breath. "I came to get your promise," she whispered.

"All right," Sloan answered. "You've got it."

McCall didn't laugh. "This is no light matter, sir."

"Nothing with you is, my general."

She placed her hand on his arm, and Sloan smiled,
thinking he was getting accustomed to her slight touch.
But he still couldn't keep his muscles from tightening as
the warmth of her hand passed through his shirt. He had
spoken the truth before. Whatever she asked him to

promise, he would. She had a manner about her that made "no" fall out of his vocabulary.

"You have to promise me that you'll go on as soon as the children can travel. Miss Alyce says she knows the way. She believes the rest of Black Kettle's people are deep into the Palo Duro Canyon, where caves offer shelter and the stream never freezes. She says all we have to do is reach the south rim of the canyon and follow it. The tribe will find us from there."

"Why didn't you tell me this before?"

"It wasn't necessary for you to know." She lowered herself beside him, bracing her side against the saddle where his head had been only a moment ago.

"Right, General," he answered, harsher than he'd intended. How many times had he not known where he was headed until all hell broke loose? You'd think he'd be used to it by now.

"I'm sorry," she sounded tired. "I just . . ."

Without finishing, she leaned against the saddle he'd been using for a pillow and lowered her face.

"McCall?" Sloan brushed her shoulder. "McCall, are you all right?"

She didn't answer.

He pushed her hair back and touched her face.

"McCall?" Pulling her into his arms, he brushed his cheek to hers.

With sudden panic, Sloan lifted her up and walked through the darkness toward the camp, yelling for Miss Alyce.

"What?" the old woman answered, running from the shelter. "Stop that yelling or you'll wake the children and anyone within a hundred miles."

Sloan moved into the light and lowered his voice only slightly. "She's got the fever."

To his utter surprise, Miss Alyce turned her back and began wetting strips of cloth with her potion. "I know that, young man. I've been watching her for hours. I also knew there was no use in trying to make her stop until she dropped. Not my McCallie. She could outrun the wind, that one, when she was a child. I can't say she's slowed down much over the years."

Sloan lowered McCall onto a blanket. She looked almost peaceful in sleep and that frightened him more than the fever. "Do something," he ordered Alyce, who still seemed far more interested in her work than in McCall.

The old woman looked at him with eyes as hard as a tombstone. "I'm not in the habit of helping folks with no wish to live. She's been running and fighting every battle she can to get herself killed. I guess now is as good a time as any. I'm too old and tired to fight both her and Death's Angel. If she dies, she gets her wish. Death comes to us all. You should know that by now, young fellow."

Sloan couldn't believe what he was hearing. "You're her friend! She told me you were there when she was born. You've helped her all her life."

"Well, I don't have time to help her now. I've got the children to think of. I'm not doctoring someone who longs to lie beside her husband. It's been three years since her man died and she's still wearing black. I guess we can bury her in it."

"You've got to help."

"I'm too old," Miss Alyce answered. "Maybe I love her too much to see her go on living, trying to walk in the shadow of her husband. He wasn't that good, anyway. Not like all of them thought. He was just a man. A man who cared more about honor and glory than he did about his wife. If he had cared, he would have brought my McCallie home and got her busy having babies instead of having her follow him from one battleground to another."

Sloan brushed the damp hair off McCall's cheek. "We've got to do something."

"No, young man." Alyce Wren crossed her arms. "*You* got to do something. 'Cause I'm not lifting a hand."

He had a feeling there was little time to argue. "What do I do, old woman?" He decided he'd strangle Alyce Wren after he helped McCall.

Alyce smiled a wicked smile that made Sloan more angry, but he held his tongue.

"First, you take her between the wagons. There's a space there that will be warm enough and out of the way of the children. I don't want them seeing her sick. They have enough to worry about."

Sloan lifted McCall as he stood. "Then you start washing her down with cool water. Not so cold she gets the chills, but cool enough to bring the fever down. Once she's resting comfortably, lay a few strips of these over her chest." Alyce handed him a cotton strip she'd soaked in her pot of herbs. "When she heats up again, wipe her down with the water. When she wakes, try and get her to drink. I'll make some of that tea she likes if I have time."

"That's all?" Sloan moved slowly toward the space where the two wagons formed a vee. "What else?"

"That'll keep you busy, young man." Alyce took several blankets and followed him. "Except if she dies, I'm holding you responsible."

The old woman didn't help him spread out the blankets, but tossed them on a pile of dried grass and walked away, leaving Sloan to fend for himself.

He lowered McCall against one of the wheels and spread the blankets. Then he rolled his jacket into a pillow.

When he lowered her onto the bed he'd made, she moaned softly and whispered, "Promise."

"I don't need to promise," he mumbled as he worked. "You're not dying on me, General, and that's an order."

Seven

MCCALL MADE NO protest as Sloan removed first her jacket, then her blouse. Calling her name, he tried to coax her into opening her eyes, but the fever had clouded her mind. He swore angrily at the softness of her skin and the beauty of her body laced beneath a thin camisole. He told himself he didn't want to touch her, that he was only doing what was necessary. Sloan couldn't stop himself from circling the wet cloth gently over her flesh even though he was sure he'd done it enough.

Again and again he dipped the cloth in the pan of cool water and moved it over her forehead, face, and arms. The night grew colder, but she still burned with fever beneath his touch. Alyce brought tea and helped him remove McCall's heavy skirt and boots to make her more comfortable under the blanket. But the old woman wouldn't stay. She seemed determined to leave McCall's life in Sloan's care.

He tried to explain that he was no nurse. His hands were awkward and calloused. Alyce turned a deaf ear and McCall seemed beyond hearing. So Sloan did his best with sometimes clumsy, sometimes frustrated, but always persistent attempts.

Finally, near dawn, McCall cooled slightly and he

tossed the cloth in the pan of water for the last time. Lifting her up, he began wrapping the strips of smelly cloth around her rib cage. McCall's head leaned against his chest as he worked. The light of the campfire danced off her creamy camisole, making it almost transparent.

Slowing his progress, Sloan told himself not to look at her. But how could a man deny the perfection in his arms? He'd seen a few overly made-up, underdressed saloon girls in his day. He'd seen paintings, mostly over bars, of nude women. But he'd never seen anything like McCall in his life.

Sloan closed his free hand into a fist, determined not to touch her. She'd made it plain she wanted no part of any advance he might make. A woman like her would never allow a man such as him to hold her. She hadn't let his hand rest on hers earlier when they'd sat by the campfire. How would she react if she knew he was so near now?

But he was holding Heaven. His fingers still closed in a fist, Sloan brushed her throat with his knuckles. Slowly, as if fighting a battle he couldn't win, his fist moved lower to the skin of her shoulders and along her bare arm. The warmth of her flesh was setting his blood afire.

Sloan felt as if he had twice the fever of McCall. He lowered his hand and held her against his side, listening to her breath, filling his senses with the smell and feel of her.

When she moved against him, settling into a deeper sleep, Sloan raised his hand once more, but this time not in so tight a fist. Gently, he touched her face, stroking to her throat with the back of his hand. With light brushings, he ventured lower until his fingers rested in the valley between her breasts. He could feel her heart beating against his touch. The softness that lay on either side of his fingers pressed lightly against his hand with each breath she took.

"Touch her, young fellow," Alyce Wren whispered from

just behind Sloan. "You're already caressing her with your stare. Go ahead and see what she feels like."

He jerked his hand away and looked up. "What did you say?"

"I said touch her. She's a young woman. She needs to feel a man's caress, if only while she dreams."

"I can't," he answered.

"No matter how much you want to?" Alyce asked.

"No matter how much I want to," he answered. "She wouldn't welcome the touch if she were awake."

"How do you know? I think you sell yourself short. You're one of the valued ones in this life, just as she is. I knew it the moment I saw you. You're one of the few men I've ever seen who might just be worth enough to stand beside my McCallie." The old woman looked at him closely. "Or bed her," she mumbled.

"I know she doesn't want me within three feet of her," he answered bitterly, remembering that first night out when he'd tried to kiss her. "I know how she reacts, and you're crazy to suggest such a thing."

Alyce snorted a laugh. "I only wish I'd been more crazy in my life. McCall's never been allowed to be wild a moment in all her days. First that father of hers wouldn't let her. He made her march around the house like she was a little toy soldier and not a girl. Then her husband, who thought she'd enlisted when she married him. Now the worse jailer . . . herself. But there's a passion in her bloodline. A passion that needs a lover's touch."

"That's the way she wants it. It's not my place to change it, old woman." He couldn't believe Alyce Wren, who called herself McCall's friend, would suggest such a thing as him touching McCall while she slept. The beautiful general would probably shoot him if she knew he was even thinking of such a thing.

"Well, you'll have to change your mind if you're going to keep her alive, because I'm not doctoring her. Before this fever breaks she'll have to be bathed and cooled a dozen more times. The more of her you touch with that cloth the faster she'll cool. Then you'll have to keep the herb across her chest so she can breathe it. Hold her up from time to time so she can drink the tea. When her fever starts to cool, you'll have to keep her warm with your body."

Alyce folded her arms in challenge. "You're going to have to touch her, or she'll die, so there's no use you acting like I've asked you to commit a crime."

Without another word, Alyce lowered the blanket Sloan had rigged as a curtain from the others. He wanted to go after the old buzzard and shake her until her last few teeth fell out, but he couldn't leave McCall.

Dawn came and went in shaded light but Sloan didn't sleep. He did as the old woman had told him until his arms ached. Slowly, an inch at a time, he became used to her body, reacting to the need to help more than his need to touch. As the day passed he worked, bathing when she was hot, wrapping when she cooled, and forcing as much liquid down her as he could whenever she moaned.

By nightfall, he was too exhausted to move. If an army of men rode into the camp, he wasn't sure he had the energy to lift his Colt. Alyce checked on him now and again, telling him that two of the children's fevers had broken. But when he mentioned her helping, she informed him she still had no time and that McCall was in danger. He'd better stay close and keep doing the best he could.

Around midnight McCall slipped into a peaceful sleep and Sloan lay down beside her, curling around her still-hot body. He pulled the blankets to her chin and placed his arm across her shoulders to keep them there.

"Good night, General," he whispered, too tired to even care that she'd probably kill him for sleeping beside her if she lived.

They both slept until first light, McCall moved only a few times during the night, thrashing the covers off when her fever broke and pulling them near when her body cooled. Days of going without sleep caught up with Sloan. He moved instinctively to cover her without waking her, letting his hand slide over the blankets atop her breasts as though he'd touched her a thousand times.

The light filtered into their tiny space. Sloan could hear the children waking just beyond the blanket curtain. McCall moaned in her sleep and his arms pulled her into their warmth.

"Shhh," he whispered, moving his arm beneath the layers of wool. "Sleep now, General."

His hand moved along her bare shoulder and arm. McCall sighed again at the dream she was enjoying and turned slightly. Sloan's next passing captured her breast with a gentle stroke. The light camisole did nothing to bar the warmth of his hand as his fingers molded around her flesh.

McCall bowed her back slightly so that she pressed harder against his open palm. His hand fit her breast to perfection.

Somewhere in the midnight of sleep, Sloan's mind fought to awaken. At first he thought he was dreaming, but he'd never had such a dream. The feel of her full breast beneath his touch was too real. He moved his fingers slowly, caressing the peak beneath the silk, testing the fullness, enjoying the softness.

She rocked, pressing herself hard against his hand, and Sloan came full awake. In the shadowy light he could see McCall relaxed in sleep only inches from him. She looked like an angel, with her face so pale and her dark hair fanned out around her. Her hands rested just above her head as her body rocked in pleasure against him.

She sighed softly and moved again, begging him to continue touching her.

Sloan closed his fingers once more around the perfect mound. He pressed his palm against the center and circled, tugging at the tender flesh.

McCall made a sound almost like that of a cat content in the sunshine. Her lips parted slightly in sleep.

He stroked again and her mouth opened more . . . begging to be kissed.

The heat within Sloan felt like it might explode through his skin. He'd never touched anything so soft, so full, so addictive to feel. A hunger to place his mouth where his hand rested was greater than any hunger he'd ever known. He wanted to taste the peak with his tongue and tug against her softness with his open mouth.

He brushed the thin silk aside, loving the softness beneath . . . loving the way she responded. All his life he'd been afraid to touch people. A simple handshake was something he did with a moment's hesitation. And women—women were definitely off limits. He could never bring himself even to think of forcing himself on a woman as he'd seen other soldiers do. He didn't figure many respectable women would welcome his advances. So he was left thinking he'd live his life without such pleasure. But McCall was accepting his touch as a gift, responding to it with only joy.

Hesitantly, he kissed her forehead and smiled as he realized the fever had passed. She wasn't delirious. With his lips still brushing her temple, he moved his hand again, enjoying the bolt of pleasure that shot through his arm and filled his body with lightning's fire.

She leaned against him, pressing the length of him. He

stroked her breast with slightly more pressure, and she moved once more. Slowly, like a man learning an instrument one string at a time, he played across her breast, responding to her moves of pleasure with more of what her entire body seemed to be begging him for.

Her arms stretched above her head to give him full range of the needy mounds. He kissed her on the cheek gently in thanks, tasting her skin with the tip of his tongue. This gift she was so willing to give him was more priceless than she'd ever know. His hand slid across her chest to her other breast and tugged at the material still covering what he longed to touch. He fanned his fingers over the silk and pressed, branding her lightly with his touch. When she didn't respond, he cupped her breast and tightened his grip slightly, capturing the warm fullness in his hand.

She moaned with the pleasure he'd waited to hear. But he didn't pull the material away. He wanted to make her move against him once more with only a light touch. He wanted her mouth to open again and silently beg for more. His palm circled above her camisole in feather-light brushes while his fingers stroked the side of her silk-covered breast until her head turned back and forth as though pleading for more. Tightening his grip, he smiled at the response she gave. He was stirring a fire deep within her with his touch, and he planned to enjoy every step as it built.

Slowly, he pulled the material from her breast and covered her peak with his lips. She moaned once more and began to move her entire body in a rhythm against him as he sucked gently at her tender flesh.

Sloan leaned above her and cupped the sides of her breasts as he tasted first one, then the other. He was so close he could feel her body moving beneath his, but he didn't lower himself. His fingers fumbled with the ribbons

of her camisole until he pulled them free and exposed her
chest to the waistband of her petticoat. For a long moment
he could only stare. She was so beautiful she took his
breath away. No, he thought, she took far more than that.
The sight of her shoved all thought, all reason from his
mind. How could he ever tell her that the look of her was
the first beauty he'd ever seen in this world?

Slowly his hands spread wide and moved from shoulder
to waist. She arched her back with each passing, and with
each passing he increased the pressure over her breasts,
loving the way she welcomed him. Alyce had been right,
he thought, a passion did run in her blood. A passion she
allowed to surface only while sleeping.

As she cried out softly when his fingers covered her,
Sloan lowered his weight over her body and captured her
open mouth with his. Mindless to all else but the feel of
her, the taste of her, he kissed her deeply and passionately.
When she moved beneath him, he raised his hands to her
hair and buried his fingers into the mass of softness about
her face.

Sloan's passion-drugged mind took a minute to register
that she was no longer moving in pleasure, but shoving and
pushing away from him.

He released her immediately and rolled to his side just
as the full blow of her fist slammed into his face.

She jerked away from him, pulling the blanket around
her as she stood. "How dare you!" she screamed as she
stumbled backward.

Sloan plowed his hand into his own hair and tried to get
his brain to work. Another few minutes and he would have
done what Alyce had talked about. He would have bedded
McCall.

"Alyce!" McCall shouted as she shoved her hair from
her eyes. "Bring me a gun!"

"McCall." Sloan stared at her in shock. She looked like an angry warrior searching for a knife to scalp him. "McCall, I was just . . ."

She pulled the blanket closer. "Don't tell me what you were doing. I'm fully aware of the fact that you were raping me. I plan to kill you and leave your body for the buzzards to feast on. Alyce! The gun!"

All the words Sloan knew were logjammed in his mind. "I hadn't planned . . . I didn't mean to . . . I was only doing . . ."

"Spare me, sir. I'm no virgin you stumbled across after a battle. I know what you were trying to do." She looked down. "Where are my clothes? What have you done to me already?" She raised her voice one notch above her hysteria. "Alyce, bring me the gun!"

Sloan stood. "I thought you were enjoying it as much as I was."

McCall was so angry she forgot about the blanket and stormed at him.

She was so beautiful he forgot to duck.

The blow almost knocked him down.

"I told you I'm dead inside. *Dead!* Do you understand that? What makes you think I'd welcome you on top of me?"

Sloan rubbed his jaw. "Well, asleep you're not dead. You may have thought you were dreaming, but you were sure enjoying the dream. You can tell yourself you're dead all day, but that body responding was very much alive to my every touch."

McCall pulled the blanket up. "You touched me!"

"You know I did."

"Where?"

"Everywhere, just about." Sloan wasn't going into detail about where he'd touched her. Not while she was in a killing mood. "You were sick with the fever. I had to bathe you or you would have died."

McCall's voice lowered to a deadly level. "You call fondling me and lying atop me taking care of my fever? Rather odd nursing."

Sloan felt an embarrassed flush climbing up his collar. "Well, no. That just happened. Before I was bathing you with a rag to keep you cool and trying to get tea down you. I had to hold you most of the past two nights to keep you warm." He was so tired he wasn't even making sense to himself, so he knew he had no hope of convincing her.

"And why were you touching me just now? To heat me back up?"

"No, I . . ."

"You were what?" she snapped. "Trying to keep me warm with a blanket of your body? Or breathing heat into me with your hot kiss? Or were you sucking on my skin to pull heat from me?"

"Alyce!" Sloan yelled. "Bring the woman the damn gun so she can shoot me. I'm tired of arguing with her."

They both opened their mouths to scream the old woman's name again, then both suddenly stopped.

McCall stomped in anger and dropped the blanket as she turned her back to him and began lacing up her camisole. "I'll get the gun myself. Alyce must have gone deaf. I can have you dead and buried before she answers."

"Why turn around?" Sloan figured if he was already sentenced to death there was no harm in asking for a last request. "I've already seen you—and felt you rather thoroughly, for that matter. You might as well let me watch you dress now."

"I'll shoot you in the legs and let you watch yourself die." McCall didn't turn around. "I've never been handled so. I can still feel places where you kissed my body."

"What places?"

McCall shot him a stare that was meant to wound. "Murdering you is too peaceful a way to allow you to die after what you did. You know very well what places."

"So you do remember." At this point he didn't care if she shot him as long as he could take the memory of her in his arms with him to the afterlife. "Then you must know you were enjoying every touch, every kiss."

She glanced over her shoulder. "I thought I was dreaming. All I want to recall now is the way you will look bleeding from several bullet holes."

"You were loving the way I caressed you," Sloan teased. "Every time my fingers tightened, you—"

"I was not."

"You were moving against me, begging for more," he whispered, figuring if he was about to be shot he might as well enjoy the last few minutes of life. "Your nipples got so hard every time my hand—"

The panful of water flew toward him.

Sloan ducked.

"Every time, time and again, as my fingers—"

McCall's fist swung.

Sloan ducked this time and grabbed her around the waist, pulling her against him so she couldn't swing again.

"You were so soft," he whispered against her hair, knowing his words were making her madder. "The softest things I've ever felt, or tasted."

"And you, sir, are no gentleman to mention such a thing." She fought to hit or kick him.

"Things," he corrected as she struggled. "There were two, as I remember. No woman in all of time could have tasted as good as you did." He pinned her still against him and whispered, "The feel of you moving against me almost drove me mad."

McCall's words were whispered between clenched teeth. "I hate you with every drop of blood in me."

"I thought you couldn't feel?" he whispered again, so near her ear his cheek brushed hers.

"I was wrong. I hate you and what you did to me while I was asleep."

"You felt the same need I did, McCall. You wanted me to touch you. In your dreaming, you were begging for more. You're more angry with yourself than me."

"No!" she screamed and struggled free of his arms. "I only want you dead and out of my life. I've never been so dishonored. If my father or the major were alive, they'd kill you for me."

Sloan reached between the wagon wheel's spokes and pulled his Colt from its holster. "Then shoot me. But I didn't do anything you didn't want me to do. And I wasn't dishonoring you."

McCall took the gun and raised it to his chest. As she braced herself for the kick, the sound of footsteps, running fast toward her from somewhere beyond the curtain, reached her ears.

"Mrs. McCall!" Winter shouted. "Mr. Sloan!"

Sloan turned and lifted the curtain as Winter fell into the area. McCall lowered the gun to her side so the boy wouldn't see it.

"Come quick!" he said between gulps of breaths. "Miss Alyce took us all down to the stream at sunup. When it got light, I saw a full band of Apaches camped not a mile from us." He stood and held his side. "And they're dressed for war."

Sloan grabbed his coat and tossed it to McCall, then lifted the rifle from the wagon seat.

As McCall slipped into his coat, he took the Colt from her hand.

For a second their gazes met. Fiery anger mirrored the spark of passion still in his eyes.

Slowly her finger moved from the trigger. She whispered, "I'll kill you later."

Eight

SLOAN CROSSED THE shallow creek bed and slid through the mud behind Winter until they could just see over the far bank. A half mile down, near a bend in the creek, a dozen young braves waited as if for a signal. A few were tending their horses, but most just stood watching the far horizon.

"They're breaking camp," Winter whispered. "I'm the one who spotted them when Miss Alyce told us to wash up this morning."

Glancing at the boy, Sloan doubted he'd washed in days, maybe even weeks. His hair was starting to resemble roots growing out of his head, and his face looked as if it had been layered in brown war paint.

Winter and Sloan watched as the Apache mounted.

"They're traveling too light to be hunting," the boy whispered. "If they were after game, they'd have a few packhorses for the meat."

Nodding, Sloan watched silently.

"You think they might be tracking that troop of soldiers we saw the other day?"

"Maybe," Sloan mumbled. "But if they are, they're far behind the army and they seem in no hurry. If they were trying to make up time, they'd have left at first light, not full sunup."

"Maybe they're hunting us?" Winter whispered.

Sloan shook his head. If the Apache had been after the wagons, they'd have taken them by now. There was a chance that the war party hadn't noticed the wagons, but more than likely a scout had seen them and thought Sloan and his little band were not worth the trouble. To the fearless Apache, two wagons of women and children must seem no more bother than gnats.

Reminding himself they were past the hundredth parallel and all Indians would be considered hostile by any army, Sloan checked his Colt. This was the land where both soldiers and braves thought of life as cheap and both sides kept score in body count.

"We going to fight, mister?" Winter's eyes sparkled with excitement. "I never did have much fondness for Apache. I'll stand with you to the end."

Sloan smiled, knowing the boy was just repeating a phrase he'd heard someone say. "They're not bothering us," Sloan whispered. "I see no need to bother them. It's not worth risking your life."

"But we'd fight them if they come?"

"Not unless we had to," Sloan corrected. "There's not much in this world worth fighting for, or dying for. I've seen men fight over words and die over which flag flies in a field. In the end, they all thought they were right, and they were all just as dead."

Winter looked at Sloan and raised his chin slightly. "When I'm a man I'll fight for what's mine. No one will take anything away from me. I'll have a camp that only a man with a death wish will enter unwelcomed."

Sloan nodded once. "You do what you think is right, Winter. That's the best any man can do. But don't make a lot of noise about what you'll do someday. Do what has to be done and be finished with it. Don't waste any time telling folks what you're going to do or making tales out of what you did."

"I'll remember that, mister," Winter promised. "But could you tell me what we are going to do now? If we're not going to fight and die, I need to get some food. Hunger's been wrestling my stomach for an hour."

Sloan smiled and acted like he didn't hear the slight crack in the little boy's voice. "We're going to crawl back across that creek and get the others. If they do come, we can defend ourselves better back at the wagons."

Winter nodded. "I'll lead them."

"And I'll follow when everything is safe. Until then, I think I'll stay here. If I should yell out or fire a shot, you make the others run as fast as they can to the wagons and don't look back."

"Mister?"

"Yes." Sloan glanced at the boy, already several feet away.

"I'm glad I didn't slit your throat when I had the chance."

"So am I," Sloan answered, thinking that he now had one less person who wanted to kill him.

After several hours, Sloan watched the Apache disappear to the east and guessed that the children were safe. The scouting party might be looking for war, but they seemed willing to leave him alone. If he were guessing, he'd have said they were waiting for something or someone who never showed up. But what, or who, would meet a band of warriors out here in the middle of nowhere?

He stood and walked slowly back to the wagons.

When he was within ten feet, Winter appeared at the entrance to their makeshift fort. "Are they gone?"

"Yes," Sloan said and noticed the disappointment in the boy's eyes. "You weren't looking to fight, were you, son?"

"No." Winter kicked at the rocks. "Mrs. McCall just told me that I had to go down to the creek and take a bath if we were safe. I was kind of hoping we were still in a little danger."

Sloan laughed. "A bath wouldn't hurt you much."

Winter shot him an angry stare. "It wouldn't do you any harm either, mister."

Sloan looked down at his muddy clothes. The boy was right. He'd been so worried about the Apache he'd forgotten about how much dirt he must have collected crawling around the creek bank. "Tell you what," he winked at Winter, "you take a bath now, then I'll leave you on guard here at the wagons while I take one later."

Winter smiled. "Agreed."

The boy ran off toward the creek as Sloan moved into the light of the campfire. Alyce handed him a cup of coffee, and one of the children gave him a plate of food. He could see McCall moving about in her little space between the wagons, but she didn't look at him.

He smiled, thinking how she'd react if he asked if he could sleep beside her again tonight. His shoulders felt tight from waiting for the bullet he'd half expected she'd fire all day. He guessed the only thing keeping her from shooting him was the fact that gunfire might draw more attention than they wanted right now.

He waited several minutes for her to look in his direction, or come close enough so that he could talk to her, but she never did. Winter returned, his hair dripping. The boy looked several shades of brown lighter and his hair was brown, not black as Sloan had thought.

Winter stationed himself at the entrance to their camp.

Crossing his arms, he stared at Sloan. "It's your turn now. Be sure and take some soap."

Sloan wanted nothing more than to curl up on the ground and go to sleep, but he'd told the boy he'd bathe. He guessed Winter cared more about being left in charge than about anyone else's cleanliness, so Sloan would keep his word.

Grabbing one of the blankets to use as a towel and his only clean set of clothes, Sloan moved away from the warmth and toward the creek.

McCall watched him go out of the corner of her eye. She'd made a grand effort to not look at him, but he'd never been out of her line of vision since he'd returned.

She'd spent the day alternately wishing him dead and worrying about his safety. By now she'd come to the conclusion that she was completely mad. Never had anything upset her so. Her life had always been black or white, right or wrong. Sloan had introduced gray.

While the children bedded down, McCall lifted the rifle from its resting place on the wagon seat. She'd lived all her life by rules. Rules never broken. Rules never compromised. Infringements never tolerated. The voices of her grandfather, her father, her husband were clear in McCall's mind. She had to take action.

Silently, she moved through the darkness to the creek.

The air was cold against her cheeks. The moon full and bright. Tears bubbled in her eyes, but she wouldn't let them fall. She had to complete her mission, no matter how painful. If Sloan had been right . . . if he hadn't been raping her . . . then she had felt something—and McCall had sworn never to feel anything good again.

She slowed and shoved a stray strand of hair from her eyes. What did it matter? she wondered. Had he attacked her or made her want to live again? One was as bad as the other. If she were alive again, she'd have to feel, and if she felt she'd only be hurt. No one was ever going to hurt her again. She'd already lived her lifetime of hurt, and now all she wanted to do was feel nothing.

"A good soldier does what's right without feelings being involved," she reminded herself aloud.

As she neared the creek, she saw Sloan standing in waist-deep water. His hands were in his hair, scrubbing. Pale soapsuds haloed his head as McCall raised the rifle.

The first shot hit the water a foot from Sloan, and he dove backward. A second seemed even closer, as he swam toward a tree that sloped along the shoreline. A third shattered the bark of his hiding place.

Then silence.

McCall jerked at the rifle's handle, but the weapon jammed. Frantically she worked, trying to make the lever shove the next bullet forward. But the darkness and her panicked fingers didn't cooperate. Despite all her days with her husband, she'd handled a rifle very little. She could take a handgun apart in the dark, but a rifle had always been a bother, too heavy to hold for long and bruising her shoulder unless she held it just right. Suddenly, she wished she'd taken the time to learn.

Tears streamed down her face. Frustrated, angry tears that blurred her vision.

A twig snapped behind her and she heard the loose, rocky ground being scuffed.

McCall turned, preparing to face an angry Sloan. She'd use the rifle as a club if she had to.

But before her eyes could focus on the form behind her, a fist slammed into her cheek, shattering the silence with its impact and sending stars across her brain. The useless rifle fell away as she closed her arms around her face for protection.

Another blow struck with no more warning than the first. McCall tumbled into the grass and rolled along the incline leading to the creek. As she rolled she could hear someone storming toward her, grabbing at her clothes, trying to pull her back.

She shoved herself further, fighting away from each grasp.

A low voice swore as huge hands grabbed her by the throat and stopped her flight.

"I'll teach you to shoot at me!" he yelled as the shadow jerked her to him and raised his hand in anger once more.

McCall screamed and jerked with all her power away from the hand that swung toward her.

His fist grazed her cheek, missing its mark by a fraction of an inch. He twisted his hand around the material of her blouse, ripping the buttons and seams as he pulled.

"Stand still and take it!" he grumbled. "I'll show you what I do to trash who try to kill me! You'll be wishing you were dead soon."

McCall's feet slipped on the wet grass as she fought to break free. The shadow's hand raised again to deliver another blow, and this time his hold was too strong to pull away from.

Closing her eyes, McCall fought at the arm that gripped her with one hand while she tried to deflect the coming blow with the other. She bit down hard on her bottom lip as her own scream exploded inside her.

Suddenly, the fist was loosened from the material across her chest. She opened her eyes in time to see her attacker being pulled backward by another.

For a moment she wanted to shout to her savior to stop. For if it was Alyce Wren or Winter, they would be no more a match for an insanely angry Sloan than she was.

McCall staggered forward and watched the two struggling. The attacker and her defender were equal in height, the defender slimmer and bare-chested, the attacker bearded and barrel-chested. Whoever was fighting her attacker was far too tall to be Miss Alyce or Winter.

Suddenly, her defender had the upper hand, pinning the larger man to the ground. She could hear the bearded man being choked until his breath seemed almost gone. He fought wildly, but the bare-chested man seemed stronger.

"Had enough?" Sloan shouted from above the man. "I've no wish to kill you."

The man on the bottom relaxed and Sloan slowly pulled back, allowing McCall to see for the first time the face of the man who'd hit her. He seemed more bear than human, with long scraggly hair and a beard fanning his face. A crimson line cut his cheek just below his left eye. Blood flowed into his beard like a tiny waterfall. His clothes marked him as a buckskinner, or maybe a buffalo hunter.

The man raised to one elbow and gripped his throat, choking out his words one at a time. "First she tries to shoot me and now you try to choke me. What kind of people are you folks?"

Sloan glanced at McCall with worry in his eyes. "Did he hurt you?"

McCall lied with a shake of her head.

He turned his attention to the stranger. "She wasn't shooting at you. She was shooting at me."

The man looked even more confused. "And you stopped me from killing her?"

Sloan's smile flashed white in the moonlight. "Does sound a little crazy, but I can't allow you to beat her even if she is trying to kill me."

"Are there any more of you folks around?" The mountain man retrieved his hat and slapped it against his leg.

Sloan and McCall exchanged a glance. "No," McCall said. "We're alone."

Moving slightly so that the view of the campsite would not be behind him when he spoke to the stranger, Sloan added, "That's right. My . . . wife and I are on our way to a ranch just south of the Indian territory. We had a little fight an hour back, and she was just taking out her anger while I took a bath."

"She could have killed you!" The stranger looked at Sloan as though he were a little too dense to be left alone.

"He'd be dead by now if I were trying to kill him. I'm a better shot than that," McCall added.

Sloan raised an eyebrow, telling her he remembered just how close she'd come.

The stranger watched Sloan closely. "Don't I know you? My name's Willis, but most call me Bull. I'm not real good with names, but I never forget a face."

Sloan looked back at the man, but in the moonlight he couldn't see beyond the beard. "No, I don't think so." He saw no point in giving his name.

"I never forget a man and you sure do look like we've crossed paths before," the man mumbled. "You fight for the North, or South?"

"North," Sloan answered slowly.

The stranger shook his head. "No, couldn't have been the war. I was a Reb. Spent most of the time in a Yankee prison. You weren't one of the guards or I'd remember you for sure. Their faces are tattooed on my brain. Since the war, I've been riding with some old buddies. There's money to be made in killing buffalo, if you can do it fast enough. I'd just stopped to water my horse, across the creek there, when your wife almost clipped my ear with her first shot."

The stranger took a step closer. "You been in Texas long?"

Sloan fought to not look away or step back. "No," he said.

Bull scratched his beard as though the action helped him think.

"I don't think we've ever met, Bull." Sloan's tone left no room for discussion. "I was on the frontier most of the time after the war, and I only arrived in Texas a short time ago."

The stranger seemed to stare closely, then suddenly moved restlessly. "Well, I don't want to come between a married couple." He glanced at McCall as if just remembering she was near. "Sorry to have hit your wife. I don't usually fight with women. Especially ones using bullets." He didn't seem to feel any need to say he was sorry to McCall. "I'll just be on my way."

"Where are you headed?" Sloan asked the question casually, almost.

"South," the man answered. "I was supposed to meet up with some men, but I reckon I'm a day late and a dollar short, as they say." The man's dark eyes stared hard at Sloan as he continued, "Who knows, they may be staked out somewhere, left to dry in the sun with their hearts cut out."

The stranger disappeared back into the night as quickly as he'd appeared.

Nine

SLOAN WATCHED THE mountain man walk back into the night. He knew that under normal circumstances travelers would offer to share a campsite. But Sloan hadn't offered and the stranger hadn't suggested. The Apache they'd seen at dawn came to mind, and Sloan wondered if they were the men the stranger had been expecting to find, or were they, like the mountain of a man, both waiting for someone else?

Instinctively, Sloan stepped in front of McCall in case a bullet should come out of the darkness from the direction the stranger had gone. Had the man's last words been just something he'd heard somewhere, or was he one of the Satan's Seven who'd ruled the prison camp years ago? The odds were that he wasn't, but Sloan couldn't be sure until he saw the man more clearly.

Sloan tried to relax, but he had the feeling, after three years, that his oldest nightmare was about to come to life. The image of the first Confederate to say he'd changed sides flashed in Sloan's memory. They had staked the man out near the front gate, blatantly showing their work to all the Union guards. The man's mouth was gagged and he had bloodied the ropes binding his hands and feet trying to pull free. His heart lay atop his chest, already collecting flies by the time the rest of the prisoners had awakened.

Glancing at McCall, Sloan pulled himself back to the present and whispered, "Let's get out of here tomorrow."

He didn't know if the man recognized him or not, but Sloan wasn't taking any chances.

McCall straightened her clothes. "That man almost killed me," she whispered. "He would have if you hadn't stopped him." Her hands shook as she moved them over the folds of her skirt. "He hit me!"

She reminded him of a first battle warrior . . . all brave during the fighting, then falling apart as soon as they realized they were safe.

"Let me take a look at that chin. I could hear the smack he gave you from across the creek."

McCall made no protest as Sloan touched her cheek and turned her face to the moonlight. The moon shone a lantern's worth of brightness.

"You've never been hit before, have you?" he asked, thinking of the times he'd been slugged by his stepfather, before the man kicked him out at fifteen. By then Sloan had reached a point where he'd stand and take the blows without giving his stepfather the satisfaction of knowing how much each one hurt.

"No," she answered. "No slaps and no hugs. That seemed to be my family's code of conduct. My father could punish with a look and reward with a word."

"Well, since you've had a hit tonight, how about the other—a hug?" Without thinking of how she might react, he opened his arms.

McCall moved into his embrace. He held her tightly, guessing that it wouldn't have hurt her father to have done so a few times.

"Thank you," she whispered against his shoulder as she pulled away. "For the hug and for saving my life."

Sloan lightly brushed at the bruise forming as if he could sweep away the pain. "You wouldn't have been in danger if you hadn't been shooting at me, so I guess the whole thing was my fault."

"I'm glad I missed." She stepped out of reach and he didn't try to stop her. *If* she ever allowed him to touch her again, he knew it would be of her doing and not from any advance he'd make. She was a person who had to set the boundaries, even in relating to another.

"I'm glad you missed, too," he answered. "Next time you try to kill me, you might think of borrowing Winter's knife. Maybe that way no one else will get involved in the murder. I hate it when strangers come uninvited to my killing." He smiled, but noticed she didn't catch the humor of his words.

"I don't think I'll try again." She held her chin up an inch, as if negotiating a deal. "If you'll promise to forget this morning ever happened, I'll promise I won't try to kill you."

"Nothing happened this morning," he lied, knowing he could never forget touching her. "Only don't be afraid of me, McCall. Half the time you act as though I'm going to grab you if you pass within five feet of me."

"Maybe I'm reacting from experience," McCall suggested. It was her turn to smile.

Sloan opened his mouth to argue, but she raised her hand in protest.

Taking a deep breath, he stepped another foot away from her. "I'll try once more." He bowed slightly. "I'd like to accept that friendship you offered me earlier. You saved my life the night we met, and maybe I saved yours just now." He didn't want to think about what might have happened if he hadn't been so close. "It's time we stopped looking at each other as the enemy."

McCall nodded. "All right," she finally said, "but you have to try to understand that I am the way I am, and you haven't the time to change me. Nothing you can do or Alyce Wren can say will make me any different than what I've become."

Sloan smiled and tried to make out her expression in the shadows. He lifted one eyebrow, thinking of both the women he knew who seemed to share this lovely body before him. One was as straight as any West Point officer he'd ever known, the other curved and molded to his touch.

He walked a few feet toward the creek and retrieved his shirt, thinking how he'd like to get to know both women better. When he returned, he handed her the rifle he'd found.

She accepted the weapon and watched as he pulled his shirt over a tightly muscled body. He hadn't been as big as the mountain man, but he'd been stronger. Suddenly, McCall was curious about this man she'd hired. "Have you fought in a great many battles?"

"A few," he said as he combed his wet hair back with his fingers.

She couldn't help but notice, even in the moonlight, the long scar that crossed over his shoulder from collarbone to arm. Another one cut just above the waistband of his pants.

When he glanced up and saw the direction of her gaze, he quickly closed his shirt and looked away, as though distancing himself from any questions about the scars.

"Most men talk about their battles." She'd grown up on dinner table conversations of war. The men in her family would never have seemed ashamed of a scar won in battle.

In fact her grandfather's favorite after-dinner game was to count the bullet holes in his leg he'd collected in the war of 1812.

"I never found killing a man something to brag about, and I'm not old enough to believe the war was an adventure." Sloan didn't look at her as he finished buttoning his shirt.

"Then why did you join?" she asked as she fell into step with him as they headed back toward the camp.

"My mother remarried when I was fourteen, and I didn't really belong at home anymore. I lied about my age and joined up, more for the three square meals than the glory of fighting."

He was silent for several steps, then added, "The three squares weren't too regular in coming. Supplies were always short when I fought for the South. In prison we were lucky to count one meal a day. And on the frontier, we were in the saddle before sunup and didn't stop until after dark. Most nights the cook was too tired to strike a fire. Some days I wasn't sure I was eating the dried meat he passed out, or my tack."

They were halfway back to the camp and both slowed as if wanting to prolong the conversation.

"Is your mother still alive?" McCall couldn't imagine a mother letting her son go to war early.

Sloan shrugged. "I'm not sure. The night I left she met me about a mile down the road with a knapsack and probably all the money she had. She handed me the food and told me not to ever come back. She had a new man and a new family on the way. There was no room for me."

"But didn't you write her, or return?"

"Once," he whispered. "The troop was passing through my hometown in Kansas, and I saw my mom come out of the mercantile not six feet from me. She had a baby in her arms and another one following behind her. I started toward her, but she moved away. She didn't recognize me. Or if she did, she wished she hadn't."

McCall could tell he was uncomfortable talking about himself and wondered if he'd ever told another what he was telling her now.

"But where do you call home?" She knew she was prying, but she had to ask.

"Anywhere, nowhere." Sloan shrugged. "Does it matter? An hour ago you were trying to kill me. Does it bother you that you wouldn't know where to send the body?"

McCall stepped slightly ahead of him so he could no longer see her face.

"No, I'd already had that planned out. I'd pack you in the back of the wagon and take you to the nearest town or fort. Then I'd put you in a crate, marked fragile, of course, and ship you to New Orleans. It's so hot down there, someone would smell you setting on the dock and they'd bury you for me."

"That's a plan? General, you're slipping."

"Or I thought of rolling you in the mud so thick you'd look like a log and then I'd tell the children you disappeared."

He caught up with her. "You're kidding? That's an even lamer idea."

The moment he looked in her eyes, he knew he was right. She was teasing him. "Maybe I'm not so easy to kill, General."

"That would be a change from every man I've ever met," she answered honestly. "Should I try again?"

"No." Sloan held the flap open for her to enter the campsite. "Not until you come up with a better way to dispose of my body."

They were both laughing as they stepped into the circle of light around the fire.

Alyce Wren looked up at the pair and huffed in anger. "You're both late for supper. I'm stuck out here in the middle of nowhere with folks who are no better than my tomcat at guessing what time to come in after dark. They leave with murder in their eyes and return laughing, when I'm the one who is doing all the work."

Sloan couldn't tell if Alyce Wren was sorry he'd touched McCall, or sorry McCall hadn't killed him. The old woman made him nervous, always looking at him as though she were waiting for him to do something. It almost seemed as if she'd read a book on his life and was just sitting around waiting for him to get to a page she found interesting.

Winter moved near Sloan as Sloan knelt to pour a cup of coffee. "Mr. Sloan?" he whispered.

"Yes, Winter."

"We've all been talking and we think Miss Alyce's mind may have flown a little close to the sun today. Some of it sure seems melted away. She's been talking to herself so much, half of the children have decided it's their eyes that have the problem and not Miss Alyce."

Sloan nodded, and the boy seemed relieved to have told an adult his problem.

"Want to help me pack up in the morning?" He handed the child a cup half full of coffee.

"We're leaving?" Winter took the drink.

"At first light. This place seems to be the crossroads. The sooner we make it to your mother the better. Every day we wait is just one more chance we'll hit bad weather."

Winter agreed. "I'm ready. My mother can't sleep without me close. She likes to pat my blankets a few times each night. I'm too old to need such comfort, but I let her. I bet she's missing me bad right about now. Since my father died, I'm all she's got in this world."

The boy swallowed hard and poked at the fire with a stick as if it were something important to do.

"Want to go out on watch with me tonight?" Sloan asked without looking too closely at Winter. The boy didn't need to add that his mother was all he had. "I get kind of lonesome out there by myself."

"All right." Winter stood. "I guess I could help you out."

"Thanks." Sloan smiled at McCall, who'd been listening. "Everyone should sleep better knowing we're both on guard."

An hour later Sloan pulled the covers over a sleeping Winter. The boy looked so small curled up on the ground. Sloan didn't want to think about the sadness Winter was about to find. For he had a feeling that if they discovered the tribe, Winter's mother wouldn't be among them.

He kept watch all night, and at dawn everyone helped load the wagons. They moved out across the open land for two days without seeing anything of life other than nature's. On the third day, McCall crossed solitary wagon tracks and decided to follow them.

Sloan grumbled for a hour, hoping she'd reconsider. To him she seemed to be doing a lousy job of staying out of sight. The woman never waited for trouble, but went hunting for it harder than a son-in-law looks for a husband for his newly widowed mother-in-law. He couldn't convince her that if they followed the trail of another wagon, they might run into anything. From the tracks, he knew it couldn't be a troop supply wagon. Two sets of footprints walked beside the wheels, and only one horse seemed to be following. Any army wagon would have been guarded by several mounted men. A single wagon of settlers wouldn't be this far north, away from a fort.

But McCall wanted to follow, so follow they did. The children stayed in the wagons during the day, and at night Sloan made sure he kept watch. They traveled three days before they caught up to the maker of the tracks.

McCall stopped her wagon so fast a half-asleep Sloan jolted awake as his team also slowed. He handed Winter the reins and climbed down, warning the children to stay quiet. Walking up beside her, he stared into the distance at a long column of smoke rising from below the bluff just beyond.

She lifted her arms for him to help her down, and they silently moved to the rise in front of her wagon. The sight before them made McCall halt suddenly and grip Sloan's arm.

"What is it?" she whispered, as if the people a hundred yards away could hear her.

"A hidetown," Sloan answered, only a few inches from her ear. He'd seen them a few times before. Hunters set up a camp near water and plenty of game. Within a few weeks they'd completely stripped the area of any animal whose fur drew a price. They'd leave the rotting carcasses of the kill where they fell and move on to the next campsite. The wagon McCall had followed must have returned with supplies while the other people worked. Hides of all sizes were staked and stretched out around the campsite—coyote, fox, deer, and several buffalo. Half a dozen men and two women moved around the area, each busy with his or her own work and seemingly paying no attention to the others.

So many buzzards circled further downstream from the hidetown that the birds looked almost like a black twister.

"I don't like these people already," McCall whispered.

Her gaze seemed to be moving from hide to hide, stretched out in the sun.

If they were anything like the hunters he'd met, Sloan had to agree. For the most part they traveled in small bands, living little better than animals. They were a dirty, lawless lot who wouldn't survive in civilization. They trashed the land without regard of who might come next, thinking nothing of killing all the game in an area or chopping down the last tree for firewood. Now that buffalo hide was becoming more valuable, Sloan guessed skinners would infest the land in larger numbers.

"These aren't like the trappers I've seen in the mountains." Sloan could smell the camp and was suddenly in a hurry to leave. "Let's go."

McCall nodded without hesitation. When they turned to leave, the sun reflected off the barrel of a rifle.

Sloan blinked and focused on the man holding the weapon. He was lean and looked to be made of last summer's jerky. His clothes were filthy buckskin, and after one breath, Sloan couldn't believe the man had gotten within five feet of him without being smelled.

"Evening." The stranger took a step forward, fouling the air like an angry skunk. Sloan doubted even a starving insect would bother such a man. His rifle rested in the fold of his arm, not pointing at Sloan, but not directed away. "You folks need something?"

Sloan moved in front of McCall. "We just saw your tracks and thought we'd follow awhile. We're headed further north."

"There ain't nothin' further north till you get in Kansas, and there's safer ways to get there than by this route. You folks alone?" He glanced over his shoulder at the two wagons.

"We have my grandmother with us," McCall answered.

"And my son," Sloan added. If the stranger had come up from behind them, there was a good chance he'd been close enough to the wagons to see Winter and Alyce Wren.

The stranger squinted at them a moment as if sizing up the possibility they were robbers. Then he chuckled to himself. "I guess you wouldn't be planning to jump the camp with your boy and grandmother along."

Sloan relaxed a little as he noticed the barrel of the gun move away. "We don't mean to bother," he said. "We'll just be moving on."

McCall didn't budge. First he tugged at her arm, then tried to pull her toward the wagons, but McCall seemed to have taken root in one spot.

She jerked her elbow from his grip. "Before we go," she glared at Sloan, "I thought I'd ask the man if he's seen any Cheyenne."

All Sloan could think about was leaving. Every minute they were in the man's presence was a minute longer than he'd like.

The stranger rubbed his thin beard and stared at her as if debating talking with her. Finally, he shrugged. "I seen a party of braves several days back. They were looking for something other than me, or I'd be low on ammunition and probably blood by now. Other than that, I don't go looking for trouble. I've survived out here by leaving everything on two legs alone."

He looked at Sloan. "My name's Moses, Moses Sneed, and I travel with my brothers and our women. You're welcome to share our camp tonight if your woman is afraid. We don't invite many, but we've plenty of meat."

Sloan almost laughed. "His woman"—she'd never be that, and he'd guess she'd never be afraid.

"Thank you for the offer," Sloan gripped McCall's arm

so tight he heard her give out a little yelp, "but we'll be moving on."

Moses Sneed raised the rifle slightly. "I insist."

Sloan turned loose of McCall's arm and opened his mouth to object. She jabbed her elbow into his ribs before he could speak.

"Thank you kindly, Mr. Sneed. We'd love to."

Ten

MCCALL MARCHED AHEAD of the men toward her wagon. She knew the children in the back were well hidden by now. "Grandma!" she shouted when several feet away. "We've been invited to supper by this man. Are you feeling up to coming?"

Alyce Wren took the clue as McCall knew she would. "What did you say, sweetie? I'm feeling poorly."

"I was afraid of that." McCall glanced over her shoulder. "Bad water a few days back."

The man called Moses nodded in understanding.

McCall patted Alyce's hand and winked. "I said, would you like to go to supper down at the camp? These folks are hunters and there will be hides drying everywhere."

"You know how I hate that smell." Alyce wrinkled up her face at the man who stood behind Sloan. "Makes me want to lose my breakfast just thinking about it. I'm not coming."

"Suit yourself," the man mumbled, clearly in no hurry to have Alyce as a dinner guest.

McCall turned toward the men. "Will there be enough that we might bring her back something?"

She could tell by Sloan's expression that he thought they

would probably be killed and skinned as soon as they got into camp, so what difference did it make? His gaze kept darting to the rifle, as though trying to silently warn her that they were about to be shot.

Moses nodded again. "We've got plenty. My woman cooks more than we can eat."

Alyce pointed her finger at McCall. "You remember I'm real hungry, child. I feel like I could eat enough for a baker's dozen."

McCall swore she'd remember.

Sloan glanced toward the other wagon where Winter sat, still holding the reins. "My boy will stay here with the old woman. I wouldn't want her to be alone, sick and all."

Moses shrugged. "Your boy looks part Indian."

Sloan watched the barrel of the gun move slightly toward Winter. He quickly drew the stranger's attention back to himself. "Does that bother you?"

The filthy man shook his head. "Hell, after sleeping with my woman, nothing bothers me."

Sloan smiled. He could hardly wait to meet the missus.

McCall disappeared into the wagon for a minute, then reappeared with something wrapped in a bandanna. She stuffed the secret into her pocket and jumped to the ground. "I'm ready," she said, as if they were going to a picnic.

Moses marched a step behind them, down the rise to the camp. He didn't say a word, but everyone stopped working and gathered to see what he'd trapped.

McCall slipped her hand into Sloan's. Not, she told herself, because she was afraid, but because she wanted him to know that he didn't stand alone in this. She was willing to fight at his side. These people looked like they might war to the death over a bone.

They didn't seem to be of the same race, nationality, or

even species as her. They looked like they belonged to a time a million years ago when man lived in caves. Their skin was leather, hardened by the sun, and the men seemed to be hairier than the animals they'd skinned. The women were stout, with long mud-colored hair. Their bodies were as shapeless as their dresses. McCall wasn't sure she could eat anything handed to her by a person so dirty.

"These are my brothers. Noah, Adam, James, and Peter."

The brothers didn't offer hands or say a word. They just stared at McCall as if they'd never seen anything like her.

"And this is Adam's woman."

The woman nearest Sloan grunted in recognition.

"And this here is May. She don't talk, but we all think it was May when we found her. Most of the time she forgets which brother's woman she is."

The one called May grinned and moved a little closer to Sloan. She leaned toward him and seemed to be smelling his shirt. When he looked at her, she smiled, and Sloan noticed half her teeth were missing.

McCall felt Sloan's fingers tighten around her hand and she almost giggled.

"Woman!" Moses yelled suddenly, making everyone jump. "Where are you?"

Before his voice finished echoing in the valley, a short woman stormed from beneath a tent of hides. She couldn't have been much over four feet tall, but she was full of fire. Her hair whirled around her like a shaggy sand-colored tumbleweed, and her straight leather dress bulged and bounced with a fullness that was all woman despite her height.

"Stop bellering at me, Moses!" she shouted in a voice louder than his had been. "I was just getting ready for our company."

McCall looked the woman up and down, but for the life of her she could see nothing that Moses' lady had done in weeks that might be an improvement in her appearance.

Moses patted her on the head and smiled at McCall and Sloan. "My Eppie do love company."

The look on his face seemed to say that he'd do anything for this little woman, for she was his treasure.

"Nice to meet you, Eppie." McCall smiled at the stranger with dancing eyes. "I'm McCall."

Eppie looked to be in her late twenties, but her movements were free and childlike. "We got lots of food. Come sit a spell and I'll boil some coffee. My mama used to say coffee and company were created to go together."

McCall turned loose of Sloan's hand and followed the little woman into the shade of a hide lean-to. The others just stared with dull eyes, not enough interest to join, not enough curiosity to care that they hadn't been invited.

Moses seemed content just to stand in the late day sun and watch his Eppie. Sloan relaxed as he noticed, for the first time, the barrel of the rifle wasn't pointed toward him. He folded his arms, widened his stance, and joined Moses in watching while the others wandered off.

Eppie asked question after question. She was curious about everything. Her face reacted to every story to the point that Sloan found himself watching her more than listening to what the women were talking about. She even cried when she heard McCall's first man died in a war. Then she lightened and bragged on McCall's new man as if they were looking at horses and not humans who could hear them. McCall returned the favor and bragged on how tall and strong Moses looked. Eppie seemed pleased.

But the little woman's delight was complete when McCall pulled the bandanna from her pocket and handed it to Eppie.

Bouncing with excitement, Eppie opened the gift and screamed with delight. "Look, Moses, look what the company done brought me!"

Moses raised an eyebrow at the ball of soap Eppie shoved in his face.

"It's soap," she added. "All cut in the shape of a rose. Did you ever see anything so pretty?"

"Nope." Moses looked doubtful.

Sloan fought to keep from laughing. To the hunter, soap was of little use to begin with. To cut it in the shape of a rose seemed down the road to foolishness and heading full speed into absurdity. But if it made his Eppie happy, the man meant to understand.

"Smell." She pushed it beneath his nose once more. "Don't it smell wonderful? I can just close my eyes and think for sure it's a flower."

Moses took a deep snort, then rubbed his face with the back of his hand. "Sure does, woman. Smells real nice."

Eppie plopped down beside McCall once more. "Where'd you ever get such a thing? Are you sure you want to give it to me?"

McCall smiled, knowing not to make too light of the gift she put little value on but this woman seemed to treasure. "From the time I was a little girl my grandfather used to bring it back to me from New Orleans. He said my mother loved the smell of roses, but could never get them to grow on our land. So if I bathe in rose soap, I'll be her growing rose. He'd have named me Rose if my father hadn't objected."

"You use this when you take a bath?" Eppie seemed shocked. "You put this pretty thing in the water?"

McCall nodded slowly. "It makes your skin smell like petals."

"I could never use it like that. If I did, it would be gone in a few years after a handful of baths."

"You could use it just a little when you wash your face," McCall suggested. "That way I'd guess it might last a long, long time."

Eppie smelled the soap once more, then leaned close to McCall and smelled her. "Every time I smell this, I'll think of you. Ain't no company ever gave me something so nice."

McCall was touched by the woman's warmth. Despite her dirty clothes and unkempt appearance, she had the heart of a lady. Moses was a very lucky man indeed.

The women talked while Sloan and Moses built a fire and cut deer meat into thick steaks for roasting. Moses didn't say a word for almost an hour. Sloan gave up any attempt to communicate after a few tries.

It was almost dark when Moses turned and faced Sloan. They were far enough away from the others that no one could overhear the conversation.

"Your woman asked me if I'd seen any Cheyenne. I didn't reckon she was talking about those children you got hid in your wagons."

Sloan's fingers brushed the handle of his Colt as Moses continued, "I didn't say nothing about them, not even to my brothers. I probably would have, but that woman of yours was powerful nice to my Eppie, so I figure I owe you something, and silence seems a proper thing to offer."

"Thanks." Sloan didn't like taking a gift, even silence, without knowing the price expected in return. "How'd you know about the children?"

"My brothers like to stay close to camp, but I like to scout around. Can't sleep without knowing who's breathing within a mile of me. I seen your fire last night and knew you was heading my way."

He stared hard at Sloan. "If it had been just you, I'd have

guessed you were kidnapping them kids and taking them back to the reservation for a fee. But they ain't tied up, and the old woman you left them with could never stop a Comanche cub from leaving if he had a mind to. Besides, we both know you're heading in the wrong direction if you're looking for the reservation."

Moses paused. Sloan didn't say a word but waited for him to finish.

"If you ain't taking them to the reservation, you're taking them somewhere else, and I'm guessing it's to their parents."

"If I am, do you plan on trying to stop me?"

Rubbing his whiskers, Moses answered, "No. I told you I don't interfere with two-legged creatures. If you're crazy enough to try such a thing, I'll not bother you."

"Thanks again," Sloan answered.

Moses nodded once. "At first I thought it was your idea, and for some reason you were dragging your woman and her grandma into this. But when I met your woman, I figured it were her notion and you were just going along."

"Good guess." Sloan had a feeling Moses had been talked into a few things before.

"I don't want to frighten your woman, but there's others looking for them children."

Sloan raised an eyebrow.

"I met up with three men a few nights ago. They weren't too friendly and the Apache with them were downright mean. There's a price on any Comanche scalp in these parts, and the boys plan to make some quick money on the children. Only from the way they talked, they think the band is traveling on foot with an old medicine man."

"Did one of the men have a cut just under one eye?"

Moses raised one eyebrow almost into his hairline. "You know him?"

"We crossed paths a few nights back," Sloan answered.

"Then you know his kind. You can skin him to the bone, but it's all bad meat."

"I guessed that."

"Does he know about your cargo?"

"No," Sloan said. "If he did, he'd have made a move."

"Or rounded up his friends." Moses looked almost sorry for Sloan. "Dogs like him always hunt in packs."

"I'll move out at first light," Sloan whispered, more to himself than Moses.

"Cross our trail tomorrow, then move ahead of that buffalo herd. You'll be harder to track from this point on. I'll see to it after you've left." Moses lifted a wooden platter of meat. "But first we best feed those kids. They're safe enough tonight."

"Thanks," Sloan said for the third time. "I'm in your debt."

"Good." Moses walked ahead of him. "Then you and your woman will stay at our fire tonight. My Eppie do love company, even if all they're doing is snoring."

Sloan missed a step and almost dropped the pot of beans he was carrying. "Me and my woman?" He couldn't say no after just thanking the man three times, but he didn't even want to think about what McCall would say when she learned she would be sleeping in the smelly hidetown . . . and as his woman.

Eleven

"YOU'VE GOT TO be kidding!" McCall whispered as they walked toward their wagons in the dark.

"I wish I was," Sloan replied as he crammed his fists into his pockets.

"But the children?"

"The children will be fine with Alyce Wren. I made sure they had plenty of wood for the fire and I left my extra Colt with Winter. I'm not sure he's ever fired a gun, but he said he knew enough to point it at the moon and shoot to sound an alarm. We'll check on them now and be back by first light."

"I'm not sleeping with you." She stormed ahead as though walking beside him was too close a contact.

"All right." Sloan didn't increase his pace, but raised his voice slightly. "I'm sure May will loan you one of the single brothers. Sleep beside whoever you like, but we are spending the night at their fire."

McCall seemed to turn to stone.

Sloan slowly walked past her. "I'm only guessing, but I'd think Moses would be a man you wouldn't want to make mad."

"I'm not sleeping with you!" she whispered between

clenched teeth, as though the idea were too foul to say aloud.

"Fine," he answered only a few inches away from her. "How about sleeping beside me? From the way the woman smelled me, I'd guess I will be in more danger of being attacked by May than you will be of being bothered by the brothers. You'll be safest close to me, and maybe I'll be safe with you by my side."

He fought down his anger. She was acting as if she'd been picked as the sacrifice. "I won't even touch you, General. Hell, I wouldn't touch you if you wanted me to. What do you think I am, some starved man who'll take a woman against her will? I should be the one upset. I'm the one who has to sleep next to a woman who spends most of her free time thinking of where to ship my body after she kills me!"

"I don't know what you are or who you are," she answered, "but you'll never touch me again and that is final."

Sloan took a deep breath. After what had happened between them, he doubted he'd ever convince her he wasn't the kind of man she seemed to think he was. All right, he had kissed her once when she hadn't expected it. And he had touched her, so intimately he ached inside just remembering it. But he'd never attack her. Couldn't she see that somewhere layered beneath years of life's dust was a man of honor? Or did she think that only the brave generals and majors had honor? Was it too impossible to believe that a man who'd fought and lost, a man who'd been in prison, a man who'd changed sides in the middle of a war, could still have integrity?

"Sleep with me at hidetown." He lifted his hands in surrender from a battle not fought. "I'll not bother you, I swear. Come morning, we'll be on our way and I'll keep as much distance between us as possible for the rest of the trip."

They had reached the wagons. McCall didn't answer as she hugged several of the children and covered others already asleep. Sloan just stood watching her, knowing she was a woman who hated being manipulated. But couldn't she see that he was a victim here, too? He had no more choice in the matter than she did. Moses could help them out a great deal if they stayed on friendly terms with him.

"The steaks were too tough," Alyce grumbled as she pulled a blanket around herself.

Sloan knelt beside her and put another log on the fire. "That was all they had." He wasn't sure if the old woman was talking to him, or mumbling in her sleep.

"Sometimes," she continued, "you bite off more than you can swallow when the meat's tough."

He looked at her, but her eyes were closed.

McCall climbed into the wagon and pulled out two extra blankets. She threw them at him and jumped back down before he had time to offer help. "Bite anything tonight, soldier, and I'll—"

Sloan stepped aside for her to lead the way back to hidetown. "Don't go threatening me again, General."

McCall stormed ahead of him. "I'm not threatening, I'm promising. Keep your hands to yourself *all night* if you value your fingers."

He followed her. "I should have been a little more careful picking a better-tempered female. You'd think you'd be happy to be my woman. After all, I've bathed in the past season."

She stopped so quickly, he bumped into her in the darkness. "Don't ever call me 'my woman' again."

"Or what?" Sloan just had to push it. Like a boy playing with a porcupine, he had to poke once more.

"Or I'll make myself your *surviving* woman," she answered.

Sloan laughed. "I'd bet the brothers will be glad to hear you're free again. Tell me, what does a widow wear when her second man dies?"

"Blood-red," she whispered. "Your blood."

Sloan was getting so used to being threatened, he was starting to enjoy it.

He reached across the darkness and took her hand. Forcing her fingers to bend over his arm, he marched into the circle of the hunters' camp.

McCall dug her fingers into his arm as tightly as she could while he pulled her along one step at a time. She'd never met a man she disliked more. He didn't seem to care that what they were about to do would raise every eyebrow in town back home. Even if he didn't touch her, just the idea of agreeing to sleep beside a man she hardly knew broke the rules. She thought of telling him that she'd never slept beside any man, not even the major, but she doubted he'd believe her. When she'd been married and they'd been home where the beds were wide, the major liked his privacy in slumber. She'd always been a bedroll, or a bunk, or a room away from Holden in sleep.

The others already circled the campfire and McCall bit back her anger as she noticed one buffalo hide had been spread out for company. Two of Moses' brothers looked asleep already. Adam and his woman were already spread out on another hide, as usual showing no interest in each other or what was going on around them. The fourth brother sat with his legs wide apart on a hide by himself. As she watched, May moved from the fire where she'd been warming and joined him, cuddling into the space between his outstretched legs. She leaned against the dirty shirt covering his chest as if she'd found her nest. He grunted loudly and circled his arms around her.

Sloan spread out one of the blankets on the buffalo hide. "Nice of you to ask us to share your fire," he said to the brothers, but none acted like they had the sense of hearing.

"You're welcome," Moses said as he pulled Eppie from the shadows. She'd washed her face and smiled with pride as she passed McCall. "We don't waste much time after dark, but my Eppie sometimes sings to us."

Eppie shook her head as if suddenly shy.

Moses lowered himself on a blanket and pulled Eppie gently down to her knees beside him. His wide rough hands moved over the back of her buckskin dress. "She'll sing." He sounded grumpy, but his hands were gentle. "Sing us one of those songs you've known all your life."

Eppie shook her head.

His fingers spread wider and continued to move over her back, dropping low atop her hips and then reaching high into her hair. The movement was slow, caressing. His hands pulled at the material covering her full body and pressed hard enough to sink slightly into the flesh beneath her dress. Eppie arched her back, flattening her full breasts against his chest as his hands continued to move over her from throat to hip.

McCall felt her mouth go dry. She'd never watched a man touch a woman so. She could almost feel what Eppie must feel. The fire of needy fingers moving over her. The longing for more.

Glancing at Sloan, McCall was surprised to find that he was watching her, not Moses and Eppie. His eyes were so dark they looked black and his stare was haunting.

McCall looked away, afraid of what she might see if she met his gaze.

Moses stopped his hand over the fullness of Eppie's hip.

His fingers pressed against her dress, imprinting deep into her flesh and pulling her hard against him. "Make yourselves comfortable; my Eppie will sing."

Sloan removed his jacket and gun belt, then lowered to one knee on what was to be their bed. When she didn't move, he raised his hand toward McCall.

She wanted to run. She wanted to stay. She wanted to watch this couple more, and she wished she'd never seen as much as she'd seen already. When her fingers slipped into Sloan's palm, he pulled her gently toward him. McCall knew it was their time to perform some strange ritual as they bedded down.

While she knelt, unsure of what to do, he shoved her coat from her shoulders and let it fall beside his. Then he took both her hands and pulled her slowly down to sit in front of him. She leaned against the inside of his knee as he reached behind her and pulled the ribbon holding her hair.

She wanted to pull away, but she knew the others were watching. If she was to act the part of his woman tonight, she'd have to play along. Somehow they had to make the others believe that she and Sloan were a couple.

When her hair was free, he lifted it over one shoulder and twisted it around his fist, pulling her head slightly toward his shoulder with the action.

Glancing up at him, McCall saw a smile touch the corner of his lip. He tugged again and she leaned into his leg.

"Close your eyes," he whispered, so close she could feel his words against her cheek. "Lean back against me and relax."

McCall's body felt like it might break from being held so tightly in check, but she did as he'd asked. If he touches me the way Moses touched Eppie, I'll scream, she thought,

TEXAS LOVE SONG   121

then wondered who would save her in this gathering of the
scrapings from the bottom of humanity?

Eppie's sweet voice began to sing, a song she must have
heard her mother sing. The words were blurred, a mixture
of English and some other tongue forgotten generations
ago. But the song had survived, passed down from one
mother to another in lullaby.

Slowly, McCall relaxed as Sloan's hands began to braid
her hair into one long rope. With each turn of the braid, he
pulled the remaining hair through his fingers, carefully
avoiding any tangles.

When he finished, he lowered to the blanket and waited
for her to join him. His eyes were so dark she couldn't read
his thoughts. Only the slight twitch of a smile told her he
was enjoying the evening.

The song continued, sweet and light like a cool breeze,
rocking everyone to sleep as if they were still children.
McCall carefully lay beside Sloan, an inch away. She
could feel the warmth of him on one side of her and the
heat of the fire on the other. All the fears of the day slipped
away. Sloan turned on his side and offered her his arm for
a pillow. His eyes were still dark with a fire she didn't understand, but he made no attempt to touch her.

McCall rested her head on his arm and closed her eyes
as Eppie's song ended. Despite all the threats and fights,
she felt safer than she had in years. He pulled the extra
blanket over her shoulder as her thoughts turned to dreams.

Deep into the night, McCall heard noises and twisted in
her sleep, fighting to awaken.

Sloan brushed her arm gently and whispered, "Hush,
now, darling. Don't be afraid. It's only May, moving
through the prophets."

McCall, still half asleep, giggled and rolled over, not
wanting to witness any of May's romances. She rested her

head against the solid wall of Sloan's chest and relaxed to the steady pounding of his heart.

Just before first light, she felt Sloan jerk suddenly. McCall raised to one elbow above him and saw that he was still sound asleep. In the dying firelight, his face twisted in pain and his lips tightened as though he refused to cry out, even in sleep.

"Sloan?" McCall whispered, frightened by a dream that could cut him so deeply. "Wake up! You're dreaming." Her hand rested lightly on his shoulder.

With a violent jolt, he shook and came full awake. For a second, he seemed confused, as though he had to blink away nightmares before he could see reality.

"Sloan?" McCall thought fear overcast his eyes. For the first time since they'd met, she realized how young he must be. Ten, maybe fifteen years younger than her husband, the major. Almost her age. In waking, a hint of the boy remained before the man could shove him aside.

Then he blinked again and the hardness was back, aging his face with memories more than years. The boy in him disappeared.

"McCall," he whispered hoarsely. "Is something wrong?"

"No," she answered, glancing around to make sure everyone else was still asleep. "I just felt you fighting a nightmare and thought you'd want to be awakened."

"It doesn't matter." Sloan lay on his back and stared up at the night sky. "The dream will be waiting for me when I sleep again."

McCall brushed her fingers along the side of his face, remembering the fear she'd seen. "I'm sorry."

"Don't be," he answered coldly. "It has nothing to do with you."

Wondering if she'd embarrassed him by having seen

him sleeping, she whispered with more kindness than she usually allowed in her voice, "My father used to make me tell him my nightmares so they'd go away. He'd sit beside my bed and listen to my dreams, then walk over and open the window as if he'd sent them away. Then he'd turn out the light and tell me the nightmare wouldn't bother me again."

Sloan didn't answer. In his silence, with his hair falling over his forehead, he almost looked like the little boy she thought she'd caught sight of before. She couldn't resist touching the thick brown mass that never seemed to stay in place.

He refused to look at her or acknowledge that she was touching him. "My nightmare hasn't gone away in three years of running. I doubt telling you will help, no matter how many windows you open."

McCall continued to stroke his hair. There was such a sadness about this man, a sadness deeper than any fatal wound. She'd lost her husband in the war, but Sloan had lost any peace even in dreaming.

Maybe it was because she couldn't think of anything to say. Or just because there were times when actions must replace words so that souls can talk. Or maybe, for tonight, there was a need that had no reason. McCall didn't want to examine the questions, but only to continue to brush his cheek with her fingers. She wanted to touch this man. The need to feel someone alive in her world of numbness was so strong, she was suddenly willing to risk the safety of her self-made confinement.

He closed his eyes and didn't move. Had he turned an inch away, she would have stopped. Turning an inch toward her would have frightened her. But he stayed perfectly still as she moved her fingers through his hair, then down again to brush over the rough thickness of his day-old beard.

She told herself her actions were aiding a worried mind, helping him fight back a nightmare that was too terrible to voice. But she knew she was lying to herself. In truth, she'd sometimes wondered what it would be like to touch a man so boldly. She wanted to feel the texture of this lost warrior, both in the softness of his hair and the roughness of his jaw. McCall had to be honest enough with herself to admit that it wasn't just any man, but Sloan she longed to touch as she was now. Men had always been strange creatures to her. Creatures hard to understand and impossible to predict.

As he remained stone, she brushed her knuckles over his cheek and raked her fingernails gently across his throat. His eyelashes tickled the tips of her fingers, and his mouth opened slightly as she brushed the corner of his lips where he allowed a smile to sometimes break through the hardness.

The major would have thought her ridiculous if she'd have touched him so, but McCall guessed Sloan would not only allow her folly, but understand.

For a moment, she thought he might be asleep. Her hand moved to his chest and she laid her fingers gently over his heart. The rapid pounding told her he was very much awake.

"I remember when you touched me like that the first night we met," Sloan whispered, so low it was almost to himself. "I wondered how a woman could test for life so easily."

"I thought you were asleep."

"How could I be?" he asked. "I think if I'd been near death that first night I would have come back at your touch."

First light warmed the horizon and McCall smiled. "You kept your word. You slept beside me without touching me. I'm afraid I'm the one who broke the bargain."

He opened his eyes and turned his head slightly toward her. "You sound surprised. Did you doubt me so completely?"

"Yes."

"But you made no such promise to me, so you haven't broken any word."

She smiled. "So you don't mind?" She trailed a finger from his sideburn to his chin.

"I don't mind," he repeated as he closed his eyes and added, "I don't mind at all."

McCall forced her hand to return to his chest. "I owe you an apology." Her father had always insisted she own up to being wrong when proven so. "I didn't believe you'd hold to your word." She thought of telling him about the derringer in her pocket, but she couldn't bring herself to prove her words. She'd admitted them; that was enough.

Sloan gently placed his hand over hers. "Go back to sleep, General. I'll wake you at full light."

McCall snuggled down at his side and closed her eyes, thinking he'd never have to know of the gun.

Twelve

SLOAN TRIED TO lie perfectly still as McCall's breathing slowed and deepened. But the corner of his mouth couldn't help but lift a fraction. He'd won a battle. She trusted him more, and for some reason that was important to him. Over the past few years he'd given up caring what people thought of him. But she'd changed that by stepping into the middle of his beating in the station house.

He wanted nothing more than to roll toward her and kiss her fully on the mouth, but he would wait. Someday the girl in the tintype would return, and he wanted to be near when she smiled again, truly smiled. For the first time in his life, he had something to look forward to and wait for. By the way she'd touched him, he knew she'd someday come to him. Then he'd see again the passion in her blood that Alyce Wren thought was there. He only hoped he lived long enough to see the day.

As thoughts of the dangers they still must face crossed his mind, a shot rang out from the direction of the wagons.

"Winter!" Sloan shouted.

McCall's hand fell from his chest. She jumped up beside him, grabbing for her coat as he strapped on his gun belt.

The brothers and May remained asleep, but Moses was

on his feet as well, listening to the morning air like an animal who'd heard a twig snap. He glanced at a waking Eppie. "Stay here in camp," he ordered, then turned to Sloan and lifted his rifle.

"Trouble," Sloan whispered as he grabbed his Winchester and glanced at McCall. "Stay here with the others. We'll be back."

McCall was already a step ahead of him. "No," she answered simply and broke into a run toward the children's camp.

Moses and Sloan passed her within a few yards, but neither tried to stop her. Sloan broke the crest and slowed as he saw the wagons. Nothing seemed amiss. The camp seemed still asleep, or in hiding.

"I'll circle around," Moses said as he veered to the right.

Sloan glanced toward McCall and knew it would be useless to order her to stay out of range. She was storming in and there was nothing he could do but hope he might block any bullet meant for her. "Stay behind me!" he snapped in what he hoped was the tone of a death threat.

McCall hesitated, then nodded. She slipped her hand into her pocket, and Sloan knew without asking that she was armed.

They walked slowly toward the camp. When they were close enough to be seen clearly, Winter stepped from his hiding place and ran toward them.

Sloan handed the rifle to McCall as he went down on one knee and caught the boy as he ran full speed into Sloan's arms.

For a moment Winter hugged Sloan so tightly he couldn't breathe, then the boy turned him loose and stepped back.

"I killed him, I think! I didn't mean to kill nothing, but I think I did."

"Who?"

Winter pointed to the east. "I was keeping guard, just like I said I would. I heard something and walked to see what it was. He was lying in the grass and I shot him before I thought."

The boy was gulping for air, fighting down fear along with adrenaline. "I just pointed and pulled the trigger. Just like you told me."

Sloan put his hand on the boy's shoulder, thinking that he must have been a fool to give the child his gun. The boy probably killed the first rabbit that jumped. But Winter had seemed a better choice than Alyce Wren. "What did you shoot, Winter?"

Winter faced him, eyes wide without tears. "A man. I think I shot a man."

Sloan and McCall looked at one another over the boy's head. Without a word they started moving in the direction Winter had pointed. Within a few steps they were running.

Moses was already kneeling in the tall grass where Winter led them. "The boy shot something or someone, all right." Moses rubbed a drop of blood between his fingers. "Hit him, too, I'd say from the drops of blood leading off in that direction. I can't tell if he was white or Indian, of course."

"It doesn't matter," Winter whispered. "I killed him just the same."

McCall knelt beside Winter. "No, you didn't," she squared his shoulders with her hands. "You shot him. He's still alive or there'd be a body in this grass. And what you did may have saved a life. Anyone crawling up to a camp can be judged to be an enemy fair enough."

Moses stood and balanced his huge rifle over his shoulders. "You wanta follow the blood trail, Sloan?"

Sloan nodded, then turned to McCall. "Will you stay

with the wagons?" He knew better than to order her to stay. "This may take a while."

"I will," she answered. "Be careful."

Sloan touched his hat in salute as he hurried after Moses, who looked like a human bloodhound hot on a fresh trail.

McCall felt Winter's hand slide into hers as they watched the men disappear. She guessed Winter had waited until the men weren't watching before he took her hand.

"I didn't mean to kill anyone," he mumbled to himself. "I only saw something crawling through the grass, and the gun went off before I thought about it."

"Never mind." McCall turned and started walking back to the wagons. "You didn't hurt him badly, or he couldn't have run away so fast."

Winter's huge eyes constantly looked back toward where the men had gone. He didn't say a word. When they reached the wagons, he perched himself on one of the wagon benches and waited.

Alyce Wren's constant grumbling made up for Winter's silence. She talked in riddles of a race of people who'd lived on this land for thousands of years. A race half human, half wolf who roamed the open prairie since a time before any Europeans thought of this place. Alyce told of how she and her father traveled over this land years ago and talked with old men who'd seen the beings. They could outrun the wind, the old men said, and steal a man's soul in the darkness of a moonless night.

McCall found the stories haunting, and when the day turned cloudy, Alyce's mood darkened even more. As the sky turned from gray to black and the men still hadn't returned, Alyce's mind also turned to the dark side. Not even Eppie's visit could change her mood.

So McCall built a fire, and Eppie gave Alyce the audience McCall and Winter would not.

"The half men," Alyce Wren began, "can slither through the grass like snakes, then jump and run like a wolf. My father tried to help a woman once who'd seen one while she was pregnant. Her baby turned sideways and refused to come out. The woman died screaming."

Eppie hugged herself and moved closer to the fire. The children around her might be curling into their beds, but Eppie's eyes were wide with excitement.

McCall thought of screaming for Alyce to be quiet, but the old woman loved her stories. Her words twisting around sorrow or joy made a music she seemed to need to survive.

"My father didn't believe the stories, but the people of the plains believed. I'd forgotten the tales until Winter told of shooting one of the creatures. If he killed the half man, half wolf, others will come the first dark night to get us. They'll lift our thoughts right out of our heads and leave us senseless beasts to stumble around without being able to talk or think."

Eppie didn't breathe.

"Then they'll run across the plains and scatter our minds over the horizon like smoke. We'll only be able to see at dusk. That is, if they don't decide to claw our eyes out."

"Stop!" McCall could take no more. "You'll frighten the children."

"They can't understand," Alyce answered. "Only Winter, and he needs to know what to expect."

McCall glanced over at Winter's back. She couldn't tell if the boy was listening to the stories or not. He hadn't moved all day from his guard. She'd placed a plate beside him, but she couldn't tell if he'd eaten a bite.

"She's scaring me," Eppie whispered. "I'm waiting until my Moses comes back before I go to our camp."

"Won't the brothers miss you?" McCall was surprised they hadn't been over to check on her by now.

"No," she laughed. "They don't care. Maybe the half men already visited Moses' brothers. They're downright senseless most of the time. Last year we were hit by a flash flood in the middle of the night. Come morning, we found two of them still asleep, floating in three inches of water."

McCall smiled and didn't doubt the story. "You're welcome to stay with us. We don't have anything as comfortable as the buffalo hides that you sleep on, but we have plenty of blankets."

As McCall reached in the wagon to get Eppie a blanket, she saw Winter jump from the bench and run into the darkness. A moment later Moses and Sloan materialized from the shadows.

Before she thought about how it might look to Alyce Wren, McCall stepped over the wagon tongue and ran toward the men. Eppie was no more than three paces behind her.

Sloan bent down and lifted Winter off the ground in a hug. "It's all right, son," he said as Winter hugged him. "We didn't find anything, so you didn't kill anyone."

"Are you sure? Not a man or something that looked like a wolf?"

"Nothing," Sloan laughed. "The blood only went a few drops, then the trail ended. We crossed every path for miles and found no one injured or dead."

The boy stepped away, almost dancing. "I got to run tell the others."

"You do that," Sloan said as Winter almost ran into McCall, coming from the campsite.

She paused a few feet before Sloan, suddenly not knowing what to do. She was glad to see him, but running into his arms seemed far beyond her ability.

Sloan solved the awkwardness by offering his free hand to her.

When their fingers laced, McCall fell into step beside him, silently letting him know that she was glad to have him back.

Eppie showed no such reserve with Moses. She jumped into his arms, hugging him wildly as her arms and legs wrapped around his body. He staggered a few steps and widened his stance to take the weight of his woman. She was still kissing on Moses when they entered the light of the camp.

"What did you find?" Alyce Wren asked, her eyes looking directly at Sloan.

"Nothing," he answered, but could tell by her huff that she didn't believe him.

"There's something out there," she mumbled as she crawled into the wagon to sleep. "I can feel it. I can almost smell it." Her voice continued, even though she'd disappeared inside. "I can hear it breathing."

Sloan raised an eyebrow at McCall, as if in silent question, but McCall only shrugged in answer.

"We best be getting back to camp." Moses peeled Eppie off his chest. "It's getting late."

"You're welcome to join our fire," Sloan volunteered without looking at McCall.

"No, thanks," Moses laughed. "My woman and I have a little sparking to do before we sleep."

Eppie's nearness to him left no doubt of what Moses was talking about. Sloan thought they'd be lucky to make it back to their fire before the sparks started flying. He glanced at McCall, but she showed no sign of understanding what the men were talking about.

She hugged Eppie and said good night while Sloan thanked Moses once more for his help. Winter gave Eppie a small medicine pouch he'd made from part of a rabbit hide. He told her it was just like his mother's and would protect her should the night people come.

After the couple left, McCall poured Sloan the last of the coffee and handed him a plate of meat and skillet bread they'd kept warm over the coals. She moved around the children, making sure all were warm in their blankets. He was half finished eating when she finally knelt beside him.

"You really found nothing?" she whispered.

Sloan shook his head. "Nothing dead, or shot. We did find signs of a camp not far from here. It must have been an Indian camp and well-covered. I would have missed any sign of it if Moses hadn't been with me."

"You think Winter shot one of his people?"

"We're all 'one of his people,'" Sloan answered before he drank the bitter brown liquid. "If I were guessing, I'd say he shot one of his mother's people. With luck the brave made it away without losing too much blood."

McCall lowered her head. "He's been so worried. And Alyce Wren hasn't helped, filling his head with stories of half men who walk the night."

Sloan suddenly looked very tired. "I'll talk to him tomorrow, but tonight we'd better get some sleep. I think it best if we leave as soon as we can in the morning. If the brave did make it back to a camp somewhere, they may come looking for us."

McCall agreed.

"Talk to me now," Winter whispered from the shadows. "Not tomorrow, but now."

Sloan watched the boy move around the fire. He motioned for Winter to take the empty space between McCall and himself.

Winter carried his blanket across his shoulders. "Alyce Wren says they'll come for me in the blackness of night if I killed a half man."

Studying Sloan carefully, McCall wondered how he would erase the boy's fears.

Sloan stood slowly and removed his gun belt. He spread a blanket beside Winter and laid his gun between them. "Anything coming to get you, son, will have to cross me first. I've had a long day and I'm in no mood to be crossed."

McCall followed his lead. She put her bedroll on the other side of Winter and laid the rifle beside her. "I'll feel safer sleeping next to you, Winter. I might not be able to stop someone, but I'll yell real loud if man or beast tries to get past me."

Winter leaned back between them and smiled. All the tension of the day seemed to pass from him in a sigh and he closed his eyes.

Looking across the boy's blanket to McCall, Sloan silently stretched his arm out. She did the same. Their fingers touched just above Winter's head.

"Good night, General," he said as he gripped her hand tightly, silently wishing he could pull her closer.

McCall didn't answer, for she suddenly felt safe as well. Not even Alyce Wren's mumblings from the wagon frightened her.

The wind blew across the land as midnight neared, howling its way up the ravines and lifting the earthy smell of dampness high in the air.

Sloan rose twice during the night to make sure the fire was strong and the children covered. Each time he passed McCall, he couldn't help but kneel beside her as she slept.

A strand of hair crossed her cheek. Sloan carefully lifted it aside, wishing he could lean and kiss her as lightly as her hair touched her without waking her. But she'd made it plain she wanted no part of him, and if he stepped past the boundaries once more, he wasn't sure she'd forgive him again.

Sloan smiled. Knowing her was like walking a breath away from the kill line. In the prison camps, the guards had constructed a rope barrier ten feet inside the prison walls. The inmates called it the kill line, because if anyone stepped over it, he was killed before he could reach the wall. Sometimes Sloan found himself walking the line, tempting fate by stepping as close as he could without touching the rope.

Now, in the shadows of night, he felt the same excitement with McCall. She'd be angry if she even knew he was watching her, but he couldn't move away. Adrenaline pumped through his blood at the thought that she slept only a few inches away. He wished he could hold her and make her remember how it felt to be alive. But it had been so long since he'd thought about living, he wasn't sure he could ever be her teacher. If she did know his dream and came willingly to his arms, he had nothing to offer her come morning.

Standing, Sloan walked to the opening between the wagons and looked out into the night. The air seemed thick with moisture, and scattered clouds blocked the stars. He thought of how McCall had changed his life, shifting his world ever so slightly until he could see a life he'd never known existed.

With her, he could almost dream of tomorrow. He could almost see himself settling down. But to what? He wasn't sure he knew how to do anything but soldier, and that was no life for a family man. He'd hated the year of farming he'd done with his stepfather. When he'd been in the cavalry he'd enjoyed working with the horses, but being a stable boy didn't seem like it would pay well. Besides, if he settled down it would only be a matter of time before one of the Satan's Seven found him. Three years wasn't enough time for the hatred to die.

"Couldn't sleep?" Her voice drifted from just behind him.

Sloan turned slowly. She was leaning against the wagon, only inches away. The collar of her white blouse was open a few buttons, exposing her throat, and she'd pulled on a wool shawl for warmth. He thought most ladies would have had trouble traveling for days, but McCall always looked fresh and comfortable.

"I was thinking," he answered, trying not to think about how rough and unkempt he must look next to her. He hadn't bothered to shave in two days. "What woke you?"

"A nightmare." She stretched, pushing her back against the wood of the wagon. "I must have listened to too many of Alyce Wren's stories today."

"You don't believe in the half-man, half-wolf tale, do you?"

He'd expected her to say no, but she only shrugged.

Sloan smiled slightly. "You probably think I'm one of them, the way I grabbed you and kissed you that night. I assure you I don't slither through the grass or howl at the moon."

"No, I didn't think you were one." She looked beyond him at the clouds. "Sometimes I'm not too sure of Alyce Wren, though the way she snores almost sounds like a howl."

Sloan agreed and leaned back against the wagon, so close they were almost touching. He tried to think of small talk, but he guessed he was no better at it than she seemed to be.

McCall closed her eyes and took a deep breath. When she finally looked at him, there was a question in her gaze, as though she needed to ask him something but couldn't find the words.

She took another breath and began slowly. "I married a man almost twenty years older than me," she whispered, as if just telling a story and not her life. "He was a good man—a great man, some folks said. But he never kissed me. Not on the mouth, anyway. Not anywhere except my cheek, the way a father might kiss his child."

Sloan found her story impossible to believe. But he said nothing.

"He'd lived alone since his school days and he didn't like to touch people, not in public or in private. He wouldn't even drink from the same cup as another unless he had to. Once, when cannon fire had been pounding only a few miles away for what seemed like days, I asked him to hold my hand. The look he gave me was one of disgust. As if I were showing some great weakness. I never asked again."

"Why are you telling me this?" Sloan whispered from the shadows beside her. He closed his fingers around the wood of the wagon, fighting back the urge to touch her now. He couldn't imagine a man married to such a woman and not touching her at every opportunity.

McCall shrugged again. "I don't know. Maybe I just need to talk to someone. I never told anyone that about Holden before. It seemed a silly thing to complain about."

"Did you love him?"

"Deeply," she answered quickly. Almost too quickly. "But sometimes I wanted to matter more to him. I wanted him to just hold me like you did last night. Or take my hand until I fell asleep. Alyce Wren says folks are wrong when they say a person doesn't miss what they don't have. Sometimes, I think, there's a need so deep inside a person that he longs for something all his life, even though he doesn't know what it is."

"And what is that need for you?" Sloan understood how she felt.

"I'd like to feel a man hold me. Hold me so tight, yesterday and tomorrow vanish. I'd like to feel like I was all that mattered when I was in his arms."

"Any man?" Sloan turned toward her.

Damn! he almost screamed aloud as she shrugged again. Why couldn't she say *him*? Hell, he'd hold her all night again if she'd just say the word. But she didn't. Her slight movement had said it all. She wanted to try something and any man would do.

Sloan felt his heart tighten, hardening against the world until he could feel nothing. If he had any sense, he'd hold her and give the lady what she wanted; but somewhere through the years, all the sense must have been beaten out of him. He didn't want to touch a woman who wanted any man. He wanted someone who wanted him, just him, with all his past and nightmares and scars.

He moved a few inches away. "Maybe if you walk back to the hidetown, May won't have made it to all the brothers tonight. I'm sure they'll hold you if that's all you want and any man's arms will do."

Anger fired, battling embarrassment, McCall raised her hand and struck his cheek before Sloan had time to move.

He reached for her, but she was gone, storming back to her bedroll with enough rage to keep the camp warm for the rest of the night.

Sloan leaned against the wagon and swore to himself. He must be losing his mind to have passed up such an opportunity. He slammed his head against the wagon and swore again. Why couldn't he have settled for being the "just any man" she wanted to hold her?

"Not too bright, are you, son?" Alyce Wren giggled as she poked her face out of the wagon. "I've seen crickets in the flour with more wisdom than you."

Sloan glanced at her, hoping she'd take his stern stare as a hint.

"That girl needs a lover, son, and you don't seem to be measuring up to the task." Alyce Wren looked into the night and smiled. "I could give you a few pointers if you like. This trip isn't going to last forever, and you're not making much progress. What you know about women won't hold a raindrop and what you don't know may drown us all."

Sloan frowned at her. The old woman was crazy, but she must see that what she was talking about was far left of proper. She might be an old friend of the family, but that didn't give her the right to pick a lover for McCall and then pester him into considering taking action.

The old woman didn't notice his silence. She climbed out of her sleeping quarters and sat down on the wagon bench just above him as if she'd been invited. "I heard tell once of a coyote that fell in love with a little red fox. He followed that critter everywhere, but every time he got close, the fox darted away. Finally one day the fox was swimming the river and the coyote jumped in the water at her side. That fox didn't want to swim nearer to the coyote, even though she had to if she was going to get ashore. The coyote didn't want the fox going ashore, 'cause she'd just outrun him again. In the water she wasn't any faster than he. So they both swam on and on until finally they drowned together."

Sloan lifted his hat from the brake handle and put it on, even though there was no reason to. "Is there a point to this story?"

"Sure," Alyce snorted. "Don't fall in love with a red fox unless you're a real good swimmer."

Thirteen

❦

FOR THE NEXT three days McCall pushed the small band as hard as she could across the open country. At first she was angry at Sloan for turning her down when all she'd asked for was a hug; then finally she twisted her anger within, knowing that she'd been a fool. She'd always felt she hadn't been good enough to be Holden Harrison's wife. He'd taken several opportunities over the years to patiently point out her shortcomings in little lectures. She should have listened more closely, for something was very wrong with her.

"Morning," Sloan startled her as he passed. "You're up early."

McCall turned from the sunrise and faced him. It was the first word he'd said to her in three days that hadn't been absolutely necessary.

"Morning," she echoed. He smelled of soap and she guessed he'd just shaved. His hair was slightly damp and he'd combed it back.

He shifted his stance, as if nervous. "I thought I'd ride out early and scout ahead. Why don't you let everyone sleep another hour, then take their time with breakfast?

We've been moving these children pretty hard the past few days."

"All right," she answered, and noticed he looked surprised, as though he'd expected an argument. "I could use the time to wash a few things."

He tipped his hat slightly and swung into the saddle. Without another word, he rode off. McCall watched him go, wondering what it was about this man that drew her. Or maybe what it was about her that made her always pull away.

By midafternoon, when Sloan hadn't returned, McCall decided he had abandoned them. She couldn't blame him; she'd done everything wrong, including shooting at him. As the hours passed, she waited, hoping she was wrong.

At sunset, Alyce Wren stood beside her, watching the horizon where Sloan had disappeared. "He'll be back," she whispered. "I feel it."

"I don't know." McCall fought down any emotion from her voice. "Maybe he's dead. Maybe he met up with others and decided to leave us behind. Not all men honor a bargain made. You talk about him as if he were a knight, but he was just a drifter, nothing more."

"He'll come back," Alyce whispered. "Not because of a bargain or honor, but because of you. He'd die for you, child."

McCall looked at the old woman. "You're wrong. I mean nothing to him."

"You're blind, my McCallie, if you can't see the hunger he has for you in his eyes. A hunger so deep it will take him a lifetime to get his fill. Some men look at women and see someone they'd like to step out with, or have children with, or grow old with. He looks at you as though he knows he'll be buried next to you."

"You mean buried by," McCall corrected.

"No." Alyce shook her head. "I mean next to."

McCall didn't argue, though she knew Alyce had to be wrong. She remembered her husband saying once that he'd like to be buried next to his best friend, her father. She'd agreed to do so if something happened without realizing that he'd fill the last space in the row, allowing no space for her to be with her parents or beside him.

A movement on the horizon drew her attention. A man walked beside a horse, fading in and out of the cloudy night's shadows.

For a few minutes McCall couldn't figure out who it was, then she recognized Sloan's lean form. His shoulders slumped with exhaustion and it seemed to take great effort for him to keep moving.

She broke into a run and was within twenty feet of him before she noticed the figure on the horse behind him. She walked the last few feet, seeing Sloan straighten, hiding his tiredness when he heard her approach.

"Evening, General." Sloan looped his arm over her shoulder and pulled her hard against his side. "You miss me today?" He leaned on her as though needing her support.

His body seemed cold and the smell of blood and dirt filled her senses. "Are you hurt?"

"I'm fine," he said. "But I'd be dead if it hadn't been for this little lady."

McCall looked behind him to the person on the horse. "Eppie!" she cried and ran to the woman's side. The odor of dirt and blood was more potent. The two smelled like they'd been rolled in blood and battered with mud.

Eppie slid from the saddle, barely able to stand. "Evenin', lady," she whispered. "I thought I'd come stay a while, if you're up to company."

Before McCall could answer, the short woman began

melting to the ground as if she were made of wax and the
sun had grown too warm.

"What happened?" McCall asked as Sloan handed her
the reins and lifted Eppie into his arms. Even in the darkness, McCall could tell the woman was hurt.

"I found her a few hours after I left," he said as he
moved toward the wagons. "She's mostly just bruised, but
she's got a few cuts that need tending. I tried to stop the
bleeding, but I'm afraid I'm not much of a doctor."

He carried her into the camp and gently laid her down
where the light of the campfire was brightest. McCall
wanted to hear the whole story, but Eppie needed care first.
While Winter helped Sloan take care of his horse, Alyce
Wren bathed and doctored the tiny woman. For once Eppie
was silent, allowing them to do whatever needed doing
without protest.

Three wounds on her legs and one on her arm needed
bandaging. Alyce doctored while McCall wrapped. Just
having the wounds covered seemed to make Eppie
stronger. She managed to sit up while Alyce tried to get a
comb through her matted hair.

McCall stepped behind the wagon where Sloan was
washing up. She stood beside the basin, silently handing
him first a towel then his clean shirt.

When he took the shirt, his fingers covered hers.
"Thanks for washing this," he whispered. "But you didn't
have to."

"I was worried about you," she answered, not wanting
to talk about the laundry when other things were more important. "I thought you'd left us." She could feel the
warmth of his hand covering hers. "I wouldn't have
blamed you."

The pressure of his fingers on hers increased slightly.
She wanted to take the step toward him and fold into his

arms but wasn't sure he was offering an invitation. She refused to show a need when she knew men saw need as weakness.

"If I ever don't come back," he whispered as he took the shirt from her, "look for my body." His voice trailed off as though he'd only just become aware of how true his words were.

"I'll remember that." McCall turned away and moved back to the fire, forcing back tears. There seemed to be a thousand words that needed to be said between them and no time or privacy to say anything. First must come the children and Alyce and now Eppie.

McCall poured a cup of soup they'd made from potatoes and sat down beside their tiny guest.

With her arm in a sling and one leg bandaged past her knee, she accepted her second cupful of soup. McCall sat on one side of her and Sloan on the other as she began to talk.

"It was the morning after you left," she said between bites. "My Moses and his brother Adam decided to take a load of hides back to the fort. I figured they'd only be gone four or five days, and by then the rest of us could have finished up and gotten ready to move camp. So I didn't tag along with him like I usually do.

"They hadn't been gone an hour when Indians hit us. Apache, I think, maybe Cheyenne. The funny thing was I could swear there was a white man or two with them. The brothers ran them off, and me and May ran into the tall grass to hide. About the time I decided it had been quiet long enough and was safe to go back, a brave rode out of nowhere through the grass and picked me up like I was nothing more important than a sack of flour. I screamed and looked back, but May didn't try to help me or yell or nothing. She just watched." Eppie wiped a tear from her cheek. "I thought I was never going to see my Moses again so I fought like crazy. But he wouldn't turn loose of me. About then another one caught May, still standing there with her mouth open watching me. She looked like a wide-mouth bass waiting for the hook."

Winter moved closer. "Were the men Apache?"

Eppie looked at the boy. "I thought so at first, but they weren't like the others and they didn't try to hurt me or May. They just wanted to take us back to their camp. But I can tell you I was mighty disagreeable as company. May wasn't so choosy. By the time we made it to camp she was riding behind the man who caught her, holding on to him like he was her long-lost kin. I lost track of them after a time.

"The one who caught me carried me to a canyon where a whole bunch of them were camped and dumped me on the ground so hard I hurt my arm. I figured they were going to kill me, but all they did was talk to me in words I couldn't understand and keep pulling on this necklace Winter gave me. One woman about fifty came up to me and grabbed the pouch and started screaming at me like I'd done something terrible."

"Maybe they recognized the pouch as Winter's," McCall volunteered.

"Or maybe they thought you'd taken the pouch from my mother. She has one just like it," Winter whispered. "You could have been with some of my people. They wouldn't have hurt you none. Not my people."

"Well, they weren't too friendly, boy. After dark, they tied me to a pole and didn't bother to feed me. It took me until almost dawn to work free, then I ran. I looked around for May, but didn't see any sign of her. I can't remember how many times I fell and tumbled in the mud. I was about ready to give up when I spotted Sloan."

Eppie leaned back to take a long drink of coffee and Sloan picked up the story. "I wanted to bring her back here, but first I had to retrace her steps and find the camp. I figured you'd want to head that direction come morning, General." He winked at McCall, but she didn't respond. "By the time I found the camp and we headed back, it was midafternoon and Eppie was starting to worry me because she wouldn't stop bleeding. Twice we had to lay low to avoid being seen, but we made it."

"She'll be fine now." Alyce Wren folded her herbs away. "As fine as any of us are."

"I got to get back to my Moses. He'll go crazy if I'm not there when he gets back from the fort."

"We'll talk about it in the morning." McCall patted her hand. "You get some rest."

Eppie curled into her blanket like a child and closed her eyes. McCall helped Alyce get all the children down, then walked to the head of the first wagon where Sloan had set up guard.

"You really need to sleep," she whispered as she folded her shawl around her shoulders. "I'll stand watch for a while."

He pointed with his hand toward his saddle. "Have a seat."

McCall sank onto the blanket and used the saddle to brace her back. Sloan handed her his rifle.

"Normally, I'd argue with you, but I could use a few hours' rest." He sat beside her and leaned his chin on one knee. "What's your plan for tomorrow?"

McCall was suddenly glad to have someone to talk to. "I don't know. If we don't find the camp fast, they may move and we'll never find the parents—if that is the right tribe. But I know Eppie wants to get back to Moses as fast as possible."

"You'll figure it out, General," he said as he reclined back and rested his head in her lap. "You always do."

McCall felt her body stiffen, but she didn't say anything or push him away. He seemed to be trying hard to make his nearness natural, but his actions weren't smooth enough to be casual. She reminded herself that she was the one who came to him tonight.

"I wish you wouldn't call me that," she whispered, very much aware of the man now using her for a pillow.

"It fits you. You're so proper and in charge. You would have made a great general." Sloan closed his eyes and moved his head slightly. "I know I'd have followed you."

"But I'm not a man," she answered.

He nestled his face against her middle. "A fact I'm very much aware of at the moment. You smell so good. You remind me of a dress shop I stepped into by accident once. All starch and fresh-washed."

McCall brushed her fingers over his hair. "You need sleep," she whispered. "I didn't come out here to talk about the way I smell."

Sloan's arms circled her waist and pulled her a few inches down as he moved up. The action left them face to face. "I need a lot of things, McCall, and talk is far down the list. Right here, right now, I need to feel you next to me so badly I can't think of anything else." He made no effort to kiss her, though their faces were only an inch apart.

"I . . ."

"Don't say anything!" he ordered. "Don't tell me of how dead you are inside or how you'll kill me in the morning. I don't want to hear any of what you think you should say."

McCall's heart felt like it was pounding all the way to her throat but she didn't move.

His fingers moved through her hair and pulled the band holding her bun free. He pressed his face into her curls as his body spread out over the length of her. "Don't fight me tonight, McCall. I'm not going to hurt you. I only want to hold you close. I thought of having you this near all day. Sleep beside me like you did in the hidetown. Just sleep next to me."

She didn't move. His chest pressed so hard against her she could barely breathe, but she didn't try to push him away. She liked the feel of him blanketing her and the roughness of his whiskers against her chin.

He rolled to his side, pulling her against him. He kissed her forehead, then her eyelids, then her cheeks. "You want me near as much as I want you," he mumbled against her throat. "If not, go now. Otherwise, I plan to hold you all night. I want to feel your heart pounding against my chest until sunrise."

McCall placed her hands on either side of her and gripped the blanket in tight fists. Her heart was racing, her breath was coming in shallow gulps, but she wasn't moving.

Sloan leaned away slightly, giving her a chance to escape. When she didn't, he ran the back of his fingers slowly down her arm. "Close your eyes, McCall. You might even learn to feel again."

She knew all she had to do was move away. He wouldn't try to stop her. But instead she followed his instructions and closed her eyes.

Sloan lay beside her, watching her for several seconds. Everything about her told him she was afraid, but she wasn't moving away. For some unknown reason, this woman seemed to want him near. *Go slow,* he reminded himself, though most of his body wanted nothing more than to make love to her. But this was not the time or the place. He'd not take her on the ground with the children and Alyce Wren within hearing distance. She deserved more than that, far more.

"You're staying, then," he whispered as he curled her into his side.

"I'm staying," she answered, and it was almost a challenge.

At first her body was stiff against him, but slowly she relaxed. He stroked her arm gently and played with her hair. As she softened, he placed his arm around her waist and pulled her closer, enjoying the feel of her breasts pressing against his side.

"Are you cold?" he whispered, pulling the blanket over them both.

"No," she answered, as she looked up at him with eyes near panic. "I'm staying," she repeated with determination.

Sloan laughed softly. "All right," he answered. "I believe you."

When she was almost asleep her mouth opened slightly and he played with her full lips with light kisses. She didn't respond, but he knew she was aware of his kiss, for the pulse along her throat quickened.

With his arm circling her waist and her head atop his chest, he fell asleep. For once the nightmare didn't bother him. Several times during the night, he reached for her, running his hand over her back, moving his face against her hair, closing his fingers over hers as they rested on his chest.

He didn't remember her moving all night, but when McCall sat up suddenly, he also came full awake. Sloan blinked away sleep and looked around him. The children surrounded them. All were dressed, their hair combed and their faces scrubbed.

"How late is it?" McCall stretched.

"Barely dawn," Sloan answered as Winter moved closer. The boy had plaited his long hair into two equal braids.

"We want to go home," he said simply. "We've been ready since before first light. If our people are within a day of here then today is the day we will reach them. I could go slow, but I know my mother will want to wait no longer."

"But what of Eppie?" McCall asked.

Winter folded his hands behind him as though he were the parent talking to a child. "Miss Alyce says we can make Eppie a bed in the wagon. If we leave one wagon here and we all walk, I think we can make good time. Eppie will be safe among my people. They will help her get back to her Moses tomorrow."

McCall looked at Sloan.

Sloan shrugged. "It's as good a plan as any I could come up with."

"I can be ready in a few minutes." McCall was already buttoning up the few buttons at the top of her collar.

"I'll hitch the horses." Sloan helped her to her feet as Winter translated to the others. They all ran to tell Miss Alyce and help break camp.

For a moment Sloan faced McCall.

"About last night . . ." he whispered.

"Don't say anything," she interrupted. "Last night can't alter our original campaign. We don't matter; only the children do."

"If that's the way you want it," Sloan forced the anger from his voice, but his last word, though whispered, was a swear, "General."

She squared her shoulders and moved away without another word. Sloan watched her go with his hands balled into fists inside his pockets. Someday, he thought, what happens between us will change everything. Someday soon. I swear.

Fourteen

❧

THE SUN WAS low in the sky by the time the wagon neared where Sloan had seen the Indian camp. A long ravine ran across the open land, a shallow stream winding along its base. The survivors of the battle along the Washita were camped amid trees, camouflaged among white pine and cottonwood.

When Sloan saw the outline of the camp, he climbed down from his horse and walked ahead of the others with Winter by his side. He could tell they were Cheyenne. The chances were good this was Winter's tribe.

"My people won't shoot you if they see me," Winter whispered. He was so excited he was almost dancing in circles around Sloan.

"They've been through a lot these past few months. My hope is if the pouch you made drew so much attention, maybe the sight of you will keep them from assuming I'm their enemy." Sloan opened and closed his hands, feeling suddenly naked without his rifle.

"Eppie says they were mean to her, so it might not be my people. I've never known my mother's family to be cruel to human or beast."

Before Sloan could answer, shadows rose almost like

smoke from the grass between them and the camp. Before he could have pulled his weapon a line of men blocked their progress. Each was armed and braced for battle.

Small groups of women waited just beyond, ready to run for the ravine if a battle erupted.

Sloan took another step, then another. He could see the men tensing, ready to pull bows but waiting for a command. Some already had their fingers around the handles of long knives they kept strapped to their legs in the manner Winter did. When Sloan was close enough to see the hatred in their eyes, they saw the children climbing from the wagon.

Suddenly the always quiet, solemn children were laughing and running. Fully armed warriors dropped their weapons and forgot about Sloan. The children's shouts were echoed by others behind the braves. Where the men had to turn from war to joy, the women just beyond bore no such hesitation. They ran past the braves with their arms outstretched to catch their children. All at once the clearing was filled with crying and shouting and laughter.

Winter ran from one man to the other, greeting each in a way that told Sloan he'd known the warriors all his life. He stopped for a few minutes and talked with one older man, then ran to the group of women. Silently, amid the reunion, four men surrounded Sloan, boxing him into a prison. He glanced at the wagon. Several had done the same to McCall. The children might be celebrating, but he and McCall were still in danger.

The older man walked toward Sloan with a limp. His hair was almost solid white, but his body had not yet surrendered to age. "The boy told me you brought the children back to us. What price do you ask?" His words were broken and hard to understand but commanded attention.

Sloan kept his hands away from his Colt. "I ask no price."

The leader didn't believe him. He'd learned to hate the "yu ne ga" too much to trust Sloan's words.

Sloan looked around at the four walls of warriors surrounding him. They were simply waiting for the order to kill him; he could feel it. Winter might believe his people were not capable of killing them, but Sloan had no such illusion.

Slowly, Sloan took a step toward the wagon. He wanted to get closer to McCall for two reasons. One, to calm her fears. And two, if they couldn't talk themselves out of this, at least he could reach for his rifle and take a few men down with him. The human prison moved with him, allowing him progress but no freedom.

"Easy now, McCall," he whispered as he reached the side of the wagon. "Don't worry."

"They don't look too friendly," McCall whispered back.

"Keep a tight rein on the horses. If trouble breaks, don't worry about me, just get out of here as fast as you can." He looked from face to face. None of the men understood what he was saying, and the older man, who seemed to be the leader, was several feet away.

"If any one of these men takes a step closer to me, do you think you could throw me the rifle, darlin'?" He smiled as if his words had all been sweet-talking her.

"My hand's already on it," she answered. "Alyce is kneeling just behind me with that extra Colt of yours. She'll take down the first man who moves toward you."

"That sounds great, but try to look relaxed. We may not have to fight our way out of this."

The older man seemed to be arguing with two younger braves.

Sloan motioned with a slight nod of his head. "Looks

like we've got someone in our corner; I just wish I knew which one."

"Sloan!" Winter yelled from thirty yards away. "Sloan!"

Sloan turned as Winter barreled through the warriors and flew into his arms. He caught the boy in a bear hug as he'd done before when Winter needed him, without thinking that he was now off guard and unable to draw.

"What is it, son?" Sloan asked as Winter's huge gulps of pain vibrated through his own chest and shook his heart with the boy's anguish.

"She's dead!" he cried as Sloan held him tighter. "My mother's dead!" The words of two languages blended in sorrow. "She must have been dead before I reached the water that day. I've been thinking she was worried about me, and she's been dead all this time."

Sloan forgot about the men surrounding him. He dropped to one knee and held Winter as tight as he could.

All the times Winter had been too brave to cry melted away as tears streamed down the little boy's face. "One of the women said they saw her fall. She was shot in the chest and blood covered her, then a soldier rode by and put another bullet in her head.

He wished he knew words to comfort. But how could he tell the boy that everything was going to be all right when it had never been more wrong?

"I didn't look back when I heard the shooting. I didn't look back. She might have been looking for me when she died. I didn't think that one of the screams I heard could have been hers. I would have run back to be with her if I'd known."

His words were a jumble of languages, but Sloan understood the sorrow. All of Winter's energy had been focused on reaching his mother, and she hadn't even been waiting for him.

Sloan held the crying boy as he fought back his own tears. The boy's sobs filled the clearing and everyone around was shaken by his cries.

The warriors lowered their weapons and relaxed their stance as they stood watching, absorbing his sorrow like slow rain falling over them.

"Get out of my way!" Alyce Wren shouted as she pushed one of the six-foot braves aside as though he were a gate and not a wall. "Go find something to do and stop trying to frighten me."

The man moved back.

Winter turned when Alyce called his name. He tried to stop the tears, but it was hopeless.

"Boy," she looked right into Winter's eyes, "you've got things to do before you let grief take you. I need to know if any of the others can't find their parents. I'll not leave them out here alone with no kin. Also, you'd better tell these kind folks fixing to kill us that we're trying to help. There'll be time for tears later. Right now I need you."

Sloan stood beside the boy and put his hand on the thin shoulder. He wished he could tell Winter to go ahead and cry, but no matter how small the shoulders, they had to hold the load. "I'll be right beside you, son," Sloan whispered. "You can get through this. Miss Alyce is right; we've got to take care of things first."

For the second time in his few years of life, the boy shoved the pain of a parent's death aside in order to do what must be done. There was no doubt in Sloan's mind that he'd be a strong man one day. He barely passed Sloan's belt buckle, but he had a man's job to do and he'd better do it fast or there would be more dead.

Winter moved among the children, then he spoke with the adults. Finally, he walked with the leader back to camp. The braves still watched Sloan and the women, but they

kept their distance now and their knives were no longer
drawn. Sloan tied his horse to the wagon and followed
Winter.

By the time they were in the Indian camp, they were
welcomed. The word had spread. Many women hugged
Alyce and McCall, crying as they thanked them for bringing back their children. Eppie refused to leave the wagon
and screamed for help every time one of the people tried to
enter. She wanted nothing to do with these people, friendly
or otherwise. Winter tried to explain to her that his people
had thought she'd killed him and stolen the bag. She still
couldn't forgive the way they'd treated her.

They were invited to supper. To Sloan's surprise, all the
children except Winter gathered around them to eat, instead of mixing with their families. Winter had walked into
the night with the leader. After they'd eaten, one by one the
children said good night to them and left to join their families. Sloan knew he'd never see any of them again. Several gave him presents. Morning Dove gave him her most
valued possession—her pouch of rocks.

When the leader returned to the campfire, he was alone.
In his broken English he invited Sloan and the women to
sleep in his teepee. Alyce refused, saying simply that she
and McCall would sleep in the wagon with Eppie.

McCall looked at Sloan. He could still see the edge of
fright in her eyes and guessed she wanted him close
tonight.

"I sleep under the wagon," he said slowly so the leader
could understand the words. "I'm used to the open air."

The leader nodded as if he thought them odd, but didn't
have time to try to understand.

When he turned to move away, Sloan stepped in his
path. "Winter?" he asked. "Where is Winter?"

The leader pointed to the ravine and shook his head. "He

would not come back. If you look, you'll find him near the stream."

Sloan glanced at McCall. Before he could say a word, she said, "No, I'll not stay. I'm going with you."

They walked together through the shadows of the trees along the shallow creek bed. Sloan took her hand, leading her slowly while he listened for any sound.

They must have walked a half mile before they heard the sound of something pounding the ground. Sloan motioned for her to be silent and they moved on.

After several more steps they came to a small clearing where Winter knelt. His back was to them, and again and again they saw him raise his knife in the air and strike the earth in front of him.

Sloan moved slowly around Winter's side.

"Winter," he whispered, not wanting to frighten the boy.

Winter looked up suddenly, his knife high in the air.

"Sloan?"

"Yes." Sloan moved in front of him and knelt. "I was worried about you, son. It's time to turn in for the night."

"I'm fine," Winter said as he drove the knife into the hole he was digging. "My mother's dead." The pain in his voice was liquid in the night air. In an hour the night would be frosty, but nothing would numb the boy's heartache.

"Yes, I know." Sloan watched the knife fall again. "What happened to her was wrong, very wrong." How could he explain to this little boy that killings were done on both sides and there would be more before it was settled?

McCall knelt on the other side of Winter. "What are you doing?" she whispered.

"I'm digging a hole," Winter answered and let his knife fall once more into the ground. "White Wolf tells me I can't stay with The People any longer. He says I must go back to my father's world. He says I'm not one of them anymore."

"But . . ."

Winter's blade hit the earth again. "He says the sun is setting on the Indian, but it is only rising on the white man's time. He says my tomorrows have to be in my father's world."

Sloan rubbed his eyes. He could see the logic in the old leader's advice. If Winter stayed here he might not live to be an adult, but if he went back he'd be going back to the very people who killed his mother. The old leader was sending the boy into the bear's cave to sleep.

"He says I'm not one of them. He says I can't be. Not ever again." Winter raised his other hand. "He did this to me."

Sloan reached out and took what Winter handed him. Hair. He looked closer. White Wolf had cut the boy's braids just below each ear.

"I don't want to go," Winter whispered. "But I have no choice." He took the hair from Sloan's hand. "So I'm going to bury the Indian part of me in the earth where my mother is. One woman told me the soldiers came back and buried the dead at Washita. I'm never going to be of the people again, but I'm never going to be white, either."

He shoved the dirt over his hair. "I belong nowhere."

McCall gently placed her arm around his shoulder. "Yes, you do," she whispered, but he was crying too hard to hear.

"Yes, you do, Winter," she repeated over and over. "From this night on you belong to us."

Fifteen

SILENTLY, SLOAN WATCHED Winter cry until there were no more tears in him, then he wiped his face with Sloan's bandanna and swore, "I'll never cry again. Not as long as I live."

Sloan lifted him from the ground. Winter wrapped his arms and legs around the tall man as though he were hanging on during a violent storm. They walked slowly through the blackness of night back to camp. McCall followed so close beside Sloan her skirt brushed his pant leg with each step. The wind howled in the trees and cool air circled around them, stealing warmth.

Choosing his footing carefully, Sloan knew if he tripped, they'd all fall. By the time they reached the campfires, Alyce Wren and Eppie were asleep. A few of the tribe members moved in the distance, banking fires for the night and securing boundaries.

Sloan lowered Winter onto his own bedroll beneath the wagon and stood. "In a minute or two he'll be too much of a man to allow me to carry him."

"He has had so much grief for such a little one." McCall kissed Winter gently on the forehead and brushed the now short hair away from his eyes. "I don't want him to think he doesn't belong. He belongs to us, now, and always will."

"He's young and strong," Sloan whispered. "He'll survive. But as for belonging to us . . ." Sloan didn't know how to say what had to be said without hurting her. She must be blind not to notice that he was on the run, avoiding invisible bullets until one day the real one came. What kind of father would he make for a boy who'd have more than his share of battles just because of his blood?

"Are you trying to tell me you don't want him?" McCall seemed to be fighting to keep her voice low as she stood and faced Sloan. The wind whirled a single strand of hair across her cheek like one streak of war paint.

Her question demanded his full attention. Sloan jammed his fists into his pockets to keep from touching her. "I didn't say that." Sloan backed a step away from her and the wagon. "But children aren't something you pick up along the road and decide to keep. Maybe we should look around for folks who want to bring him up proper. You know, with a farm and a school down the road." He knew it would be a long shot, but they might find someone.

"You know as well as I do that most of the folks who'd agree to take him would use him as a slave until he ran away or died from a beating. I don't know of a family that doesn't have more kids than they can feed already."

He didn't argue. The war had pushed many children on the streets when a widow couldn't take care of them. But Sloan was no more a father than McCall was a mother. Did she think she could keep Winter with her while she wandered from adventure to adventure? She was looking for a reason to die more than one to live, but he'd never confront her with such a fact. "I never thought about having kids, and if I had, I always guessed it would be the usual way."

"The usual way?" McCall answered.

"You know, by sleeping with his mother." Sloan was glad it was dark, for her question embarrassed him. He might not know much about men and women, but he knew enough to guess that folks didn't go around talking about such things as having children. He moved another step away and mumbled to himself, "Seems to me we skipped the fun part."

"Well," McCall followed him into the shadows, "I'm Winter's mother and you've already slept with me."

She wasn't making it easy. If he were turning down this huge responsibility she'd so lightly tossed at him, he'd have to do so with more directness. "I mean . . ." All the words that came to mind were gutter talk men used when no women were listening. Not the kind of things he'd ever be able to say to McCall. "I mean, a man becomes a father when he . . ."

She stared directly at him with that warrior stance that said she'd fight to the death, and he might as well surrender while he was still breathing.

"Do you mean that if you bedded me and I were Winter's mother, then you'd take on the responsibility?"

"Of course," he answered. "It would be the only right thing to do."

"Then bed me and be done with it, for I am Winter's mother from this time on and there seems to be no other man to serve as his father. My grandfather always told me a child must have a man to look to as he grows."

Anger boiled over his embarrassment. "Are you asking me to sleep with you just so I'll be a father to Winter?"

"If that's the price you ask." McCall straightened her clothes.

"Even if I wanted to share a night with you, McCall, I wouldn't do it because you were sacrificing yourself for the child. I care as much about Winter as you do."

"Then you don't want to make love to me?" She was charging again like a warring general opening up another line of attack. Even in the darkness he could see the fire in her eyes. A fire that would probably burn him to cinders at any moment.

"I didn't say that." Sloan could never be that big a liar to her, or to himself. "I've thought about making love to you. Hell, the thought occupies most of my time, when I'm not worrying about staying alive. But I'm not bedding any woman just so I can be tied down."

McCall stomped in frustration. "You're mad. First you won't sleep with me, then you tell me you think about it every waking moment. What's the great dilemma? I'm no untouched flower. Several times a year when I was married, my husband asked me to raise my hem for a few minutes so he could do what he called 'his duty.' I never minded all that much, and it doesn't hurt but a moment before it's over. My own father told me the day before I married not to go on about such a thing, like most women do."

Sloan didn't hear any thunder, but he sure felt the lightning strike him as her words registered. He always thought women valued their virtue over all else. Here she was using it like a card in a deck she played, telling him it would be no great thing if he had her. She seemed to think the act was no more important than making soap. Just part of life, nothing else. The idea not only astonished him, it hurt his pride. "Have you ever made anyone else such an offer?"

"I've never had a child who needed a father before," McCall answered. "Plus, I've never known a man I thought I could tolerate atop me even for a few minutes beside Holden and maybe you."

"Thanks for the compliment," Sloan said. The sarcasm

curdled in his voice. "But come hell or high water, I'm not sleeping with you for such a reason."

Her lips pressed together. Sloan knew she was debating. What would she try next, pulling a rifle on him and demanding he be Winter's father? Couldn't she see that he was barely able to stay alive himself? What kind of father would he be? *Hell,* he swore again, *what kind of lover does she think I'll be?*

Lifting her chin an inch, she turned away. Retreating silently, but as always with honor.

Sloan followed her back to the corner of the wagon. He didn't want to end their conversation like this. "Don't worry about the boy. I told you, he'll survive."

McCall leaned against the wheel. She was silent for so long, he didn't think she'd heard him. Then softly she whispered, "That's what they said about me . . . but they were wrong."

Watching her closely, Sloan suddenly realized the truth. She identified with the boy. Maybe a part of her was Winter. The little kid that had never been allowed to be a child. The girl who'd had to be a woman too soon. The young woman forced to play the part of widow before she even knew what it was like to live with love.

Without hesitation, he folded her into his arms. He'd fight the general in her, but he could never turn away from the child she needed to trust him enough to be. Like the sleeping boy at their feet, she needed to feel the warmth of arms holding her.

"It'll be all right," he whispered. "We'll find a place for Winter."

"I know." His chest muffled her words. "Just as I know there will never be a place for me."

Sloan remembered a line from a poem he'd seen once in a paper. Something about, *What do we do with the widows*

when the war is won? Their men will never come march-
ing home, but they'll go on, one by one.

Her husband had been the lucky one, Sloan realized.
He'd died a hero, but she'd had to go on with only memories. She'd been there for him, but Holden Harrison would
never be there for his wife. Sloan held her as she cried
softly. Tears for Winter, tears for herself, tears for a world
gone crazy. Her pain was so deep it left a cavern in her
he'd never be able to fill. She wanted a hero, and he was
only a man.

"Shhhh," he whispered against her hair. "You're not
dead, darlin'. You only think you are."

"I'm tired of all the sadness," she cried. "I want to feel
alive just once before I'm too old to feel anything. Walk
with me back to the clearing, then hold me like you did last
night. Hold me close."

Sloan glanced over McCall's shoulder at a movement in
the shadows of the wagon. He looked closely, not believing what he saw. Alyce Wren was holding out a blanket
and pointing with her head toward the woods.

He couldn't think of anything he'd like to do more than
take McCall into the shadows where no one would see
them. He'd like to make her feel alive again, the kind of
alive that great hero of a husband never made her feel. But
it galled him to think that Alyce Wren was pushing him.
The old woman had decided somewhere along the line that
he should be the one to bring McCall out of her mourning,
but this was going too far. He kind of wanted the decision
to make love to be his own. He didn't want to do it because
McCall needed a father for Winter, or because Alyce Wren
thought it was time.

"We can't leave the boy." He forced each word out.

Alyce shook the blanket harder.

"He'll sleep now," McCall said.

"What if Eppie wakes up and I'm not here to protect her? She goes half mad every time anyone except us gets within ten feet of her."

Alyce waved the blanket like a flag in a windstorm. She shook her finger so hard toward the trees, she rocked the entire wagon.

"Alyce Wren will comfort her." McCall snuggled beneath his arm.

He knew she'd let him make love to her tonight. She was vulnerable. Winter's grief had brought back her own. He wouldn't put it past her to be acting now, trying another strategy when her last advance failed. But he had to know that she wanted him, not just anyone. She'd come to matter too much to him. He didn't want to just bed McCall, he wanted to make love to her.

"I can't," he answered as his hands moved lovingly along her back. He must be very careful about turning her down. He had to think of some way to tell her there would be time later.

Alyce snorted from the wagon's interior and tossed the blanket out on the ground. She'd finally given up on her not-so-subtle hint.

Sloan smiled and lowered his face into McCall's hair to keep from laughing. "I'd love to walk with you," he whispered low in her ear. "I'd love to hold you in the moonlight of the clearing and lower you in the grass and make love to you. Not the kind of love where a woman only raises her hem, but the kind that blends two bodies so close together there is no beginning to one or ending to the other."

"I was only asking for a walk." McCall pulled away slightly.

Sloan's arms remained tight around her. "No, you weren't, lovely lady. You asked for more, far more. More than I may ever be able to give in this lifetime." His hands spread wide over her back and pulled her closer. He could feel the softness of her breasts against his chest and he knew she could feel the hardness of his need against her skirt.

"I won't ask again." She lightly kissed his lips as if testing.

"You won't have to," he whispered as his hands moved along her sides and warmed her through the cotton blouse. "But come to me when there's no reason besides loving. I'll do the best I can for the boy. I'll protect him with my life. But sleep with me because you want to, not out of sacrifice or duty."

She didn't answer as he kissed her lightly.

Suddenly, the need to taste her was greater than any need he'd ever known. He felt he might die of starvation if he didn't have just a little more of her. Nothing they'd said mattered. All that mattered was her.

Lifting her in his arms, he moved into the shadows. "I have to hold you and kiss you before I say good night, McCall. And for once, I plan to do it without an audience."

She didn't answer or protest as he walked away from the wagon and the lights of the campfires.

They crossed into the line of trees along the creek bed until they were so deep into the shadows that he couldn't see her face. But it didn't matter. He didn't need to see her; he only needed to feel and taste.

He lowered her feet to the ground but didn't lessen the hold around her waist. Here, the wind whirled around, rattling the leaves in a breathy whistling sound. Here, he could hold her without anyone seeing or listening. Here, he could let himself believe for a while that he belonged at her side and that she was his. He put his hands on her shoulders and moved slowly down, feeling her in front of him now that he could no longer see her.

"There's so much to loving." He kissed her bottom lip, guessing the location of her mouth. "I may not be the best teacher, but I could start you off with one lesson tonight. A lesson long overdue."

Cupping her face with both his hands, his mouth lowered to hers. The kiss was long and demanding, not tender as his others had been. He wanted her to feel him, only him. When she parted her lips to protest, the kiss deepened. He felt her body stiffen, but she didn't pull away.

He lightened the pressure until his words just brushed her lips. "I want you to remember the feel of my kiss, McCall. You'll never forget the taste of me, not after tonight. Just as I'll never forget the taste of you."

As he widened his stance for balance, he felt her lace her arms behind her back, as if willing herself not to push away or touch him except with her lips. She was silently telling him she'd take the full force of the lesson, even if she didn't feel anything inside.

He wanted to scream for her to kiss him back, or put her arms around him, or press against him, but he knew she was doing all she could. She wasn't running. He could almost hear her saying, "I'm staying," as she had last night. As if the words were a promise she'd made to herself, to be kept no matter what she must endure.

His hands moved down her throat, sliding into the open collar of her blouse so that he could wrap his fingers around her neck and feel her blood pulse just beneath. He could feel life pumping through her. She was alive, no matter how much she wanted him to believe otherwise.

The kiss turned warm and loving, but still she didn't respond. He gently nuzzled her throat and lightly brushed his lips over her eyelashes. But she didn't move.

He tasted her deep and long, memorizing every detail of the feel of her. His hands moved up from her waist until they rested just below her breasts. Her heart pounded against his fingers and the weight of her breasts rested lightly atop his hands.

She was driving him mad. She'd offered to lift her skirts and he'd adamantly refused. Now, he was bruising her lips with the force of his kisses, but she was responding with the warmth of a china doll. He had no idea what she'd do if he unbuttoned her blouse and continued the lesson. He had no idea how he'd survive if he didn't.

Sixteen

IN THE LAST remaining realms of sanity, Sloan stepped away. It was so dark he could barely discern McCall's outline, but he could hear her breathing. Shallow breaths that told him the kiss had affected her, even if she would never admit it.

"Do you want me to stop?" Sloan's words were low with longing; he barely recognized them as his own.

"What?" she whispered. Her voice shook slightly.

"Do you want more, McCall?" He'd make her see her own needs, even in the blackness. She might have buried a husband, but she was still very much alive. It was time she faced the fact. "Answer me!"

She didn't move; even her arms remained locked behind her back. Her tall frame blended with the trees, making her almost invisible.

He waited, hearing only the pounding of his own heart. If she said no, he'd walk away and never touch her again.

Finally her words came, just above the wind. "If I say yes, will you think me weak?"

"No," Sloan answered, fighting the urge to pull her to him.

"I've never been kissed or touched like that."

"Like how?" He couldn't tell by her voice if she was pleased or terrified.

"Like you'd swallow me whole if you could. Like I'm velvet and you can't get enough of the feel of me."

"Just answer the question. Do you want me to continue, McCall?"

"I don't know." Her shoulders lifted and fell slightly. "I think so."

It took every drop of control he'd ever reserved to stand still and say, "Then prove it."

She took the challenge like he'd known she would, like a fighter. "How?"

"Unbutton the top button of your blouse."

For a moment she just stood still, then he saw her silhouette move. Her hands raised to her throat. "But you can't see me. What difference does it make?"

"It doesn't matter if I can see you. I'll know," he answered, swearing that someday he'd watch her undress again in bright sunlight. "Now the next button."

"But . . ."

"Are you afraid?"

"No," she answered, her hands moving down the front of her blouse. "But I see no point."

"Now the next button, and then the next."

He watched as the shadow's hands lowered. "Is your blouse open all the way to the waist?"

"Yes," she said matter-of-factly.

"Then pull the ties on your camisole."

She complied, but he only guessed she'd followed his directions.

"Now, push the material aside until the night air touches your skin."

The shadow shifted again, then straightened and locked her hands behind her back once more.

"Are you finished?"

"Yes," she answered.

"Are you cold?"

"A little," she whispered.

"You won't be in a minute."

Very slowly, he stepped closer, until he could feel her breath at his throat. So close his knuckles brushed her as he worked, unbuttoning his shirt and spreading it wide so that his chest was bare. All she had to do was step away and he'd stop, but she didn't move.

"Tonight you're going to feel, McCall," he said against her ear as he turned her face slightly and kissed her once more.

As before, she didn't respond to his kiss, but stood frozen in his arms.

Moving his arms around her, he threaded his fingers through hers as he pulled her to him. The impact of his skin against hers sent a jolt through McCall that Sloan felt with his whole body. She stiffened, her fingers closed around his, and her mouth opened in shock.

He took advantage of her surprise as his mouth closed over hers. The softness of her skin against him was maddening, affecting him as much as it shocked her. Sloan didn't want to use his hands to touch her. He wanted to feel McCall against his heart.

Sloan tasted deeply of the inside of her mouth as she struggled slightly, causing her bare breasts to rub against his chest. He released her mouth and kissed her throat. She still struggled, pushing and turning so that the wall of his chest molded her against him, driving reason from him as passion flooded in. She didn't cry out and she didn't turn loose of his hands, now locked behind her back.

He let her twist as if she were a wild animal trapped while he captured her mouth and kissed her. The warmth of him spread into her, and she no longer felt cold against him.

"Do you feel me now, McCall?" he whispered into her ear. "Are you alive enough to feel my heart pounding against yours?"

She didn't answer, but turned her face away when he tried to capture her lips once more. Suddenly pulling her closer, he lowered his mouth to hers with more hunger than he'd meant to show. He knew she was fighting her own emotions and not him, for her fingers held his arms tightly at her back. He couldn't have stepped away from her if he'd had the will to try.

With a hungry sigh of longing, she stopped struggling. The death grip she'd had on his hands loosened. His kiss turned gentle as she rested against him, a warrior tired of fighting all feeling. As he moved his mouth to her throat, he felt her breath coming quick and hard and her chest rising, pressing again and again into his. There was a softness and a wildness about her he'd never thought the woman he called General could have.

Finally, she softened in his arms. He was able to kiss her as he longed to, showing her how warm a kiss could be. She lifted her arms and draped them over his shoulders. As he stroked her back, he felt her move against him in matching rhythm.

"Kiss me back," he pleaded.

"I can't," she answered as she cuddled into his chest, fighting her own feelings.

"Kiss me back!" The cry came from so deep inside Sloan it shattered the passion he felt. He didn't just want to kiss her, he wanted her to kiss him. He needed to know that she cared about him a fraction as much as he cared for her, and had since she'd laid her hand over his heart that first night. He wanted one corner of her love, but she wouldn't allow him even that.

"You're not dead," he whispered, holding her to him as if he could will her to feel. "You can't be, because . . . because you're the only woman I've ever wanted." Fate had played enough tricks on him, surely he wouldn't find a woman like McCall, only to discover she couldn't return his feelings. "You're the only one I've ever wanted to make love to."

"I can't," McCall answered. "I want to, but I can't."

He knew the reasons without her telling him. She'd been ordered and laced within rules so tightly, she couldn't break free. But that didn't stop him from wanting her.

"If I were—"

"If you were another, it wouldn't matter," she interrupted, pressing her cheek against his throat. "You're the first man ever to make me want to feel. I've been told it was wrong to show emotion for so long, I can't just change in a day and begin to react."

When she looked up, he pressed his forehead against hers. "I want so much to make love to you, McCall."

"I've already said you could. If it will make you Winter's father, I don't mind."

"No," he corrected. "You said I could take you. There's a difference. I can't use you. It's not my way. Most of my life I've spent not knowing on which side of the fence I stood. But this I know for fact: I'll not make love to you without you participating. I'll wait."

"I may never—"

"Then I'll wait forever." He kissed her nose. "Just promise once in a while when we're alone you'll let me hold you like this. I need to hold you, even if you don't need me."

She didn't answer, but he could feel her tears against his

chest. He wrapped his arms around her and held her so tightly he feared he might hurt her. But she said nothing.

An hour later, when they returned to camp, her head still rested on his shoulder and his arm still kept her warm.

As they moved through the shadows, they could see that White Wolf stood beside the wagon. He'd found the blanket Alyce Wren had thrown out and wrapped it around himself while he waited.

Before Sloan could stop him, White Wolf shook Winter's shoulder and awakened the boy. He whispered something to him.

Winter shoved the sleep from his eyes and rose. "White Wolf says you must talk to him."

"Now?" Sloan released McCall's shoulder with a gentle hug.

"Now." Winter yawned. "I'm to say his words. But not until the woman leaves." He glanced at McCall. "That's what he told me to say."

"The woman stays," Sloan gambled. If White Wolf was going to tell them of trouble, he'd best make sure McCall heard, or she'd never follow his advice and be careful. Sloan slid his fingers down McCall's arm and took her hand. "He'll say what he has to say to both of us."

Winter talked with the old man for a minute. White Wolf nodded. They all moved to the light of the campfire and sat down as if it were early and not after midnight.

"White Wolf says he made me go with you because you are the one I ran to when I knew my mother was dead. He says my heart made the decision of which people are now my people." Winter tried to sound very matter-of-fact, but the words tore at him.

"He says I will be a powerful man in any world, but I will never belong to you as a child belongs to his family.

He says I am a man now and must make my way. You are only my guide for a few moons."

Sloan nodded, wondering how much of what Winter said was the old man's words and how much was a boy's longing to be grown. "Tell him I agree," Sloan said, and ignored McCall, who looked like she wanted to object but didn't dare when she hadn't been invited to the meeting. She settled instead for poking him in the ribs with her elbow, a habit he found not only irritating, but painful.

"He also says a group of men are two days' ride from us. They are a mixture of both our peoples, but they all share one thing. . . ." Winter paused, looking for the right words. "They are all maggots."

Sloan understood. "Ask him if they look for his people."

Winter whispered and the old man answered. Slowly, he looked back at Sloan. "Some do," Winter said. "But three men hunt for you. One has a cut just below his eye that is your mark."

Sloan felt the blood drain from his body. He didn't have to ask why the men were coming after him. He knew. The man from the creek who'd beaten McCall—what had his name been—Bull? It must have taken him some time, but the man had figured out Sloan's identity. Now at least one of Satan's Seven had found him—maybe three. And Sloan hadn't made it hard for them by changing his name. He'd ridden into their home state as if daring them. Old Pete in prison used to say, "If you call out the devil, don't be surprised when he comes a-dancing."

Glancing at McCall, a realization struck Sloan. A month ago he'd almost been looking for the Seven, hoping they'd find him and end the worry. But now, now he'd found McCall, and suddenly wasn't in so much of a hurry to die. There were things he wanted to say to her, times he wanted to spend, and passion he needed to believe her capable of returning.

If he hadn't come to Texas, he never would have met her. He might never have found any of Satan's Seven.

An hour later Sloan had saddled his horse and was ready to leave. Half the camp had awakened and were standing around discussing his strategy.

"It's the only way, McCall," he said for the tenth time. "If I stay with you, I may get you all killed. The men who are after me have been looking for three years. They'd never leave a few women and a boy alive as witnesses. But the odds are good I can draw them further north, away from Winter's people and you."

"But you'll be alone?"

"I've been alone most of my life. It's nothing new to me. I'll survive." He glanced over his shoulder as he finished tying his saddlebags. McCall never looked as beautiful as she did right now. Her lips were a little puffy from his kisses and her eyes were wide with question. He wasn't sure he could look at her when he rode away. If he didn't, he wasn't sure he could leave.

"But you promised to stay with us until we made it back to a fort."

"I promised to keep you safe, and this is the best way. At dawn, head back to Moses' camp. White Wolf said he'd have a few men follow close to make sure you're safe. Then, have Moses take you back to the station."

McCall straightened, too proud to cry or beg him to stay. "We'll be fine."

Sloan faced her. "I'm not leaving you because I want to. I'll make it back to the station as fast as I can."

He reached to touch her, but she stepped away. "It doesn't matter," she said. "Your job is over. Thank you for helping me deliver the children."

She was dismissing him. After all they'd been through together, she was dismissing him! Sloan fought the urge to grab her by the shoulders and shake her. "Fine, General," he whispered. "It was nice knowing you."

Winter handed him a canteen he'd filled with water from the spring.

Sloan smiled down at the boy. "Take care of the women as best you can, son."

"I will," Winter answered, and brushed the handle of his knife as he'd seen Sloan do with his Colt. "I'll see that they get back to the station without any harm coming to them."

Sloan knelt and hugged the boy one last time. "I'm coming back," he whispered. "I'm not leaving you."

"I know," Winter tried to make his voice strong.

Standing, Sloan crammed his hat low and took the reins with one hand. Just before he swung into the saddle, he glanced back at McCall.

"I'll meet you at the station," he promised.

"Good-bye," she answered, as if she knew he was lying. "Take care." She turned away as he kicked his mount into action.

Seventeen

MCCALL TRIED TO sleep the few hours between when Sloan left and dawn, but couldn't. Every man she'd cared about had left her, and now Sloan was no exception. She didn't even want to care about him. He was a no-good drifter who'd never stay in one place. He couldn't even stay on the same side of a war. She'd be a fool to think he'd be back. He was probably halfway to New Mexico Territory by now. In a matter of days he'd forget her and the station, and if she was wise, she'd forget him.

Just after dawn, Alyce Wren brought McCall a warm cup of her special herb tea. The old woman insisted Mc-Call lie back down for an hour while she and Eppie took their time with breakfast.

McCall started to argue, but as the tea warmed its way down her throat, she yawned. She set the half-empty cup aside and curled into the covers inside the wagon. The canvas cover blocked out the early sun. McCall relaxed.

For a while her dreams floated aimlessly over her life, finally settling in the warmth of a man's arms. McCall smiled in her sleep as she recognized Sloan's hold. He always had a way of pulling her against his chest so she could feel the pounding of his heart. Some folks hug with their arms, or lightly with a touch, but Sloan hugged with his heart, warming her no matter how cold she'd felt a moment before.

In her dream, she raised her face and kissed him as she never could in her waking hours. With each of her responses, he stroked her hair—silently telling her of the pleasure she brought him. She liked the taste of his mouth and continued the kiss.

Her hands moved over his shoulders, loving the hard feel of his muscles beneath her touch, loving the way her touch made his breath come quicker.

McCall moaned in her sleep, wishing for more . . . dreaming for something she'd never known.

Ten miles away, Sloan finally collapsed on his bedroll. The sun was up. He'd done all he could do for one night. He'd crossed his own trail ten times, leaving signs a blind trapper could follow. If one of Satan's Seven was following him, he should have no trouble finding him after tonight. Sloan had done everything short of cutting arrows into trees to point his path.

Now it was time to rest awhile, then move on. Sloan had ridden onto rocks about a half hour back and climbed up until he'd found a place big enough to hide his horse. Then he'd left his gear several feet below and curled beneath an overhang so he could sight anyone coming, yet not be seen. The horse would warn him if anything moved within a hundred yards. He laid his rifle and Colt within easy reach and pushed deeper into the rock's trench.

Sloan pulled the bandanna from his saddlebags, then propped the bags up as a pillow. Lying back, he unfolded the bandanna until he touched McCall's picture. There she was, still smiling at him. For a long moment he stared at the tintype, wondering how the beautiful widow had come to mean so much to him.

As he closed his eyes, she came to him, all soft and wanton. Her mouth was hungry and ready for his kiss even before he lowered his lips. She pressed against him as though she longed to be closer. She touched him with hands of velvet. Unlike in life, in his dream she was the aggressor, moving against him, begging him for more.

Sloan awoke with a start. He'd dreamed of women before, but nothing so real. He could still taste her in his mouth, and the feel of her body still warmed his side. He could almost smell the rose soap she used in the cold dampness of his tiny cave. He folded the tintype back into the bandanna and placed it in his shirt pocket.

For a long while he didn't sleep, but lay awake thinking of McCall. When he did sleep, she didn't appear in his dreams again.

By the time he awoke, it was noon. He ate a hard roll and jerky McCall had packed for him, noticing she'd used one of her own clean white handkerchiefs to wrap it in. Today he'd keep riding north, leaving a trail, then tomorrow he'd backtrack and see if the bait was taken. With luck, McCall and the others would be halfway to the fort before those tracking realized they'd been fooled.

McCall watched from the wagon as Eppie jumped into Moses' arms. The moment they'd seen the camp, Eppie had climbed down and started running like a child who could wait no longer. She hadn't made it half the distance before Moses appeared from the hide lean-to. He dropped the wood he was carrying and rushed toward her with his arms outstretched. He grabbed her wildly and swung her high in the air. Their greeting made McCall envious.

"We made it back to her man," Alyce Wren said from

the rocker behind McCall. Since the children had gone she'd insisted on riding in her rocker, now that there was room to set the thing upright. She didn't seem to mind the trip so much in the chair McCall's grandfather had given her years ago.

"They look so happy." McCall smiled as she watched them. "They must really love one another."

"That they do, child, but there's something else. They got a passion for each other. She's a part of his need in this life and he's a part of hers. From the looks of them, I'd say they may be each other's only necessity in this world."

"I loved Holden," McCall said, more to herself, just because it seemed to need to be said. "But I don't remember ever thinking he was a part of my need. He was my life, though. From the time I awoke until I fell asleep, I was always thinking of taking care of him. When the army rested, I cooked and mended. When the army marched, I followed."

"Did he ever hold you wildly like that man does Eppie?" Alyce Wren asked. "Did he ever need you so badly he'd risk his life to be at your side?"

"No," McCall answered, then lifted her chin. "He had his men to think of and the war and a hundred more important things."

Alyce Wren rocked. "My father told me once that only one man in a hundred finds a woman so vital to him he can't live without her. He said maybe only one in a hundred women love enough to keep such a man."

"You're not making sense. I know lots of folks who love their mates."

"Enough to be each other's basic need? Enough to have a passion so deep it blinds? Do they have a longing so deep into their soul that they'd do anything for the other?"

"Yes," McCall answered. "I would have loved Holden

that much." The moment the words were out she realized what she'd said. "I mean, I did love Holden that much."

"Of course you did, child," Alyce Wren whispered. "But did he love you back?"

McCall opened her mouth to say yes, then stopped. In three years she'd never thought that maybe Holden didn't love her. He'd told her he did several times before they married and a few times afterward. Even to the end, she'd tried to prove her love. But it had never seemed like enough. Alyce was right—he'd never needed her the way Eppie and Moses needed one another.

"My Eppie tells me I'm supposed to get you ladies back to the fort and beyond safely," Moses interrupted McCall's thoughts. "Seems the least I can do, since your man saved her life."

"Thank you," McCall answered without correcting Moses on his choice of words.

"I'll collect a few things and be ready to move. You go ahead and get this wagon pointed in the right direction."

"I'll go with you to see them home," Eppie volunteered. "I'm not staying with the brothers again."

Moses laughed. "They're real sorry they didn't come to your aid. They thought the braves would only take you, so they didn't fight. When the last rider grabbed May, they collected their guns, but it was too late." Moses looked around. "Where is May? Did they kill her?"

"No." Eppie tried to keep from giggling. "She told us she liked the way the savages treated her. Plus she said they smelled better than your brothers."

Moses shook his head. "They'll be real sad to hear that. I think at least one of them was gettin' ready to make May his woman. Maybe her leaving saved a fight between them."

"They will be real sorry to hear from me when I get

through with them." Eppie laughed. "I'll skin them alive
for not rescuing me when I get back from helping you deliver this wagon. They'll think twice before letting some
brave ride off with me again."

Moses patted her on the bottom. "What say we stay a
day at the station? I've got enough cash that we could sleep
in a real bed and eat vittles someone else cooks."

Eppie was so excited she rocked the wagon as she
climbed in. "Let's get going."

McCall moved out while Moses ran for his gear. Within
a few minutes he'd thrown his smelly bedroll into the back
of the wagon and tied his horse to the tailgate. By nightfall
they'd covered twice the land McCall would have thought
they could. Moses knew the route and was a skilled team-
ster, plus he and Eppie seemed in a hurry to sleep in a real
bed.

The days passed in endless scenery. Only the colorful
sunsets broke the boredom of the prairie. When they made
camp each night, everyone had a job. McCall cooked,
Eppie got out the bedrolls, Winter gathered firewood, and
Moses took care of the horses. In less time than she'd
thought possible after having all the children to deal with,
everyone was bedded down for the night. McCall and
Alyce Wren slept in the wagon, Winter beneath it, and
Moses pulled Eppie into the shadows for a while each
evening before sleeping in the open by the campfire.

As she had each night since Sloan left, McCall tried to
sleep, but she could hear Eppie giggling from the distance.
She snuggled into her blankets and tried to force herself to
relax. Finally, Moses and Eppie returned to the campfire,
and all was silent.

As McCall's body warmed beneath the covers, she felt
Sloan beside her. She welcomed the dream once more,
opening her mouth to his kisses and feeling his hands mov-

ing over her body. He tickled her ear with his whispers and pulled her close so she could hear the pounding of his heart. Sloan's heart. The only sound that allowed her to relax and sleep.

Hidden in a distance of miles and night, Sloan also slept. He also dreamed. She came to him all soft and gentle, as she never had in life. Welcoming his touch and needing his warmth.

Sloan was so lost in his fantasies he didn't hear the first sounds of someone moving toward him through the night. He'd been so many years without a dream that he didn't pull himself back to reality as fast as his training should have demanded. He didn't respond to the slight sound of a blade clearing leather.

In his dream he wanted one more touch, one more kiss, one more heartbeat.

Eighteen

MCCALL JERKED AWAKE with a cry. For a moment she didn't know where she was. The wagon's canopy hid the stars, and she couldn't feel the warmth of any fire.

"What is it, child?" Alyce Wren rose on one elbow, only the width of the wagon away. "What's happened?"

"Sloan," McCall whispered. "Something's happened to Sloan." She couldn't bear to voice her dream.

"Nonsense," Alyce tried to reassure her. "Sloan can take care of himself. He promised to meet us back at the station. We'll be there in another day, two at the most if this rain keeps up. You'll see—he may even be waiting for us when we arrive."

When McCall didn't seem convinced, she added, "I'd have felt it if he were in trouble. I can always feel trouble riding in, even on a cloud."

"No." McCall shook with a fear she'd never known, not even when she'd been in the middle of the battlefield. She felt as if a part of her were dying, and she could do nothing to stop it. "He's in trouble, maybe dead already. I can feel it." All the men who ever cared about her, her grandfather, her father, her husband, had died. Since Sloan had acted like he cared, it seemed logical in this midnight hour that he might be dead also.

McCall didn't sleep the rest of the night. At dawn she tried to talk Moses into leaving to look for Sloan. But Moses was determined to see them to safety. When she wouldn't stop asking, he finally told her that no one, not even an Apache, could track in this rain. Everyone, including Winter, tried to convince her Sloan would be all right alone, but McCall wouldn't be calmed. By the time they reached the station two days later, she was ill from lack of sleep.

Pushing herself, McCall insisted on settling Winter into the room between hers and Alyce Wren's. She then weathered the icy rain with him in tow to a little store across from the station that served as mercantile, dress shop, and bakery. It was more a post for trading goods than a shop, but she managed to find the boy boots, trousers, and three shirts. Helen, the owner, gave Winter a proper haircut with her sewing scissors. Linda, her spinster sister, picked out several things she thought a boy would like—a small pocketknife, a book, several wooden toys, and a child's dressing table set. Winter showed no interest in anything but the knife.

When they returned to the station, the rain had turned to snow, blowing hard out of the north. Alyce Wren stood just inside the door as though she'd been waiting for them. "It's about time!" she shouted. "I was thinking of sending Moses out to track you two down. Didn't you notice the weather getting bad?" She helped McCall with her coat. "And you already looking all dark-eyed from no sleep. You'll catch your death."

McCall allowed the old woman to pamper her. She insisted McCall go upstairs and change into a warm cotton gown, then gave her a strong dose of herb tea.

"Sleep!" Alyce ordered as she held open the blankets to a bed that had already been warmed with a covered brick. "It will be dark in a few hours. No one will be riding in in this weather, so you might as well rest. I'll see that the boy has supper and is put to bed."

Finally, McCall slept in the warm darkness of a room that had been hers for three years. Surrounded by familiar things she treasured—her father's huge bed, her grandfather's rocker, her mother's dressing table—she closed her eyes to the world. This was as close to a home as she felt she had or would ever have.

Sometime long after dark, she awoke as wind from the window blew snow into her room. She crawled from the warm blankets and crossed the room to close off the night air. The land was covered with white silence. The wind seemed to whirl without direction. All looked at peace, she thought.

As she reached for the window's handle, something moved to her left, near the fireplace. McCall felt groggy and half asleep. She fought to awaken fully, for her life might depend on it. Her body tensed as an outline of a man lowered itself into her grandfather's chair, between her and the fire.

The wind and snow were forgotten as McCall looked around for a weapon. No one but a crazy man or a ghost would dare disturb her sleep at the station. All she had to do was cry out and twenty people would be at her door. She'd always felt safe here, never thinking of how easy it must have been for this intruder to climb the low porch and walk along its roof to her bedroom window. She'd chosen the room because it was in the back of the station, away from all views except the barn.

"I didn't want to frighten you," the shadow whispered. "I only wanted to make sure you were all right before I bedded down in the barn. I didn't think I'd wake you up, but I couldn't see you from the window."

"Sloan?" McCall whispered.

The shadow removed its soaked hat and let it plop on the floor. "At your service, General." He gave a slight salute.

McCall rushed to his side and knelt. "You're alive!" Her hand touched his snow-covered shoulder.

Sloan turned his face into the shadows, not wanting her to see the bruises. "That's the rumor, but the jury's not in yet." He leaned back in the chair, rocking away from her.

"I dreamed you were killed." McCall whispered the words she'd been afraid to tell anyone for three days. "I dreamed you were asleep, and someone jumped atop you with a long knife already raised to plunge into your chest."

"Your dream wasn't far off." His laugh was void of humor. "I was caught off guard by one of the Apache scouts looking for me just about the time this storm started. If he hadn't been alone, he would have made your dream true. When I finished with him, I hadn't the energy left to fight another." Sloan didn't want to tell her the details of how they'd fought in the darkness and that he'd killed the man without seeing his attacker's face. He didn't want to relive any of the past few days.

"You're hurt." McCall wasn't sure if her words were a question or a statement. Firelight reflected off the bloodstains on his coat and sleeves.

"No, I'm fine." He touched his jacket as if he could brush away the stains as easily as he did the melting snow. "Most of this is someone's else's blood. You were right about the long knife, but I stopped its path with my arm." He rocked back again, feeling more pain now that he was less cold. "I haven't slept for three nights while trying to get back to warn you." He clenched his teeth. Every muscle in his body throbbed. His ribs were hurting again and the cut along his arm had already soaked through the bandage he'd rigged.

"Warn me?" McCall watched him closely. A week's worth of beard covered his face since she'd seen him last, framing his strong jaw with warmth and making his eyes look darker. His hair was damp and lightened with snow at the sideburns.

"I lost something in the fight." Sloan closed his eyes, damning himself for being so careless. He didn't want to have to tell her about the tintype, but there was no other way to keep her safe. "I went back to look, but it was too late. The body and the bandanna had already been found by men who won't waste any time coming after you."

"You're talking out of your head." McCall stood and poured water into the kettle hanging on the swinging hook. As she pushed the pot over the fire she continued, "I'll go get Alyce Wren and tell her you're safe. Once you're comfortable, we'll talk about how men could possibly be looking for me."

Sloan reached for her with bloody fingers. "No!" he insisted. "Don't tell anyone I'm here. It's safest if I leave before anyone knows. And you've got to leave also. Go down south or back east or even to that ranch of yours. No one will look for you there. But promise me you'll leave, and soon."

McCall stared at his hand, dirtying the sleeve of her white nightgown. "You're not going anywhere tonight and neither am I. You're hurt."

"I'll be fine." He let his hand drop. "But your life may depend on your not telling anyone I was here tonight. Don't you see, if they took my gear, they can find you. I can disappear; no one knows me. But you—half the state knows of the brave widow of Holden Harrison."

McCall knelt and pulled at one of his muddy boots.

"You're not making any sense. How could a fight you had bring some bad men back to me? No one even knows we've been together but a handful of people, and I trust all of them with my life. Everything will make sense when you've rested."

Sloan was too exhausted to argue. He hadn't eaten or slept in almost four days. He'd been in the saddle so long he wasn't sure his legs would support him for more than a few feet. All he could think about was getting back to Mc-Call and warning her that Bull Willis and maybe others from Satan's Seven would be looking for her. Thanks to him, the man would have little trouble recognizing Mc-Call. He knew their types. If they thought they could hurt him by killing McCall, her life would be worthless.

She pulled at his other boot, then removed his socks. "You need a bath," she said without hiding her disgust at the mud caking his socks. "I'm surprised they haven't smelled you from downstairs. You are fairly dripping in mud and blood."

"Don't tell anyone I'm here," he ordered in what was meant to be a roar, but sounded more like a plea.

"All right, but you're having a bath." McCall stood and pulled on her wrapper. She went to the hallway and called down to the kitchen for someone to please bring her a tub and water for a bath.

Then she turned her attention back to Sloan. "Step around that panel and slip off those clothes. No one will see you."

"I can't," he shook his head. "I have to be going. The farther I'm away from you, the safer you'll be."

"You'll do as I say, soldier, or I'll call Miss Alyce to hold you down while I strip you myself."

Sloan was too tired to argue. He picked up his boots and

moved behind the curtain as Annie brought in the huge tin tub.

"It'll take a few minutes for enough water to boil, Mrs. Harrison, but I'm sure glad to see you up and about. We was all worried when you came in this morning, so tired and all. I checked on you a few times today, but you were sleeping away."

"Thank you, Annie." McCall kept her hands behind her so the girl wouldn't see the mud on them. "I didn't realize I'd been asleep so long. Would it be too much to ask if I could have some supper? I'm starving."

"Sure," Annie smiled. "You know there's always plenty left in the pie pantry for midnight raids. Sometimes a few of the soldiers come over from the fort for a little visit, but I doubt with the weather I'll be having any company tonight. I'll bring you something to eat right away."

Sloan moved as if he were underwater. He pulled off the dirty clothes slowly, peeling away dried blood in several spots as he undressed. Standing nude behind the thin folding panel, he tried to ease the bandage off his arm, but it wouldn't give. Parts of the blood had dried, holding the wound and bandage together, while the top layer of blood had mixed with the snow and was frozen.

"Are you undressed?" McCall called from the other side when the water had been delivered.

"Yes," he answered.

"Then come out here and get in the tub while the water's hot."

Sloan hesitated. He'd never considered himself as modest as most, but he wasn't sure he could just walk out in front of her. Asking her to turn around seemed a coward's way.

"Are you coming out or do I have to come get you?" McCall asked again.

"I'm coming, General," he grumbled in protest.

But when he stepped out from behind the wall he found he'd worried for no reason. She was busy by the fire and didn't even look in his direction.

"Get in the tub. I'll pour more water in. It'll take gallons to get you clean."

Sloan eased into the long tub. He'd never had a bath in anything so big. He could almost stretch his legs out all the way and sink plumb down to his shoulders.

"Ahh," he whispered as he lowered his tired body into the warmth.

McCall turned when he was in the water. "That tub belongs to Alyce Wren. She'll probably skin all the mud off you along with the hide if she knows you're using it. She told me once that a man gave it to her years ago. She said he brought it all the way from New Orleans." McCall stepped closer. "I'll wash your hair if you like."

"I can do it myself." Sloan dunked his head face first into the water.

He felt her hand grip his hair and pull hard. When his head cleared the water her words greeted him.

"Don't be ridiculous. Of course I can help. You couldn't possibly be as much trouble to bathe as Winter. He threatened to murder me in my sleep if I scrubbed any harder. He said he'd be lucky if he had enough skin left for anyone to tell what color he was."

McCall talked on of their days returning to the station as she lathered his hair and scrubbed. She didn't seem to notice how her wrapper had come open at the waist and that her gown was getting wet, sticking to her skin like a second layer in places.

Sloan was too tired to object at first and too interested in the sight of her to speak. Her skilled hands moved through his hair, soaping away the dirt and the worry. He didn't want to think about how she'd done this task for her husband. He didn't want to think about anything.

He leaned back and closed his eyes as she washed his hair, then his back and shoulders. When she reached his arm, she gently took the bandage off his forearm and examined the cut.

"When we're finished, I'll put salve on this and a clean dressing. It doesn't look infected, but it's deep enough to leave an ugly scar."

Sloan looked at her then. "One scar more or less doesn't matter," he mumbled as he watched her. The general was back, ordering, making plans, making decisions. And for once he was too tired to argue.

She started to wash his chest and Sloan covered her soapy hand with his. "I can do the rest," he whispered with a smile as he tried to guess just how far she planned to continue.

She dropped the soap and nodded, leaving no doubt the thought had also just crossed her mind. "I'll fill you a plate while you finish. I'm sorry I don't have any coffee up here, only tea. Will that do?"

Sloan didn't answer as he continued washing. It felt so good to get the layers of mud off.

As he rose from the tub, she handed him a stack of towels without looking at him. He wrapped one around his waist and reached for another.

"I don't have any other clothes to change into," Sloan said, realizing he'd have to put the filthy shirt and trousers back on.

"I could get you something clean to wear come morning, if you don't mind spending the night in a towel." McCall handed him a plate of food. "But clothes aren't as important as taking care of that cut. You should have stopped long enough to tend it properly."

"I had to get back," Sloan answered, thinking he should add "to you," but didn't. He sat silently in the old rocker and ate with his left hand as she doctored his right arm. He could never remember food tasting so good. Even the tea didn't seem as bad as he remembered. She looked so different in the white gown. Little of the untouchable general remained.

"Did you make it in before the storm?" he whispered as she worked. Her fingers showed the skill of having handled many field dressings.

"Barely." McCall ripped a square of cotton for bandages. "Another day and we'd have had it rough. Moses and Eppie were in one of the back rooms downstairs when I fell asleep. I hope they're still here and not out in this."

Sloan was having trouble keeping his eyes open. The warmth of the fire and her gentle touch washed over him like aged whiskey.

"Finished." She stood and ordered, "Now you need sleep."

Pulling him from the chair with gentle tugs, McCall helped him to the bed. Sloan started to object. He couldn't lie down wearing only a towel. But she had that "We're going to do this my way, soldier" look about her.

"I've slept enough. I'll stay up while you rest, and in the morning we'll talk."

Sloan knew he should tell her more about the men who were looking for her. He should warn her that they might try to get to him through her. If they had her likeness, it wouldn't take long before someone in this part of the country would point them toward the station.

She put one hand on each of his shoulders and pushed him against the sheets, then pulled the covers over him with the same indifference of a tired field nurse.

Pulling the towel from beneath the quilts, he handed it

to her. "This is damp," he mumbled as he relaxed into the soft bedding.

"You're naked?"

Sloan smiled. He'd shattered her military manner.

"I think so. Want to check?"

"No." She straightened, trying to draw back into her proper stance. "I guess I didn't know men ever slept nude."

"Of course we do." Sloan tried to think of one time in his life when he had. "Don't you?"

"I . . ." She'd been around males all her life, but they'd always worn nightshirts or long underwear. Her grandfather had said more than once that a man without wool next to his skin from September to May is a fool asking for pneumonia.

Suddenly, she realized she'd seen more of Sloan as he sat wrapped in a towel than she'd ever seen of her father or grandfather. The scars on his body interested her more than repelled her. She had a feeling each was a story.

"You don't have to answer." Sloan patted her hand. "I'd be very surprised if you ever considered the idea of sleeping without your collar button tightly closed." He yawned. "I'd like to stay up and talk, but my mind feels like it's floating in mud."

McCall gently brushed the sandy-colored hair from his forehead. "Sleep. I'll wake you at dawn."

Before she could pull her hand away, she guessed he was asleep. The worry lines began to soften and his breathing took on a slow, steady rhythm. Pulling the sheet over his shoulder, she thought of how natural it seemed to see him like this. Somehow he'd become a part of her life, almost like he'd always been there in the shadows, waiting to come forward. Reason told her she should be outraged to have a man she'd known only briefly sleeping in her room. But she wasn't.

She gathered the quilt from the foot of the bed and wrapped herself in it. McCall thought of going to tell Miss Alyce that he was here, but she didn't want to wake the old woman so late. Whatever Sloan had to say could wait till morning. Besides, Miss Alyce had never been worried about him, or doubted he'd be back.

At first she tried to sleep in the rocker, but it was too hard. Then she curled up by the low fire. But the floor was cold and drafty against her still-damp gown. She knew if she burned more coal she'd not have enough to last the night. The wind rattled the windows with icy rain and snow, making her feel cold all the way to her bones. The only other place to sit in the room was by the windows, and she knew it would be colder there.

Finally, after an hour of discomfort, she marched over to the bed and curled beneath the covers on the opposite side from Sloan. The sheets were cold and she could hear the wind howling, creating a draft even through the covers.

McCall tried to lie still, but her body didn't seem to be putting off enough heat to warm the bed. She began to shiver, drawing her arms and legs up in a ball to keep warm. Her fingers felt icy. She was sure her feet would never warm. Rubbing her hands over her arms and legs, she tried to force warmth into her cold flesh. She pushed her nose below the blankets and breathed long breaths beneath the covers, but it was hopeless. For each breath she shivered, letting more cold air in around her shoulders.

Suddenly, Sloan's arm touched her. With one mighty tug he pulled her to him, uncoiling her body and pressing it against his own for warmth. He didn't say a word, as though he'd done the action in his sleep.

McCall felt the heat come back into her as the knowledge that a nude man lay beside her registered in her mind. His leg moved over hers, pinning her in place. His arm rested over her chest. His breath came slow and warm against her throat.

She tried to remain still. All cold was forgotten. Her cheeks felt like they were on fire. The cotton of her gown did little to guard against the feel of him.

"Sloan," she whispered. "Let go of me. I wasn't all that cold."

He didn't move.

"Sloan," she repeated, turning to face him. She'd fight her way out of his arms if she had to. He couldn't just pull her against him as though she were May, wandering from bedroll to bedroll. She hadn't planned to be this close when she'd thought she'd share the bed for a few hours.

But Sloan Alexander was sound asleep.

McCall didn't know whether to be relieved or disappointed.

Nineteen

MORNING CREPT INTO the room without any warmth, but McCall didn't notice. She was curled against Sloan, half awake, thinking of how wonderful it had been to sleep with a man. All night he'd kept her warm. Slowly, their bodies had gotten accustomed to one another. When he moved, she adjusted. When he turned, she formed against him. Each time she shifted, he covered her shoulder. It was almost like they were dancing to a very slow lullaby.

"McCall?" Sloan rubbed his scratchy chin against her ear. "You awake?"

She moved her forehead against his chin. "No," she whispered.

"Good." He laughed. "I wouldn't want you to be alert enough to hear this, but I think somehow you've become a part of my life so completely I can't even dream without you. I don't ever remember sleeping so soundly."

She didn't answer and he wasn't sure she was conscious enough to respond. But it didn't matter; he needed to talk anyway. It seemed all his life he'd kept his feelings inside. Now he needed to hear the words.

"When I said I'd come back to you, I meant it. All I've thought about for days is the way you felt against me in the

dark that night with your blouse open. Every time I'd try
to sleep after I left you, I could feel you next to me like you
are now, all warm and soft. I've spent most of my life
alone, but these past few days I didn't feel like I was alone,
even out there in the middle of nowhere. I felt like you
were by my side."

He gently moved his hand along her back, until his fingers rested just below her waist, over the curve of her hip.
"Will you unbutton your gown for me now the way you
did in the dark?"

For a moment he didn't breathe. If she were sound
asleep he could probably unbutton it himself without waking her, but he wanted her to show in some way she cared,
even if she couldn't in her kisses. These feelings mixed up
in his mind had to be returned, in some small way, on her
part.

"Unbutton it for me, McCall. I want to see you in the
early light. I need to feel your heart against mine again as
it was that night."

Slowly, her fingers moved to her throat. Without a word,
she unbuttoned the top few buttons of her nightgown.

Sloan pushed the soft cotton away with his nose and
kissed the skin at her throat. "Now the next, darling."

McCall moved again, unbuttoning the next button.

"And the next," he coached as he had once before. In the
shadowy light, he could see her lying across his arm. Her
eyes were closed, her hair spread all around her, and a tiny
smile tilted the corners of her mouth.

"And the next," he whispered, loving the way she pulled
the material apart slightly as she moved down. The swell
of her breasts showed. When she moved her fingers lightly
down the valley between her breasts to the next button, he
felt his every muscle tighten in an attempt at self-control.

"Now, open your mouth," he ordered softly as he lightly kissed her bottom lip.

Still she didn't move or struggle, but her lips parted. She allowed him to taste her. She might not think she could feel, but she was allowing him to feel and taste and hold her. He accepted her gift as a treasure.

His kiss was gentle and loving, as she needed it to be. Since the night she'd dreamed he died, McCall had promised herself that if he were alive she wouldn't push him away again. She might not be able to respond to his loving, but she wouldn't deny it.

Sloan raised above her on one elbow. "Are you awake now?"

"No," she answered without opening her eyes.

"Good, because I'm having a great dream and don't want to be interrupted." He played with the button just below her bustline until it gave, and then the next. "Mind if I open a few of these?"

"No," she whispered.

When he reached her waist, he stopped and slowly spread the cotton wide so that he could look at her. As his hands moved over her bare flesh, he heard her sharp intake of breath, but she still didn't open her eyes.

He wanted to tell her how lovely she was, but he couldn't find any words. She took his breath away just by lying amid the sheets with her proper gown open wide.

"Put your hands on my shoulders," he whispered as he moved his fingers over the curve of her waist.

Timidly, McCall touched him.

"Now move down," he ordered.

Slowly, her fingers traveled along his skin, feeling every curve, every muscle, every scar. When she reached his waist, she stopped.

He leaned and kissed her lightly. Then he unbuttoned

the next button below her waist, as if allowing himself only so much pleasure at one time.

"Now lower," he whispered as he nibbled at her ear. "Touch me lower."

Her fingers didn't move.

He brushed his hand across her breast and caught her open mouth with a kiss. As he kissed her deeply, his palm moved over her tender mound and pressed lightly, moving only slightly to a rhythm of her heartbeat.

"Touch me," he whispered finally when he released her mouth. "Touch me."

Slowly, her fingers moved past his waist and along the sides of his hips.

Sloan groaned with a need deeper than life itself. He pressed his chest over hers and moved above her. Very lightly, her fingers slid to his hips and up to the small of his back. Then slowly her hands spread across him, caressing with gentle strokes.

Burying his face in her hair, he tried to endure the pure pleasure of her touch without yelling out his joy. The need to have her was a throbbing pain shaking his body, but the longing to feel her touch was stronger.

He held himself in check as she hesitantly explored his back, then his hips. Her caress was featherlight, afire with each stroke. He could feel the softness of her below him and the whisper of her breath at his throat.

Her hands grew bolder, exploring along his sides. He twisted until they were facing one another. While she continued to touch him, he pulled her gown up so that her legs were bare. Gently, with fingers as light as hers, he moved his hand across her legs.

He kissed her tenderly, as if yet afraid to move too fast and break the spell. Slowly, she relaxed in his arms, opening her mouth each time he kissed her lips and opening her legs as his hands grew bolder.

Her breasts molded to his capture and her back arched as he spread his fingers wide and moved down the length of her body. Like snow slowly melting, she began to respond to his loving. Her caresses became bolder; her body moved against him, pressing as if needing to be closer still.

Making himself wait was maddening, but Sloan forced back his own needs. Finally, she was answering his every touch with a longing of her own. Her mouth was warm from the fire he'd started. Her body moved against his with a hunger for more. Her hands explored possessively, as though each touch brought a need for more.

Sloan parted her legs wide with gentle tugs and rolled between them, loving the cry of joy she gave in response to his weight once more atop her. With a sudden plunge, he entered her, driving deep as she arched to meet him. When he moved within, she held his shoulders tightly, pulling him closer still with all her strength.

As they moved together in a rhythm of perfect timing, Sloan felt himself alive, totally alive. All the visions he'd had of making love to a woman paled in comparison. He could have never guessed how soft her body would be when she welcomed him or how great his need.

Suddenly, McCall jerked and stiffened, pulling his hips to her as she cried out his name. He pushed once more and felt all reason shatter in his mind. He wrapped his arms around her and held on tightly as they both drifted back to earth, their hearts pounding wildly against one another.

When he could think again, he rolled without turning loose of her so that she rested atop him. He loved the way she felt, all warm and satisfied. The familiar smell of her rose soap blended with the warm perfume of her hair and the slightly salty taste of her shoulder.

For a long while they lay together, both too moved by what had happened to speak.

Finally, Sloan brushed the hair away from her face and kissed her cheek. "Are you awake yet?" he laughed.

"No," she mumbled. "I think I died in my sleep. I never dreamed anything could feel so good."

"No, darling, you didn't die. I think you came alive in your sleep."

"I never knew it could be like that," she whispered against his chest. "Never."

"Neither did I," he answered honestly.

McCall let out a long sigh and snuggled her cheek against his chest. "I'm so tired now."

"Me, too," he whispered.

With a smile on his face he fell back asleep, loving the way she curled atop his chest.

Sometime long after dawn, he felt her kiss him lightly on the cheek. A few minutes later he heard the door open and close. Without rolling over, he pulled the covers over his head, knowing McCall would be back with his clothes soon, and they would have to talk. He'd never thought in terms of the future because he'd never seen one ahead, but when she returned they had to make plans. He had no idea how they could make it work, but he knew one thing— sleeping beside McCall was where he belonged.

An hour later Sloan heard a light tap on the door.

"Yes," he said as he twisted to face her.

To his shock the station manager entered. "I brought you some clothes," he mumbled. "Mrs. Harrison told me you'd need these. She also ordered breakfast for you, if you're ready."

Sloan reached for the shirt. "Thanks. Mine were covered in mud." He felt he had to explain, though he doubted the manager cared. He'd probably seen enough in his life that the fact that McCall and he had spent the night together wasn't all that shocking. "Where's McCall?"

The manager rubbed his hands on his dirty apron. "She left about an hour ago on the early stage. From the looks of things, it may be the only one out today."

"What!" Sloan forgot all about the clothes he was putting on. In his bare feet, with his shirt wide open, he stormed at the man. "She left?"

The station manager raised his eyebrows and nodded. "Said to tell you not to look for her. She believed she'd take your advice from last night and disappear for a while. She left the boy in Miss Alyce's care. As soon as the weather clears, I'm to take them out to her place."

Sloan headed out the bedroom door, still pulling on his boots. "Where was the stage headed?" he snapped.

"You can't chase the stage!" The station manager looked irritated as he tried to balance Sloan's coat and guns. "It's been snowing for half an hour."

"I'll follow the tracks. Which way did it go?"

The manager frowned. "I figure if Mrs. Harrison wanted you to know, she'd have left you a note."

"I figure if you want to stay standing, you'll volunteer the information." Sloan was in no mood to be subtle. McCall had left without any idea of how much danger she was in. He wasn't sure if he was madder at himself for not telling her or at her for walking out on him. How could the woman make love to him only hours before, then get up and pack to leave him?

"West," the manager answered. "She's going west to the next station. It's four hours in good weather from here, then another four or five to Fort Worth. But if you—"

"Don't threaten me." Sloan strapped on his gun belt. "I don't like threats."

The manager nodded. "If she hadn't cared for you some, you wouldn't have woke up in her bed."

Just as the last words trickled from his lips, Miss Alyce Wren opened her bedroom door and looked out at Sloan and the station manager, as if their conversation was disturbing her.

Sloan froze. He knew she'd heard the last words, but from the expression on her face she didn't look all that happy to see him.

"I . . ." What could he say, that he'd just slept with an angel and she'd flown at dawn? "I've got to go." He pulled his shirt closed. "Good morning, Miss Alyce."

A slow, knowing smile spread over Miss Alyce's wrinkles. "Trying to learn to swim, are you?"

"No," he answered. "I'm trying to learn to fly, and I'll do it if I have to, to get to McCall before she stumbles into any more trouble."

Miss Alyce chuckled. "You think you're going to keep her out of trouble? Son, you are just the trouble I've been hoping she'd fall into."

Sloan took the steps two at a time. "Good. It's nice to know I have your blessing."

He slammed the front door shut, cutting off her laughter.

Twenty

SLOAN PULLED UP the wool collar of his new coat and pushed the horse forward. Nothing made sense to him, not even the weather. The snow seemed to swirl without direction, making it hard to see the tracks of the stagecoach, much less follow them. From time to time, the snow would feel more like rain, then harden into cutting ice against his cheeks.

He tried to put the pieces together. He had spent the night with McCall. She made love to him as he never knew people made love. Then, she took the time to kiss him good-bye, buy him clothes, including a coat and gloves, and order breakfast. Next, she left him without a word.

The pieces didn't fit.

If she'd disappeared suddenly, he'd have sworn she'd been kidnapped. He would have searched the country for her like a madman. But she hadn't disappeared in any suspicious way. Her leaving had obviously been by her own free choice.

Sloan slowed his horse. What was he doing? She didn't want to be with him. How much plainer did she need to make it? She must have realized last night had been a big mistake. Maybe she'd cried out his name because she hated his lovemaking so much? Maybe she couldn't stand to face him again, even to tell him she never wanted to see him? Maybe she'd be like his mother and notice him on the street one day, then walk away without saying a word.

"I'm being a fool!" Sloan mumbled to no one but the wind. "I've been a fool for many reasons, but never because of a woman."

Nothing else in his life had ever made sense. Why should he have expected love to? Why couldn't he have been happy spending a few hours with a whore in some back room of a bar? Why did he have to learn what it felt like to make love to a woman who took his very soul inside when she accepted his body? How could he live on without feeling her heartbeat echo his each night?

She was just a woman, he told himself. Nothing more. They'd never said they loved one another. He hadn't offered marriage and she'd never mentioned it. She was a lady, though. A hero's widow. A wealthy landowner. While he was nothing but a soldier. He knew how to ride and shoot and fight. And last night . . . last night, for a moment, he'd thought he knew how to make love.

Suddenly smiling, Sloan remembered what old Pete used to say: "A man who thinks he understands women can be fooled into believing anything about himself."

Sloan knew he could find McCall, even in this storm. She was on a public stage and had nowhere to go but where the stage traveled. But if he found her, did he want to hear why she'd left him?

Slowly, like the cold, the answer pressed into his bones. It didn't matter why she left him or even that she never wanted to see him again. All that mattered was that he warn her against the men who might be looking for her. If she didn't want to be around him or sleep with him, that was her right, but he could never live with himself if he knew that he'd put her in danger and hadn't warned her.

He'd find her, tell her what she had to know to protect herself, and leave.

It was almost dark when the stage reached the next station along the line. Unlike the huge place at Howard's station McCall had left, the next was little more than a barn and a cabin. Normally a coach would only change horses and feed the travelers a quick meal at this stop. It wasn't set up to house guests overnight. The cabin had a fireplace on one end and a long kitchen table in the middle that looked like it might seat six. But the sleeping quarters on the other end of the room was for one. The bed was an army-issue cot. A few pegs served as wardrobe and a barrel as dresser.

The driver, Bryant, carried McCall's bag as they stepped through the door and into the shadowy warmth of the cabin. The other three passengers, a middle-aged couple and their grown daughter, were already inside, huddled around the fire. Both women were complaining to a silent husband and father about how tired they were.

"Starkie O'Ryan runs this place. He farms and picks up a little extra having fresh horses ready for the line," the driver called Bryant offered. "He's not much of a housekeeper, or cook, but he makes a cup of coffee that'll stay in your blood for hours."

McCall looked around. "Not much of a housekeeper" was an understatement. The only thing in the room that looked to be dusted regularly was a huge pair of Patterson Colts hanging next to the back door.

"I'm sorry about this, folks." Bryant removed his hat. "But it looks like we're going to have to stay here for the night."

The woman, who'd introduced herself to McCall earlier

as Reverend Rogers's wife without ever introducing Reverend Rogers beside her, charged toward the driver. "We can't sleep here tonight! It was my understanding we'd be in Fort Worth before dark."

Her daughter, a younger copy from the same mint, nodded in agreement with her mother.

The driver glanced at McCall as if to say he was sorry for the pair as well as for the room. "I can't do nothing about the weather, Mrs. Rogers."

"There's not enough room in this cabin for two, much less for all five of us." The reverend's wife looked around, becoming more disgusted by the moment.

"Six," Bryant corrected. "I don't know where Starkie is, but he's around here somewhere."

"Well, I don't know about this woman here," the wife pointed at McCall and lifted her nose, "but my daughter and I are certainly not sleeping in the same room with strange men."

The driver stepped around McCall while she fought down a laugh. He seemed to take more offense to the woman's insult to McCall than McCall did.

He was prepared to defend her honor. "Pardon me," he stared at the wife. "But maybe you don't know who this fine lady is."

McCall raised her hand to calm Bryant. She'd been expecting Mrs. Rogers to storm at her for hours. The woman was a talker who never bothered listening. When McCall politely refused to visit during the trip, Mrs. Rogers had simply changed the subject and tried again. Until finally she'd grown tired and became out of sorts with not only McCall, but her family. After hours of this, McCall could clump her conversation into two categories: the imperfections of her husband and the perfections of her daughter, Pearl.

"It's all right, Bryant. The woman has no reason to know me." She touched the driver's shoulder in a silent thank-you for his gallantry. "And she's right. We can't all sleep in here."

McCall turned her attention to the woman. "There isn't enough room, madam, but we also have the barn to use as quarters. I might suggest that the women take the cabin and the men take the barn, but, in truth, I've spent most of my life sleeping among men. I think I'd be more comfortable in the barn with Bryant and Starkie. So your husband can stay here and guard his family for the night."

Mrs. Rogers's mouth fell open as she stared at McCall.

A roar of laughter came from the cellar door in the corner. A large man in his late thirties climbed out with a sack of potatoes over one shoulder.

Before anyone in the room could recover from his sudden appearance, he tossed the sack on the table and grabbed McCall around the waist. "Well, if it ain't Major Harrison's wife!" he yelled in a voice that rattled the few unbroken dishes he had. "'Tis glad I am to see ye, ma'am."

McCall felt like a child as the big man picked her up and held her in the air like a treasure. "Hello, Stark," she laughed. "I'm glad to see you, too."

Starkie put her down. "Folks call me Starkie now. I've mellowed in me old age." His face darkened. "I heard about the major, ma'am. 'Tis sorry, I am. He was a great commander. I would have been with him that day if I hadn't been delivering horses over to Arkansas."

"I know." McCall fought down the tears. Starkie had been with her husband from the beginning of the war. The big man knew his horses and the major respected him greatly for that.

"You're Widow Harrison?" Mrs. Rogers moved closer, interrupting the reunion. "I've heard about you."

"I'm Mrs. Harrison," McCall corrected. Even after three years she hated being called widow. "I think I introduced myself when we climbed into the coach this morning."

Mrs. Rogers shook her head. "You told us you was Mc-Call Harrison. You never told us you was the widow of Major Harrison." She looked like she was angry at McCall for not filling her in on the proper details.

McCall's patience was at an end. She always hated folks who treated people different after learning who their family or husband was. Glancing at Starkie, she asked, "Can I bunk in with you and Bryant in the barn for tonight? I need to sleep among comrades."

Starkie straightened to attention. The deep dimple on his left cheek reflected his pride. "We'd be honored." He glanced at the others. "The cabin's yours. Try not to mess anything up."

Mrs. Rogers huffed, but was suddenly hesitant to show her anger. A silent woman she hardly knew was someone easily snubbed, but the famous Widow Harrison was quite another. "Excuse me, Mr. Starkie," she stepped in front of him, "but what about supper?"

"I'll be back when I get the horses in and see that Mrs. Harrison's got a place to sleep for the night. If ye're worried about food, start peeling them potatoes. If ye peel enough we'll have potato pancakes for supper, with what's left over for breakfast."

Mrs. Rogers refused to move out of the way. "There's no need for you to worry about the widow. She can sleep in here with us. My husband can sleep in the barn with the men. It wouldn't be proper for her to sleep out there with strangers."

McCall smiled. She'd sleep in the snow before she'd share a room with this woman. "No, thanks." McCall tried to sound polite. "I'll be more comfortable in the barn. And

Starkie isn't a stranger; he was my husband's trusted sergeant. To my way of thinking that makes him more family than any I've got."

Mrs. Rogers opened her mouth to argue, then thought better of it. Both Starkie and Bryant looked like they would go to hell and back to defend McCall's honor while Mr. Rogers, her husband, didn't seem like he'd go half as far to stop them. Plus, anything the widow did would be fuel for future stories.

An hour later, McCall was truly comfortable in the barn. Starkie had cleaned out one of the stalls and laid down a foot of hay. Then he'd unpacked a load of burlap bags as a mattress and used his best, half-clean quilts to make her bed.

"Bryant and I will bed down just outside this stall, so ye'll be real safe, Mrs. Harrison." Starkie looked pleased with himself. "Is there anything else I can get ye?"

McCall smiled at the man she'd known for years, yet never really talked to. "Yes. First, I'd like it if you called me McCall. It would please me greatly to think that after all these years we're friends. And second, if you feel strong enough to brave the cabin one more time, I'd love another cup of your coffee."

"I'd be honored to count ye as a friend." He started to say McCall, but couldn't quite get it out. "And I'll get us both a cup."

He disappeared without another word. McCall pulled her boots off and slid beneath the first quilt. She liked the smell of hay and horses surrounding her. This night reminded her of all the nights she'd slept out in the field with Holden. Usually they put up a tent, but when they were moving fast they often camped in barns much like this one.

"Here ye go, ma'am." Starkie handed her a cup. "I'll be saying good night now."

"Stay a minute and drink your coffee, Starkie. Seeing you brings back the days when we were traveling and fighting. I rarely get to talk to anyone about the past."

Starkie leaned against the stall railing and took a sip of his coffee. "I know how ye feel. Most days I don't want to remember, and when I do there's no one to share the memories with."

"It wasn't all terrible, was it?"

"No," he answered. "It was bad sometimes, but ye know every day a man feels totally alive when there's a war. Most days now blend into one another until I can't recall what's happened for a week sometimes. Back then, everything I did mattered. Knowing one mistake and I'd be killed sure did a lot for keeping me alive."

"I know," she answered, thinking that she'd felt dead since the night Holden died. Except for last night. Sloan had made her alive again. He'd made her aware of all she was missing and of all she'd never known.

"And the friends we made," Starkie continued. "I sometimes knew men for only a few months, but was willing to die for them, and knew they would for me. Now, I've known my neighbors for three years and couldn't even tell ye one good secret about them."

McCall laughed. "I guess secrets don't seem so important when you think you've got a few days left to live."

"True, and they did make for interesting talk around the fire the night before a battle."

McCall hugged her knees. "I learned something about the major recently I never knew." She couldn't tell Starkie of learning in Sloan's arms about loving. She'd never admit to this man how her husband hadn't known the first thing about making love to a woman. But she needed to get her thoughts in order. "But you know, Starkie, it doesn't

matter. I feel the same way about him as I did, even knowing what I know now."

Starkie's bushy eyebrows pulled together and he took a
big gulp of his coffee. "I'm mighty glad to hear ye say that,
ma'am. Me and the men were always afraid ye'd find out,
and we didn't know what ye'd do if ye did."

The words took a moment to register in McCall's tired
mind. He was talking about something and it couldn't possibly be what she was thinking. He couldn't know that
she'd spent the night with Sloan and that she'd really made
love for the first time. Starkie couldn't have known that the
major knew nothing of how to please a woman.

"All the men knew?" McCall tried to hold back her interest.

"We knew." Starkie looked down at his boots. "But none
of us would ever have told ye, 'cause it would have hurt
ye. We was keeping his secret to protect ye, not him so
much."

"I see," McCall whispered, thinking that she didn't see
or understand at all. How could she have lived among
them and not known something all the others knew?

"Ye have to know, ma'am, that it had nothing to do with
ye. He'd been with her for years, long before the war broke
out. She weren't the kind of woman an officer would
marry. She couldn't even write her own name." He thought
he was being helpful. Starkie had no idea of the earthquake
he was setting off. "The major didn't care about her the
way he did ye. He told me once that if he ever had children
he wanted ye to mother them. Bloodlines are important in
more than horses, he used to say. McCall's got good breeding in her lines."

"I see," McCall said again. She was glad she was sitting,
for his words would have knocked her off her feet.
"Starkie," she raised her chin slightly. "I don't know much

about her. Would you fill me in? Not that it matters, but I'd like to know."

Starkie hesitated. "I don't see no point to—"

"I'd just like to know." McCall fought the lump in her throat. Holden had had another woman. A lover everyone in camp, but her, knew about. Never in her wildest dreams would she have thought her proper, do-it-by-the-book husband would have kept a woman.

"There ain't much to tell," Starkie shrugged. "She stayed with the women who follow behind the army. Mostly she just did laundry, and I understand she could cook pretty fine, too. I heard tell before the major, she used to have several men visiting her after hours, but once he came along, she limited her nights to him. The last few years she stayed in a little house near Howard's station. He visited her when he could. I heard someone say that she's still there. She does some cooking for the station and takes in sewing. She's no common whore." He looked embarrassed at the word he'd used. "I mean, she might not be a lady, but she's not trash."

"Did Holden love her greatly?" McCall had to ask, though she wasn't sure she wanted to know the answer. If he did, it would hurt. If he didn't, she'd think less of a man she'd always thought was great.

"I don't know that," Starkie answered. "I know he saw that she never went hungry. A couple of times when I was moving horses and he was on a campaign somewhere, he'd have me check in on her and see if she needed anything. I always took her an envelope that had money in it and the two letters M and L. I think they must have meant something to her, because she always smiled when she saw them."

"What did she look like?" McCall tried to think, but she

could remember no young woman who had moved to Howard's station in the past few years.

Starkie shrugged. "Short, not near as tall as ye, ma'am. And she had long hair that had once been blond but was turning gray. She was maybe fifteen or twenty years older then ye, but still full of life."

"She was Holden's age." Several women of that age lived around the station. Most were widows, McCall thought, but she really hadn't spent any time visiting with them.

"I reckon. She'd had a hard life and the years wore heavy on her. She had a way about her, though, a way that said she was all woman. Even her name, Lacy, was something different."

McCall fought down the emotion. Lacy, the little woman she'd seen a few times when she'd been staying at the station. "Thank you for telling me," she managed to say. "I needed to have a picture of her in my mind." He couldn't mean the Lacy she knew. He was talking of a mistress, and the Lacy that she had met a few times was just an ordinary plump little middle-aged woman who seemed shy every time McCall spoke to her.

Starkie lifted his cup and moved away. "Good night. Try to sleep. Ye folks will be moving out at first light."

McCall snuggled down in the covers and closed her eyes. Tears fell silently down her cheeks, wetting the blankets. Whoever this Lacy woman was didn't matter. Holden hadn't been what she'd thought he was. After three years of wearing black and swearing to always keep his memory alive, she realized he hadn't loved her. He'd needed her with him, but he hadn't loved her. Her Holden had loved another while they were married.

The pain in her heart felt as if it might shatter her chest at any moment and leave her broken into a thousand pieces. She forced herself not to cry aloud as she heard Starkie and Bryant bedding down several feet away. They were talking about the day in low tones. She couldn't make a sound and let them know how deeply she hurt.

Closing her eyes tightly, McCall tried to imagine herself in Sloan's arms. She needed to feel the safety of his embrace, even though she knew they could never be together again. Before he'd come into her life, things had been so simple. Not feeling was her wall against the world. But he'd shattered that wall. She knew she'd have to run as hard and fast as she could if she were ever going to pull her life together again. He hadn't said he loved her, or talked of tomorrow. She was a forever kind of woman. And Sloan was a one night kind of man.

As she relaxed, Sloan's arms came around her in her dreams. He was there beside her as he'd been on the prairie. She was wrapped in the warmth of his hold and unafraid.

McCall smiled. He'd never again be more than a dream to her, but at least she had the dream to help her make it through the endless nights to come.

Twenty-one

❧

SLOAN PULLED THE thin bedroll blanket over his shoulder and tried to sleep. He'd found a cluster of evergreens that offered some shelter from the wind. The fire he'd built of branches pulled from the dry areas beneath the trees seemed to give off little warmth. The snow had stopped, but the air was icy and thick. The whole world seemed heavy over him . . . as heavy as his heart.

Hugging his arms around his chest, he tried to get warm enough to sleep. "Why?" he mumbled the same thing he'd thought all day. "Why'd you leave me, McCall?"

Enough hours had passed that he thought he knew the answer. He had nothing to offer her. A lady like her doesn't sleep with a drifter. If anyone knew, it would damage her spotless reputation. With the dawn, she'd come to her senses.

Yet she'd told Howard, the station manager, to give him the clothes she'd bought for him. All were the right size, down to the gloves. The coat probably cost more than he had money in his pocket to pay her back. If she cared anything about her reputation, wouldn't she have just left them, or borrowed rags no one would miss?

Nothing made sense to him anymore. In the cold loneliness of the winter night, he could almost feel her snuggling up against him. He could smell her hair and feel the weight of her head resting on his chest. If he closed his eyes tight enough, he could believe she was with him.

For the rest of his nights, Sloan knew he'd sleep next to her, if only in his mind.

The morning was crisp and clear as they loaded the stage for Fort Worth. McCall felt rested as she went over the plan of what she must do next. The Rogers women complained as they climbed into the coach. Their dresses and jackets were more for fashion than warmth. The reverend said nothing, as usual, but did manage a polite nod at McCall as they waited for the others to decide where everyone should sit. McCall surprised herself by hugging Starkie good-bye.

The big man looked like he was close to tears as he stepped away. "Now you let me know if you ever need anything, Mrs. Harrison. There ain't nothing I wouldn't do for you."

"Thanks," McCall said as she took her seat. Mrs. Rogers had announced yesterday morning that she couldn't ride facing the back of the stage, so McCall had been permanently assigned to the front window. Mr. Rogers shared the bench, since his wife and daughter had also complained about not wanting to be cramped. He placed a small case marked BIBLES in the space between him and McCall, as if to say that this chest was far too valuable to travel in the boot.

"Hold on!" Bryant yelled as he walked up from where he'd been checking on the horses. "We got another passenger."

Before McCall could say a word, Sloan stepped into the coach. He glanced at her as though the others were no more than freight. His clothes were dusty as if he'd ridden most of the night. Several days' growth of beard covered his face.

McCall caught herself remembering the way the short beard had felt two nights ago. She'd expected it to be rough and scratchy, but it was soft. She refused to look at him as he climbed in. Her fingers busily played with the flap over the window, as if adjusting it would keep out the draft. But the memory wouldn't disappear so easily.

The Rogers women made no attempt to pull their skirts aside so he could sit between them. When Sloan reached for the Bibles, the reverend lifted the case to his lap and moved closer to the side of the coach.

Without a word, Sloan planted himself in the center of the now cramped bench between McCall and the preacher.

"Roll 'em out!" Starkie yelled as Bryant whipped the reins.

The coach took a sudden rocking jerk. Sloan, with nothing to hold on to, rocked back and forth on the center seat, his shoulders hitting first the reverend, then McCall.

McCall let out half a yell before he rocked back and forth, hitting her again.

"Sorry, miss," Sloan said as if he'd never spoken to her in his life.

McCall looked in his eyes and saw no hint of sorrow in his dark gaze.

"Hold on, folks!" Bryant yelled again. "The road's a little rough when it's muddy, but we'll level out soon."

"A little!" Mrs. Rogers yelled at the roof of the coach. "We'll all be black-and-blue by the time we get to the next station. Slow this thing down or I'll send my husband up to drive."

"Can't do that, Mrs. Rogers!" Bryant's voice boomed. "I've got a schedule to try and catch up with. We'll be on harder ground before long. Just think of it as rocking aboard a ship."

Sloan twisted toward McCall just as the coach bobbed sideways, sending him against her so hard she was pinned between him and the window. Cold air cut through the gap she'd caused in the window's canvas flap.

McCall shoved with all her might, but he only budged an inch. The Rogerses were all too busy with their own problems to seem to notice.

"Change places with me," Sloan ordered.

She thought of arguing, but at this rate she would be one mass of bruises within an hour.

Without waiting for an answer, Sloan circled her waist with his hands and lifted her over his lap as he slid against the side of the coach. His wide shoulders covered the opening, halting the draft. He then braced his legs against the opposite bench and pulled her hips firmly against his side. When the coach bobbed again, she moved only slightly, like a rider who'd learned to move with a horse.

"Better?" Sloan asked as McCall rocked against his side.

She hated to admit it, but leaning against his chest was much better. His leg braced her slightly, keeping her from tumbling forward, and she no longer had the constant draft from the window on her neck and shoulder.

"Thank you," she said, admitting he was right.

"Anytime," he answered, pulling his hat low as if he had no desire to become overly friendly with anyone in the coach.

They rode on to the rhythm of Mrs. Rogers's complaining for almost an hour, then as Bryant had promised, the road straightened out and everyone relaxed. McCall moved an inch away from Sloan's chest, but she noticed he didn't move his leg, keeping it slanted so that it touched hers.

"We haven't had time to properly introduce ourselves," Mrs. Rogers began, as though she were the appointed leader of the group.

"I'm Mrs. Rogers. This is my husband, the reverend. We're on our way to San Antonio. This is our daughter, Pearl Ann."

Sloan touched his first finger to his hat. "Nice to meet you," he said without volunteering any information about himself.

"And," Mrs. Rogers frowned at him, as though she thought him beneath her but still felt the need to be proper, "the lady you seem to be sitting a bit too close to is the widow Harrison. The famous widow of Major Harrison."

Sloan raised an eyebrow. "Famous?"

Mrs. Rogers pressed her lips together as if irritated with a small child. "Don't tell me you haven't heard of Holden Harrison?"

"Can't say as I have," Sloan lied and leaned forward, encouraging the woman with his interest.

"She's a little quiet, but don't hold that against her," Mrs. Rogers said. "I'm sure she wouldn't mind my telling you who she is."

"I wouldn't hold anything against her." Sloan glanced at McCall. Only she saw his wink.

She could see the fire in his dark eyes, like slow-burning coals from a flame started long ago. McCall couldn't tell if he was laughing at her or hiding anger with his false smile. But the fire was a certainty. McCall fought down a comment. She didn't like to be gossiped about, but she didn't want to talk to either Sloan or Mrs. Rogers. Her only option was to remain silent.

"Her husband was a great man. Half the men in Texas served under him during the war. But what she did was just as brave."

"What did she do?" Pearl chimed in, tired of her mother bragging on McCall.

The younger woman had a way of opening her eyes too wide and staring hard when she was irritated. McCall couldn't help but notice that she was dressed younger than the tiny lines around her eyes told of her being. Her ringlet hair seemed out of place on a woman obviously in her twenties.

Mrs. Rogers wiggled in her seat, getting comfortable before continuing the story. "She went into battle with her husband. Lots of battles. I've heard men tell story after story of her riding through enemy lines to deliver messages, and riding like the wind through the night to carry needed word home.

"She was like one of his men, always there, always with him. When the major was dying, she held him all night while he bled all over her clothes. Then she talked the Yankees into helping her load his body into a wagon. She drove the major home all alone. Not even stopping to change from her bloody clothes."

"You did that?" Pearl looked at McCall with horror. "Wasn't it terrible, traveling with a dead body? And wearing the same clothes day after day?"

McCall could hardly hide her disgust for the girl. "He was my husband," she answered simply. "He'd asked to be buried at home."

"It took her weeks," Mrs. Rogers added. "Traveling through land where there weren't any farms to stop at for food."

"No," McCall corrected. "It took days. I don't remember much about it except the cold and how alone I felt. I don't remember thinking about food at all. My clothing seemed unimportant."

Mrs. Rogers wanted to hear details, but McCall wouldn't

volunteer any more information. She finally grew tired of trying to get McCall to talk and turned her attention to Sloan. "Were you in the war, sir?"

"Yes," Sloan answered.

"The North or the South?"

"Does it matter?"

"I guess not," she huffed. "After all, it's over. I imagine you've settled down in the three years since it ended. A wife and children? Started a whole new life and don't want to talk about the war."

"No," Sloan answered. "No wife or children."

Mrs. Rogers perked up and smiled that broad, toothy smile only mothers of overaged single daughters get. "Oh, so you're still unattached?"

Sloan slowly slid his hand along his leg. The back side of his fingers brushed against McCall's thigh, but no one but her seemed to notice. He'd removed his gloves. She could feel the warmth of his hand through the material of her skirt.

"Still unmarried," he mumbled as his hand moved back up his leg, applying slightly more pressure to McCall's thigh than before.

"What type of wife are you looking for, may I ask?" Mrs. Rogers leaned forward as her child leaned backward and opened her eyes too wide a few times toward her mother, as though the action would silence the woman.

"The kind who'll stay in bed until daybreak," Sloan answered.

Mrs. Rogers let out a huff in shock. McCall shifted slightly and swung her foot so that the toe of her boot jabbed into his calf.

Sloan fought to keep from yelling out in pain and laughing at the same time. "And a woman not overly fond of inflicting pain on me," he mumbled. "It seems I've had the misfortune to meet of late the kind of woman who has a mean side to her that'll most likely get me killed."

McCall shifted again and dug her elbow into his ribs.

When he drew in his breath suddenly, McCall flashed him what she hoped was a worried look. "Oh, I'm sorry, Mr. Alexander. Did I hurt you when I moved? We're so cramped I didn't notice."

"No, ma'am," he lied again, thinking his ribs would never heal with McCall around.

"Mr. Alexander?" the reverend's wife chimed. "Do you know this man, Widow Harrison? I was under the assumption we were all strangers here."

McCall shook her head, but she wasn't accustomed to lying. She opened her mouth, but nothing came out.

A moment later, the wheel hit a hole. Everyone in the coach rolled to one side. The stage rocked once violently and vaulted sideways as if pushed aside by some giant. Sloan swore. The reverend prayed. Pearl screamed for her mother.

McCall reached for Sloan and found herself on top of him a second later, with the reverend on top of them both. The sound of wood shattering mixed with the shouts of the passengers. Mrs. Rogers's hollering was cut off by Pearl landing atop her mother.

"Whoa!" Bryant yelled, and the stage slowed while still leaning.

Before the screams died, he was on the ground, pulling the door open. "You folks all right in there?"

Pearl crawled off her mother. Her bonnet was crumpled beside her and part of her blond curls was gone with the hat. The reverend helped his daughter out of the lopsided coach, patting her hand to calm her. Mrs. Rogers scrambled for the opening next, like a rat about to go down with the ship. Her flying arms would have pushed anyone else aside. She was screaming and crying as the men helped her to the ground.

For a moment, Sloan was alone with McCall, his back against the window. She rested on him, holding tightly to his jacket as if she didn't believe the rocking had stopped.

Sloan bent his head slightly and brushed his lips against her forehead. "You all right, darling?"

McCall took a long breath. "I think so." She moved slightly, stretching against him, testing for broken bones.

He pulled her closer with one arm as his free hand moved slowly over her from shoulder to hip, making sure she wasn't hurt. "Good. I wouldn't want you hurt before I strangle you."

She pulled away and climbed from the coach as though she hadn't heard his words.

Sloan fought the urge to swear. She was driving him completely mad. He wished she'd shot him that first night he'd touched her and put him out of his misery. Even a stagecoach wreck with McCall made him more hungry for her touch.

He crawled from the stage and joined the others a few feet away. Everyone had survived with only a few scratches. Only Pearl's bonnet, with several curls of wig hair attached to the back, looked to be a fatality.

"We've busted a wheel, folks," Bryant announced the obvious. "Make yourselves comfortable. It'll take me an hour or so to fix it. That is, if I can."

"Need any help?" Sloan offered.

Bryant shook his head. "I'll yell when I'm ready to put the new one on." He lifted a box of tools from the front boot. "You could walk the horses a little. It'd sure be lucky if we were close enough to water for them to have a drink while we wait."

Sloan nodded and began unhitching the team. He'd

worked with horses all his life and felt the action relax him
a little. He could also feel McCall watching him, but he
didn't look in her direction. She had some answering to do,
but he'd wait until they didn't have an audience. He could
just guess how much pleasure Mrs. Rogers would have
telling new stories about the famous Widow Harrison and
some drifter.

McCall watched him closely, seeing the skill in his
hands and the easy way he mastered the team. She glanced
down at the women sitting on a rock to her left. They were
both complaining as they compared scratches and rips in
their skirts. Suddenly McCall had no time for them.

"I'll help you," she said as she stepped over the coach's
tongue and joined Sloan.

He glanced at her with a look that said he needed no assistance. When she cut her gaze over to the Rogerses,
Sloan said, "Thanks, I could use a little help." He handed
her the lines to the two lead horses.

They worked together, walking the horses to a low place
where some of last night's rain still stood in one-inch pud-
dles. When they were a quarter of a mile from the others,
Sloan dropped the reins and allowed the animals to graze
on winter weeds and hardy buffalo grass.

"We have to talk," he said casually, as if only passing
the time of day.

"We've nothing to say." McCall followed his lead with
her horses, but didn't look up at him.

"Yes, we have," Sloan corrected. "I tried to explain
when I arrived at the station that night, but you wouldn't
listen. I made some powerful enemies in the army. They
swore to find me even after the war ended. They called
themselves Satan's Seven. The man we met that night you
tried to shoot me must have been one of them. Remember,
he said his name was Bull Willis. He was such a mountain

of a man. When I knew him, he was much thinner and we were in a place where names weren't important. It took him some time, but he recognized me even in the dark that night."

"Why would he want to kill you now? The war's over."

"Not for men like him. Never for men like him. He doesn't want to just kill me. He swore to cut my heart out while it was still beating and set it atop my chest. He and a few of his friends are following me. Right now they're closer than they've ever been. I thought I'd draw them away from you; you'd be safe. But the night the Apache attacked me and cut my arm, they must have found my bedroll before I could get back to it."

"So?"

"In the bedroll was a picture of you."

McCall faced him directly for the first time. "A picture of me? That's ridiculous."

"I found it at your house before we started the trip with the children. It was on the floor, like someone had thrown it away. I didn't think you'd mind. It was only a bent tintype." Sloan felt like a fool, rattling on.

"You stole a tintype of me?"

"I didn't steal it," he offered as his only defense.

"I didn't give it to you," she countered.

"That's not important. What we have to think about now is that somewhere within a day or two from us is a man who wants to kill me and has your picture."

"Would he kill me to get to you?"

Sloan closed his eyes. "If he knew you mattered to me, he'd kill you."

McCall was silent. When he opened his eyes, she was looking closely at him. "Do I matter to you?"

Sloan knew that if he said yes, even a little, he'd be opening himself up for all kinds of pain. If he said no, he'd be telling the greatest lie of his life. In truth, he would have fought to the death to get the tintype back, never mind her.

"More than life," he answered, figuring he might as well jump in head first and see how deep the well was. He was a drowning man either way.

Sloan wasn't sure what he expected her response to be, but her fist flying at his face wasn't among the top hundred guesses.

He ducked a moment before her balled fingers slammed into his cheek. With all the rage of a tornado, she swung again and again until he caught her around the waist and pulled her to him. "Damn!" he swore. *The woman has more fire in her than a cannon.*

"Stop it!" he yelled, trying not to hurt her, though she bore no such hesitance with him. "Stop it, General!"

She fought wildly, kicking, slugging with more strength than he thought a woman could muster.

Finally, he shoved her away and stepped backward. "What are you trying to do?" he shouted. "Kill me for caring about you?"

"I don't want you caring about me," she answered as she paced like a wild animal waiting for an opening to attack. "I don't want you or any other man in my life at all. I was doing fine before I met you."

"You're the most aggravating woman I've ever met. It's no wonder you never remarried. There's not enough plots in that little cemetery on your place to hold all the husbands it would take to tame you."

"It's not a problem you need to concern yourself with."

She was lifting her chin now the way she always did when she stepped into the high-and-mighty major's widow role. He'd never seen anyone, man or woman, go from being so wild to being so proper faster than he could blink. She probably murdered her enemies all the time and always got away with it. From looking at her, no one would ever guess the temper inside that body.

"I'm not concerning myself with your welfare anymore." Sloan tried to keep his anger under control. "I just wanted to warn you. Now that I've done that, I'll be on my way. I'm getting out of your sight and life as fast as I can."

He picked up the horses' reins and started back across the field. "And you, lady," he mumbled, "you can go to . . ."

"Don't you swear at me!" she whispered from a foot behind him. "I'm not the one who got us into this mess. I'm not the one who has people trying to kill me because of something I did three years ago. By the way, what exactly did you do that made these Satan's Seven hate you so much?"

Sloan stopped and stared at her. "I did what I had to do to stay alive. I took off a gray uniform and put on a blue one. And it's going to haunt me the rest of my life."

"Which may not be long," she answered as she walked ahead of him, "if you don't quit following me."

Twenty-two

❧

BRYANT WAS STANDING above the wheel when Sloan walked back over the rise to the stagecoach. The Rogers family members were camped in the shade of a rock cluster and, for once, weren't screaming at each other or anyone else.

"Problem?" Sloan asked the obvious.

Bryant scratched his head. "Wouldn't you know I broke four oak spokes and I only brought two along. If we had one more I could make do the three more hours into Fort Worth, but it would be risky."

"I could probably carve one." Sloan looked at the long piece of wood. "It wouldn't take long if I could find a hard enough wood."

"No." Bryant shook his head. "It might not last. Plus the hub's bent. I think it would be faster if I rode back to Starkie's place and brought the wagon up for you folks. We're not more than an hour out of his station. Then I could pull this empty coach into his barn for repair." He grabbed his hat off the brake lever and added, "I can be back in a few hours, at the most. We'll get this fixed and start over. It'll mean driving at night, but I'll make it."

Sloan pulled a horse away from the others. "Why don't

you rest? I'll ride back to Starkie's place. That way maybe you can sleep a few hours."

Bryant didn't argue.

Sloan grabbed the horse's mane and swung up on the animal's back. "I won't be long." He lowered his hat tight across his forehead.

"I'm going with you." McCall didn't wait for either man to answer. She chose a horse and climbed up as if she'd been riding bareback every day of her life. Her traveling dress hiked to her knees, but she didn't seem to notice.

Mrs. Rogers stood suddenly, as if she'd been called to counsel, but McCall didn't give her time to comment. She kicked the animal and was almost out of sight before Sloan managed to get his horse headed in the right direction.

When he finally reached her, he shouted. "You should have stayed with the others!"

"And listened to Mrs. Rogers all afternoon? No, thank you!" McCall shouted back. "I've spent my life avoiding women like her."

She kicked her horse to a faster pace and the ride became a race. Sloan wasn't able to say another word until they were pulling up at Starkie's barn.

"You could have killed yourself, riding like that!" he yelled, jumping from his horse and raising his arms to her.

She dismounted without his assistance. "But I didn't," she answered. "I told you before, I can take care of myself."

Starkie shouted a welcome from the corral and broke into a run toward them, ending the fight they both needed to have to clear the air.

"You come back to sit a spell and watch me whittle?" the man asked in a casual voice, even though his movements were that of a man knowing they brought a problem.

Within ten minutes Sloan hitched a team to Starkie's

wagon, Starkie collected the needed tools, and McCall packed day-old potato pancakes she swore Mrs. Rogers would love to have.

"I'll be back as soon as I can." Starkie looked at McCall. "You take care and rest. A night trip will wear you out before you get to Fort Worth."

McCall nodded, then waved until Starkie was out of sight. Suddenly the realization that she was alone with Sloan struck her. Truly alone.

Looking around, she discovered he was nowhere in sight. He obviously didn't want to be any nearer her than she did him. She guessed he'd wait until the others got back, then leave her as he'd planned. Now that he'd warned her, there was no use in him following her all the way to Fort Worth.

She rationalized that it didn't matter to her and went into the empty house. The breakfast dishes were still on the table as they'd left them. Starkie'd told her and Sloan that he'd been trying to save one of the wild mustangs he'd roped. He'd said the horse's leg was bleeding and coyotes were already following the animal by the time Starkie had spotted her, just after the stage left. He'd had his gun drawn to put the animal out of her misery when he heard them coming. Starkie had asked Sloan to do the job while he was gone.

McCall didn't want to watch or think about what Sloan had to do, so she rolled up her sleeves and went to work on the kitchen. It took three tubs of water to clean all the dishes and another to wipe everything down. She decided there were layers of grime from a hundred meals on the cookstove and almost as many on the table. It was no wonder Starkie had never married. With his lack of order and the dribbling of wood shavings everywhere he sat long enough to put a knife to wood, he showed the markings of a man hard to live with.

When she finally finished, she walked out into the sunshine and stretched her back. This probably wasn't what Starkie had meant by relaxing, but it made her feel good. She never wanted a house to clean, with meals to cook and beds to make. She'd never had one. All her adult life she'd lived on the move, eating her meals around campfires and in restaurants. Bed had been everything from fine down mattresses in the cities to hard rock when they were in the field. She wasn't sure she'd know how to run a house alone, even if she wanted to.

McCall glanced over at the barn and realized she hadn't heard the shot. Sloan must have ended the horse's suffering. As much as he seemed to care for horses, he could have never allowed the animal to be in more pain. Maybe he wrapped the gun so that she didn't have to hear the shot?

Walking toward the barn, she decided to find out. If for some reason he hadn't been able to give the animal peace, she would. Her father had made her put down a horse when she was no more than ten, explaining all the while that it was the only kind thing to do.

The barn was empty.

McCall walked around in the shadows, trying to guess what had happened. Maybe Sloan walked the animal out to the corral so that he wouldn't have to drag it so far to bury it.

The corral was empty.

She stepped up on the first rung of the fence and looked around. Nothing.

He'd left her, she decided. He somehow took the lame horse and left her. McCall straightened. "Good," she said aloud. "Go."

Just as she turned to go back to the cabin, she caught movement out of the corner of her vision. Curiosity drew her to the back of the corral and over the fence, where Sloan had left his coat, hat, and the new shirt she'd bought him.

As she moved toward the plowed field, her boots became caked in mud, but the sight before her pushed her on.

Sloan stood calf-deep in mud, leaning over the mustang's front leg.

As she neared, the horse tried to pull away to run, but the mud was too deep. Sloan's low voice came slow and easy, calming the wild animal. After a few tries, the horse stopped jerking at the rope around her neck.

"If you're going to come out here, keep your voice low and your movements slow," Sloan ordered in the same easy tone he'd used to calm the horse.

She moved around the animal. "What do you think you're doing? In this mud the horse will break the three good legs she has."

Sloan rubbed his muddy fingers along the horse's neck. "But if she doesn't, maybe I've got a chance to keep her calm enough so that I can pack this cut and wrap the wound."

McCall stood very still and watched as Sloan slowly worked with the wounded leg. The animal's eyes were wild with fright, but she didn't try to bolt. She was a shade darker brown than the mud, a horse of little beauty. Sloan's white undershirt contrasted with the horse as he leaned his shoulder against her, examining her leg. McCall had never realized how broad his shoulders were—as powerful as the wild animal he calmed.

"It took me almost an hour to get her to trust me enough to get a rope on her. The trip from the barn cost her dearly in blood. If I can stop the bleeding and pack the cut with

crushed yarrow, she just might recover." His words were
meant for McCall but his soft voice soothed the animal.

"She's a mustang," McCall whispered, trying to guess
why Sloan was fighting so hard. Most men she knew
would do as Starkie suggested and put the horse out of
pain. "A horse like her is of little value. Even tame she's
not worth ten dollars. If she does live, she'll probably go
wild again and run away."

"No," he answered calmly. "This one's a keeper. She
may be small, but she's got a wild heart. Had to . . . to have
made it this long. I'm guessing she's smart, too, coming so
close to the cabin in hopes the coyotes wouldn't follow. If
she were strong and well, she'd outrun them all."

Slowly, McCall moved closer as she caught her skirt
hem in one hand and folded the material over her belt. The
horse watched her and snorted loudly, as if not approving
of her skirt now being almost to her knees.

"I could hold the rope if you like," McCall offered.
"That would free your hand."

Sloan moved behind her, giving her the rope as he
passed. "She likes you to rub her neck with mud. I think it
must feel good on the rope burns she suffered from Starkie
trying to get her here."

McCall leaned and lifted a handful of mud. She touched
the animal gently as Sloan crushed the tiny flowers in his
hand and began applying them on the mustang's leg.

"We'll leave the mud caking the bandage. It won't be
much protection, but by the time the burlap wrap rots
enough to fall off, the cut should be healed."

Watching his fingers moving slowly over the bandaging,
McCall could almost feel his touch on her body as well.
He'd had the lightest touch. Almost as though he were
afraid of hurting her. Hesitant. Caressing. Exploring.

She forced herself to look away. It would do no good to

think of the night they'd spent together. She was only taking a fool's ride to heartache by reliving it in her mind.

Finally, he stood and touched McCall's shoulder with his dirty hand. "Pull the rope off her neck."

"Why?"

"She's got to walk out of this mud at her own pace. It's the only thing that will keep her from falling. With the amount of blood she's lost, she'll be heading right toward that trough of water."

As they watched, the mustang moved one leg at a time through the field. She hesitated each time she put weight on the injured leg.

Sloan slid his hand over McCall's and pulled her toward the barn. McCall jerked away and tried to walk. The mud sucked at her boots. After a few steps, she twisted wrong and almost fell face first in the mud.

Sloan caught her but his laughter was cut short when he almost stumbled.

To McCall's shock, he laughed as if he wouldn't have minded greatly and these weren't the only clothes he owned.

"You're insane." She tried to walk but slipped again. His arm steadied her once more. "We'll look like two escaped gingerbread men if we don't get out of here soon. If I fall, I've nothing to change into, for my bag is still on the stage."

"I was just thinking about what Mrs. Rogers would say if she could see you now." Sloan laughed deep and hard. "The daughter's eyes would probably bounce right out of her head. The great Widow Harrison, strolling in the mud."

"What about you?" McCall laughed. "You're off the list as eligible husbands." She patted his cheek, leaving her muddy handprint.

When she stumbled a third time, Sloan lifted her in his

arms. "I'm not husband material. Even Mrs. Rogers should see that." He waded through the mud with McCall. "I had a friend named Pete once. We had a lot of time to set about, talking. He used to say that before a man marries a girl he should decide if he'd want her mother moving under his roof, for it's sure to happen."

"You'd turn down sweet Pearl because of her mother?" McCall acted shocked.

"Among other things," he answered as he reached the back of the corral. "If you've no more questions, I need to check on our horse."

McCall watched as he slowly moved toward the mustang standing at the corner of the fence. The animal didn't have the energy left to run away. Sloan laced the rope over the mustang's neck and led her through the gate to the trough at the front of the barn. He let the horse drink, then released her in the corral.

McCall watched in disbelief as Sloan turned back to the trough and began pulling off his undershirt. He washed it, then himself, in the ever-dirtying water. As he turned to spread it out to dry on the fence, he noticed her watching him.

"Open your eyes any wider and they'll start calling you Pearl Ann," Sloan teased.

"What do you think you're doing?" As before, his bare chest fascinated her, with its finely carved muscles and thin white scars.

"Cleaning up," he answered as he pulled off his pants and shook the clods of mud from them.

"Out here?"

"I don't see any other place. I'd be willing to bet Starkie doesn't have a bathtub, and the stream's too cold. This way I can do my laundry at the same time."

"I can't believe you're stripping out here in front of God and everybody."

Sloan looked around. "God has seen me. As for everyone else, you appear to be the only everybody around. You've seen me bare-chested before."

McCall walked to the gate, a few feet from where he was hanging his clothes. There she propped her arms on the top rail and smiled at the sight of him standing in the bottom half of his long johns.

"What are you doing?" He eyed her carefully.

"I'm going to watch," she answered, as if irritated that he had asked. "If Mrs. Rogers makes it back soon, she'll see more of you than I'll bet she's ever seen of the reverend. I wouldn't want to miss the screaming."

Sloan turned his back and splashed water on his bare chest. He'd started this and he planned to finish, whether she watched or not. The air was chilly, the water even cooler, but with McCall so close, he felt a warmth that needed cooling if he planned to keep his senses.

When he finished, he grabbed a rag towel hanging from the pump.

"Where'd you get that scar?" McCall startled him. She'd been so quiet he'd almost fooled himself into believing she wasn't watching.

"What scar?" he answered without looking.

"The one across your shoulder."

"I don't remember."

"You mean you want to forget," she countered.

"Something like that."

"You're not going to tell me, are you?"

Sloan looked at her then, unable to ignore her any longer. "I could tell you, but it wouldn't matter. Folks spend too much time remembering when and where they were hurt." He took a step toward her. "The scars are a part of me. Some people have them on the outside, some on the inside, but they don't go away by telling about them."

"They don't need to go away," she answered, thinking that in a strange way they made him more attractive.

For a long moment they stood five feet apart, staring at one another.

He couldn't think of anything else to say.

She was afraid she'd say too much if she spoke at all. He'd think her stump-witted if she told him she found the scars added character and emotion to his body the way twists in a tree add interest.

Finally, he slung his damp hair out of his eyes and lifted his shirt from the fence. "My undershirt will be dry in an hour, long before they get back. If you like I'll clean some of that mud off your boots." He pulled his shirt on without buttoning it.

"Oh, no, I can—" Before she could finish, he lifted her atop the fence. For a moment, he studied her as she looked down from a few inches above him. He grabbed a handful of straw and began rubbing the mud off her boots.

"I don't suppose you'd want to take them off?"

"No," she answered, just imagining what the others would say if they came back and found him nude to the waist and her barefooted.

She felt a warmth climb up her neck as he continued to rub the dirt from her leather boots. His act was meant only as a kindness, but there was something very intimate about him touching her.

"Why didn't you come back into the cabin?" she asked, finally realizing that he'd been avoiding her since Starkie left.

"I didn't want to start another fight," he answered as his hand cupped her calf to keep her boot still while he finished. "In a few hours we'll be on our way. You'll never have to see me again. I don't want the last words I say to you to be said yelling."

"That was kind of you." She tried to say the words without emotion, but his fingers moved up over her boot lacings to the thin cotton of her stockings. Lightly, she felt his hands begin to caress the inside of her leg, just below her knee.

"It wasn't kind." His voice was low now, only a whisper. "I just didn't want to hurt you any more. I never meant to hurt you in the first place."

His fingers moved higher, passing her knees.

"I can't blame you for all the hurt." McCall closed her eyes. She should stop his hand before it went any farther. She should push away and go back into the cabin to wait for the stage. Soon everyone would be here, and she'd never see Sloan again. She'd never allow a man close to her again.

His fingers reached the top of her stockings. The sudden warmth of his hands on her bare skin felt like fire. Gently, he rolled the stockings a few inches downward.

"Will you give me credit for some of the pleasure?" he whispered as his hands moved over her legs, pushing the lace of her undergarments higher and her stockings lower.

McCall gripped the fence so tightly on either side of her that she could no longer feel her arms. But she could feel his hands. Moving over her, caressing in long, heated strokes, pulling her knees open with each action.

When he leaned against her, she would have fallen backward, but his hands moved around to her hips.

"Kiss me good-bye, McCall," he whispered, his voice thick with a longing far deeper than desire. "I hated your leaving without saying good-bye."

"No," she answered, thinking that leaving him asleep had been the hardest thing she'd ever done. If she kissed him again, how far would she have to run to escape feeling?

He brushed his lips over her cheek. "Kiss me goodbye," he demanded. "But do it without feeling, so I'll know that our night together meant nothing to you."

The pain in his voice was liquid between them. He was telling her that he needed the hurt of an emotionless kiss. All his life it had been the pain that made him know he was alive. He needed the pain now to walk away.

Reason shattered into need as she realized no one had ever cared for Sloan. All his life he'd wandered from battle to battle without refuge. He'd been lost in his aloneness so long he didn't know how to look for a harbor. She'd always been surrounded and advised; he'd been alone so long he saw it as his only home.

Leaning into him, she kissed him with all the passion and heartbreak inside her.

His arms tightened around her as he lifted her off the fence and into his embrace.

Twenty-three

❧

THE THUNDER OF horses' hooves whispered from far away, growing louder in Sloan's mind as if the noise had always been there. The feel of McCall's legs around his waist . . . the taste of her mouth . . . the intoxicating smell of passion swirling around his head . . . all blindfolded his instincts for caution.

The noise grew louder, shaking Sloan from paradise.

McCall cried out in surprise as he lifted her to arm's length away from him and pushed her toward the house.

"Run!" he ordered. "Bolt the door. Find Starkie's guns if you can. Then hide."

"But . . ." McCall looked toward the road as danger registered. She moved to follow his command. She could hear the horses, but her senses were still thick with the hunger Sloan had fired within her. "It's just the stage." Even as she said the words, she seemed to realize the riders were coming from the wrong direction.

"Get inside!" Sloan pulled his shirt together. "Unless my hearing has gone bad, there are only two, maybe three horses traveling toward us. They're moving far faster than a wagon."

McCall ran for the open cabin door.

Sloan strapped on his gun belt and moved to the porch. "Lock yourself in and don't come out until Starkie and Bryant get back."

McCall turned at the doorway, her mouth open to question.

"Don't argue, General! These men aren't like men you've ever dealt with. If they get past me and find out you're here alone, they'll make you wish you were dead a hundred times over before they kill you."

Stepping into the cabin, McCall threw the bolt. Sloan breathed for the first time since he'd heard the horses. The noise was getting louder. They'd be breaking the rise any moment. He checked his guns and whispered to himself, "If they make it past me, I'll be dead but they'll be fewer."

The horses broke the ridge from the southeast, traveling like a wild herd. For a twinkling of time, Sloan couldn't see the riders, only the animals. Then they were closer. He blinked again.

Only one rider! One very small rider!

"McCall!" Sloan shouted as he shoved his Colts back into place and broke into a run.

He was halfway between the cabin and the barn when the three horses slowed only a few feet before reaching him. The two riderless animals kicked and stomped as though not wanting to end the run. They were all lathered and snorting in the cool morning air.

"Winter!" Sloan cried as he pried the boy's fingers from the reins and lifted him down.

Winter fell into his arms as if he were made of rags and not bone. "I'm not too late," he whispered. "I'm not too late."

Sloan grabbed the reins of Winter's horse and noticed the boy had tied lead lines from his saddle horn to the other two horses. While holding the boy with one arm, he opened the corral and put the animals inside without bothering to untie them.

McCall was at their side. "Winter, what's happened?"

Sloan felt Winter straighten and slide from his arms. He fought down a smile. Even exhausted, the boy was growing too old to be held.

"I came to warn you," Winter said as he took deep breaths and placed a hand over each knee. "Five men came by the station last night. They were asking all kinds of questions about you. But we didn't tell them anything." He stood a little taller and his breathing slowed to almost normal. "We thought they'd left, but at dawn, after we saw Eppie and Moses off, I went into the barn and found the station manager, Howard. He'd been beat real bad and left in one of the stalls."

Sloan looked over the boy's head at McCall. There was no panic in her eyes, only worry.

"Is he dead?" McCall touched the boy's shoulder lightly.

"No," Winter shook his head so hard his hair fell into his face. "But he couldn't walk. Miss Alyce had us put him in bed. Then she worked on him for an hour, telling everybody what to do. She set his arm. Wrapped him up as best she could. And all the while he kept mumbling something no one could make sense of."

He looked directly at Sloan. "When she finished, she told me to follow her to the barn. I did. She asked if I could ride fast all morning without falling off. I laughed at her. I've been riding like that since I was four. She told me to pick out three of the station's best horses and follow the rut of tracks the stagecoaches make. She said I'd find you at the end." He lowered his voice as if afraid to even say the words. "She wasn't sure if I'd find you alive. If you were alive she thought you would need the horses. If I reached the next station without finding you, she told me to rest, then come back because there was nothing else to be done."

"How much head start did the men who beat Howard have on you, son?"

"Miss Alyce said to tell you two hours, at least." Winter had told his story; he was starting to relax now.

"Go get a drink from the well, son. I'll take care of the horses. You've done a good job."

Winter smiled proudly and moved to the well. Sloan walked toward the corral with McCall jumping around him like a puppy.

"He doesn't make sense," she whispered. "If they were headed our way, and they're not here yet, then he'd have had to pass them. Anyone could have heard him coming from a mile away."

Sloan began walking the horses as he untied the mess of ropes. "You're right," he mumbled.

"I'm right!" McCall snapped. "What kind of answer is that? Why didn't they stop him?"

He handed her the rag he'd used to dry off with only minutes before. She absently began rubbing the sweat from one of the animals.

"Maybe the manager gave them the wrong information? He could have sent them east, or south."

"Maybe," he answered.

"Or what if they saw us leave this morning and knew of a place where they could ambush the stage. They're out there, probably only a mile ahead of where we broke down, waiting for us."

"Maybe."

"What if they're right over the ridge and they were just waiting to see if Winter would lead them to us? What if the manager told them nothing and they followed Winter, thinking he'd be sent to warn us?"

"Could be."

McCall swung the towel at his head. "You're no help at all. What do you think? You must have some guess."

Sloan stopped pouring oats into the feeder. "I don't have a guess, McCall. I save that for the generals. All I *think* is that we'd better get out of here as fast and as well-armed as we can. But we can't take Winter and we can't leave him here alone, so while the animals rest, we wait for Starkie. I wait and watch and listen. You guess."

She wrinkled her eyebrows together and thought of guessing a few names to call him. So what if he was right? He could talk to her about their problem. She realized that if they needed to ride hard and fast, the boy could never stay up with them. He'd already crossed his limit of land today. Starkie would protect him with his life if she asked him. But she had to wait until he got back to ask.

As if wishing something could make it happen, a wagon came into view from the west with the stagecoach just behind. They were moving slowly, as though out for a Sunday drive.

McCall waved as relief flooded her. If trouble should come, they now had a much better chance.

"No one's waving back," Sloan whispered as he moved between the horses. "Winter, stay out of sight for a few minutes."

Winter nodded silently. A moment later he vanished.

"Keep waving, McCall," Sloan mumbled. "Still got that little derringer in your pocket?"

"Yes." She slipped her hand into her skirt pocket and felt the gun.

"Keep your fingers around it, but don't stop smiling. Just act like we're working with the horses."

"What is it? What's wrong? Maybe they just can't see me waving. Maybe some of them are asleep. Maybe they're talking."

"If we can see them, they can see us." Sloan slipped a bridle over first one horse, then the other. "Winter, can you still hear me?"

"Yes," he answered from somewhere near the well.

"Good." Sloan saddled one of the extra horses Winter had led in. "See if you can get behind these horses and open that gate back of the barn. When it's open, shoo the mustang toward me so I'll know."

"Yes, sir," Winter whispered.

He moved so quickly, McCall wasn't sure it was him darting from one shadow to another.

"What should I do?" McCall felt like she was running in the dark. She had no idea what was going on. Sloan was making no sense, but Winter didn't argue and Starkie still hadn't returned her wave.

Sloan lifted a whittled cane Starkie had left leaning against the barn. "Walk over and slowly latch the gate. Then slide this sideways over the latch. It won't stop anyone, but it'll slow them down."

McCall followed his directions.

He threw the second saddle into place and pulled the cinch. "Can you mount a moving horse without my help?"

"I think so," McCall answered, thinking she might not have much choice.

"Then take the reins of this bay and start walking toward the barn like you're putting him up. When you pass my hat and coat, throw them over the saddle."

McCall watched over her shoulder as the wagon approached. The Rogerses were sitting on the back bench as if they were straw people.

She wrapped the reins around her hand, ready to mount the horse if Sloan yelled.

Suddenly everyone in the wagon seemed to melt into the buckboard. Starkie slapped the horses into a gallop as the stage stopped abruptly, blocking the road a hundred yards from the cabin. Bryant dropped down into the front boot of the stage and pulled a rifle to his shoulder.

"Take cover!" Starkie yelled as soon as he thought Sloan could hear him. He almost toppled the wagon as he swung it around only a few feet from the cabin. "Trouble's right behind us."

Sloan swung up into the saddle and grabbed the rope of the horse Winter had ridden. As he kicked his animal, McCall looked back and saw him. With her horse already dancing to run, she climbed atop the bay just as the mustang came into sight from the back of the corral.

"Ride!" Sloan yelled.

McCall pushed her horse into a full run, knowing that if the gate was closed behind the barn she'd break both her and the horse's neck trying to stop.

Winter was standing by the open gate. McCall galloped through with Sloan a length behind. As he passed the boy, he leaned in the saddle and extended his arm. Winter swung up behind Sloan as if they'd practiced the move a hundred times.

Gunfire flooded the already charged air, splattering fear into both the animals and McCall.

She glanced back in time to see Starkie standing beside the wagon with one of his Patterson Colts in each hand. He was firing so fast a man would be a fool to even lift his head enough to take aim.

As she leaned into the horse for more speed the barn blocked her view. She could still hear the guns firing and the screams of the Rogers women. She rode on as she always rode . . . fast as the wind. Holden's brag flashed through her mind. *Not even a bullet can catch my wife when she rides.*

McCall only prayed it was true.

Twenty-four

SLOAN CUT HIS horse in front of McCall's and led the way toward the stream. The recent rain had made the water almost a foot deep along the wide creek. They splashed into the water and moved east, allowing the stream to erase any trace of their passing.

They traveled fast, but they weren't moving as swiftly as they would have if Winter hadn't been with them. Sloan constantly paced himself for the boy, looking back every few minutes to make sure Winter had made the turn or climbed the ridge. He'd learned McCall could keep up with him without any trouble. In truth, she rode better than most of the men he'd served with in the cavalry. She must have been a great asset to her husband in the field.

After an hour, he pulled up and raised his hand to stop.

"We need to rest the horses," Sloan said as he swung down. He took all the mounts' reins.

McCall slipped to the ground and walked to a rise several feet away. She could see for a mile or more in all directions. She crossed her arms around her but didn't complain of the cold.

Sloan took care of the horses while Winter stretched out on the grass. McCall watched and waited. She needed to talk to Sloan, but wasn't sure where to start. Maybe he blamed her for the mess they were in. He'd said earlier that he wanted to kiss her good-bye and be on his way. He'd kissed her good-bye, but now they were trapped together for a while longer.

"We've got to go back and help the others." She settled on the only safe topic she could think of.

Sloan looked up at her as he was checking the bay's hooves. "There's no need. Starkie and Bryant can take care of trouble. I'm betting it was Bull Willis and his friends. If so, they'll try to get away from the station as fast as they can and follow us. It's me that Bull wants to kill, not those folks."

"And now me," McCall said, more to the open prairie than to him.

"I know," he answered, sounding angry again. "I should have never taken the job you offered. If I hadn't gotten involved with you and the children, even if they'd found me, it wouldn't have mattered. It was a mistake to let anyone close. You'd think I'd be old enough to know better."

"You're right." McCall felt her own anger rise. "We should have never gotten involved." She said the last word in a way that left no doubt it included the night they'd been together.

He opened his mouth to speak, but he wasn't sure where to start. Did he say, "I take it back. I'm not sorry I met you," or did he order McCall to take her words back, for she'd cut him deeply.

Staring at her, he saw the coldness returning to her blue eyes. She'd built the wall around herself once more, and it wouldn't be so easy to scale again. He wished he could say that he would never be sorry for the time they'd spent together. He wanted to tell her that the hours with her in his arms were the only hours he'd lived. But he wasn't sure she would listen. After all, she'd been the one who left him. She walked out without bothering to explain.

"What's happened has happened," he finally said. "Right now, we've got to figure out how best to stay alive."

"And keep Winter safe."

Winter raised up and leaned on his knee. "Don't worry about me. I can take care of myself."

Neither McCall nor Sloan seemed to hear him.

"They'll think we're going back to Howard's station." McCall began to pace. "Or to Fort Worth." She walked, turning sharp corners as if framing a room. "We've got to think of an alternate plan. I could go one direction, you another."

Sloan stood directly in her path. He wasn't letting her have her way this time. "We go together! I'm not taking the chance of them following you and not me."

Fire darkened her eyes. "I'm going," her words were almost calm, "where I decide to go. No one . . . no man has the right to order me."

"I can find my way back to the station by myself," Winter volunteered.

Again no one listened.

Sloan fought the urge to grab her, tie her up, and throw her over the saddle. She was the most frustrating woman he'd ever met. It didn't matter that she thought he had no right to tell her what to do. It didn't matter that she would be riding right into trouble. Even the fact that Winter might watch him kidnap her wasn't what stopped him, Sloan realized.

He hesitated because he knew that eventually he'd have to untie her. When he did, she'd either kill him or, at the least, hate him for the rest of her life.

McCall folded her arms as if waiting for a battle, but

Sloan turned and walked away. He could say he didn't want to fight with her a thousand times, but she still kept drawing lines in the sand, daring him to step over. Well, this time he wasn't taking the challenge.

"I know the way back from here," Winter said loudly for the second time. "We're not far from the station."

McCall raised her face to the noon sun. "Are you sure you know the way?"

"Yes," Winter answered. "We crossed here when we were alone, after the old medicine man died. The station is beyond that rise where the trees shield the sunrise. We camped there before moving on. It took all morning on foot to make it to Miss Alyce, but on horseback I could make it in half the time."

Sloan turned and walked back to Winter. "He's right. He does know the way."

"I know he's right!" McCall snapped. "I grew up in this country."

"I could go back alone," Winter offered. "No one's looking for me. It seems to me I'd be safer away from the two of you."

Sloan touched the boy's shoulder. "Then go. Find Miss Alyce and tell her to meet us at McCall's place. Tell her to bring any supplies she thinks we'll need." He looked up at McCall. "Then we could ride a wide circle around the settlement so no one would see us."

"I haven't spent the night on the ranch since my husband died." McCall took a step closer to Sloan.

"It would only be a few days. It's the only place where we'll be comfortable and safe without endangering anyone else. No one will look for us there." He could tell she was thinking of agreeing. She might be angry, but she wasn't foolish.

"Then what? We hide like rats forever?"

"No." Sloan forced himself to stay calm. "I'll rest up and get a fresh horse. Then I'll go looking for them, once I know you're safe."

McCall took a deep breath. "It appears to be the only sensible thing to do."

Sloan couldn't believe she was agreeing so easily. He could almost see the wheels turning in her mind. She was up to something, but he'd just have to wait and find out what. Or maybe, like him, she was exhausted. Going home, even to a house she hated, sounded good.

They mounted in silence and rode together to where the trees marked the ridge. When Winter headed toward the station, Sloan and McCall began their circle to the ranch.

Sloan was careful to cover their trail, riding on hard ground when they could find any and staying to well-trod paths other times. McCall was an easy partner, for they paced themselves very much the same. She rode like a seasoned soldier, never complaining.

It was midafternoon when they reached her place. He watched her carefully. She showed no sign of being happy to be home. She didn't pause or glance into the cemetery as they passed it. The place might as well have been unknown to her and not the place where she'd grown up.

When they stopped in front of the barn, Sloan broke the silence. "I'll take care of the horses if you want to go on in." The sky had clouded up, making the air cold once more. He'd offered her his coat five times in the past hour, but she'd always insisted her jacket was warm enough.

"I'll start a fire." She didn't look at him as she turned and walked away.

Sloan led the horses into the huge barn. As he worked, he glanced around, noticing how neglected the barn looked. Only one of the stalls had been used in years, and most of the equipment hanging on the walls was in need of oiling. He tried to remember what McCall had told him about the place. Something about an old couple living out here as overseers until a few months ago, but she hadn't lived here in years.

It was a shame she'd neglected the place. The land was good, grassy and laced with streams. Her ranch would make a grand place for raising horses. From the number of wild ones they'd seen, Holden must have done what most men did when there was no one left to run the place. He'd turned his cattle and horses loose. With work, the ranch could be productive once more.

Sloan crossed the yard to the back porch. Though the house was a good size, it seemed to be standing at attention like a toy headquarters, not a home. There were no curves or softness in the design. As he'd noticed before, there was no welcoming warmth about the house McCall grew up in. It reminded him of one of the hundreds of buildings he'd seen inside forts.

When he entered the kitchen, he found her sitting by a cold fireplace. A layer of dust covered what must have once been a spotless kitchen.

"McCall?" Sloan knelt by her chair.

"I don't want to stay here." She looked at him with an expression in her eyes he'd never seen. "I hate this place," she whispered, as though someone might hear her. "There are too many ghosts. I thought I could come back for a day or two, but now I'm not sure."

"There's nothing to be afraid of," Sloan said as he glanced at the empty box of matches in her hand. "If ghosts could hurt anyone, I'd be long dead."

"I'm not afraid," McCall answered. "I just feel myself going back in time. By stepping into this house, I step back into the role I played until Holden died. I don't want to be that person anymore."

Sloan took her hand. "What person?" He couldn't allow her to let a house break her. He cared for her too much.

"The perfect daughter, the perfect wife." McCall glanced around the room as if expecting someone to jump out of the shadows. "My father couldn't have a son who'd go to West Point and be an officer, so he did the next best thing. He raised me to be the perfect officer's wife."

Sloan pulled her toward the doorway. "And you were, weren't you? Everything in order, follow a timetable, reason out strategies, never show your feelings, never complain."

She looked up at him as if seeing the truth of his words.

"You can dress a wound, fire a gun, ride better than any messenger sent, therefore saving a man for the battle. What more could an officer want of a wife?"

McCall followed him into the hallway.

"You were raised by two military men to know your duty. And you did it to the end. You were perfect to have in camp to take care of Holden's needs, and the only one who could have brought him through the lines so he could be buried back here." Sloan continued as he pulled her into the main entry. "It's no wonder Holden Harrison married you on sight."

"But he—"

"He what?" Sloan raised his voice, suddenly angry at her family. They'd tried to take all the woman out of this beautiful creature. "But did he really love you? But did he cherish you as a husband should cherish a wife? Did he want you as a woman and not as a major's second?"

McCall didn't answer.

"Or maybe he just wanted you to have his children. Men like him are usually worried about leaving part of themselves to carry on."

McCall looked at him then with anger to match his own. "He did want me to have his children. He told Starkie so."

"So he could breed more soldiers for wars in the future." Sloan stormed into the room he guessed to have been the study. "Why didn't you, McCall? Why didn't you have a dozen little Holdens? You were married long enough. I'm sure it would have made your father happy."

A tear ran unnoticed down her cheek. "I don't know. I couldn't. After every time he touched me, I'd wait, hoping, but it never happened."

Sloan saw it then, what drove her forever on into danger. "So, you weren't perfect? You couldn't have his children. But you made up for it, didn't you, McCall? You rode into danger again and again. You became a legend as great as the famous Major Harrison."

McCall turned her back. She didn't want to face the truth.

Sloan wouldn't stop. "But he died, didn't he? He died with honor, and you lived on. So you locked up all the emotion and let only the legend live. You've been riding in honor's shadow for three years."

"That's all still—"

"Don't say it!" Sloan turned her to face him. "That's not all of you that is still alive! There's a woman inside you. A breathing, needing, passionate woman. You can run away from me, but you can't run away from the truth."

She stared at him, dry-eyed, as if weighing everything he'd said.

"I have to go," she finally whispered. "There's someone I have to see."

Sloan released the grip he had on her arms. He could fight her when she was fiery. He would argue until morning. But he didn't know how to react when she became so cold and factual, like a puppet who was being controlled by invisible strings.

"As soon as the supplies arrive, I'll go with you."

"There's no need."

"I'll go with you," he repeated.

Sloan had to shatter the cold manner about her, but he wasn't sure how. He walked around the room, picking up objects.

"Whose room was this?" he asked.

McCall didn't seem interested in talking, but she answered, "This was my grandfather's study when I was a little girl. He never allowed me in. When he died, my father took over and taught me lessons in here. When he died, Holden used this room as his home office. Men would come here at all hours of the day and night to talk to him. The room was usually full of cigar smoke and the smell of brandy."

"Do you hate this room as you hate the rest of the house?"

McCall looked interested in the conversation for the first time. "Yes. I probably hate this room the most. When I was little and didn't do my lessons right, my father would make me stand at attention, sometimes for hours, in this room. It, more than any other room, has always been a place I didn't belong."

"Good." Sloan opened one of the long windows. The afternoon air was warmer than the interior of the house. "Then let's start here. This is your house, McCall. You shouldn't hate it. It's only a house."

He picked up what looked like a cannonball mounted on a board. "Do you hate this?"

"Yes," McCall answered slowly.

With one quick throw, Sloan sailed the cannonball out

the window. "It's gone." He lifted a leather-bound cigar box. "Do you hate this?"

A smile touched her lips. "Yes," she answered, more quickly than before.

The box flew out the window. "And this?" Sloan grabbed a brandy decanter.

"I always have hated that thing," she shouted.

One by one all the items sailed out the window. McCall began to laugh as she handed Sloan all the worthless things the men in her life had collected and thought too valuable for a little girl to touch. War books, old drawings of battles from long ago, spurs worn in campaigns, all hit the dirt outside the window.

Soon the room was stripped of all but the furniture. "Now the carpet."

McCall grabbed one end of the long roll to help carry it out.

"And the desk?" Sloan raised an eyebrow.

"No," McCall laughed. "I like the desk." She giggled. "I hid under it once and carved my name where no one would ever find it. My father would have killed me if he'd found out."

Sloan looked around. "Do you like this room better now?"

McCall stared at the bare shelves and walls. All the trappings were gone. "Much better."

The rattle of a wagon drew them out of the game and back to the danger they were in. Sloan pulled his Colt and moved to the window.

"Anybody home?" Annie yelled.

McCall hurried to the porch. "Where's Winter and Miss Alyce?" she asked, then thought of how rude she must sound and softened her voice. "Good to see you, Annie."

"They're back at the station. Miss Alyce said to tell you

she'd like to come out, but she needs to stay and look after my pa a bit longer. Winter thought you would want him to stay with Alyce and watch her. He's also loving helping out while Pa's in bed. So they sent me here with supplies."

Sloan holstered his weapon and walked onto the porch. "Thanks," he said simply as he started unloading the wagon.

Annie climbed down and looked at all the things cluttering the ground outside one of the windows. "What's all this? Did someone break in to rob you and his bag burst as he climbed out?"

"No," McCall laughed. "I was just cleaning house. I'm getting rid of a few things I no longer need."

Annie picked up the cigar box. "I got a fellow over at the fort who might like this."

"Take it," McCall said. "I'd like to think of someone getting some use out of these things."

"And this." Annie lifted one of the drawings.

"I'll unload a grocery box to put your finds in." McCall followed Sloan into the house. "Pick out everything else you think your fellow might need."

While Sloan unpacked, Annie pilfered and McCall made several trips upstairs. Each time she appeared on the porch with an armload more for Annie's wagon.

"I can't take so much," Annie protested when the wagon was half full. "He'll think he has to marry me if I give him all this."

"Do you want to marry him?" McCall asked.

"More than anything." Annie sighed, almost popping the buttons across her bustline.

"Then let me get some more." She disappeared and returned with a folding field desk of fine redwood and shiny new boots.

Annie squealed, and Sloan left to help with the next trip McCall made upstairs.

By the time they finished, the wagon was packed full and Annie was speechless.

"Come back in a few days." McCall smiled. "I'm sure I'll find more."

"I don't know how to thank you," Annie began.

"You don't have to," McCall answered honestly. "You've done me the favor."

As Annie took the reins, she reached in her pocket. "Oh, I almost forgot. Miss Alyce gave me this to give to you." She handed McCall a paper and slapped the horses into action.

McCall stepped beside Sloan on the porch and waved to Annie.

When the wagon was out of sight, she turned to Sloan. "Thank you." She touched his arm lightly.

"For what?" Sloan leaned against the railing.

"For helping me clean house."

"It was long overdue." He held the door for her, wishing she'd touch him again, but she didn't.

As they walked inside, she looked around. "Funny. The house is not the same now. I don't hate it so much anymore."

"Good." Sloan moved toward the kitchen. "Can we cook something? I'm starving, and we now have matches."

While Sloan rummaged through the groceries, McCall read the note from Miss Alyce. "She reminds us to be careful and be on guard," McCall began. "Then she's drawn a map that makes no sense. At the bottom, it says 'to Sanctuary.'"

Sloan had two eggs in each hand as he leaned over her shoulder. "It looks like a map starting at the barn door and moving out back of your place."

McCall turned it sideways. "If you say so. Funny, I haven't heard that word in years. My grandfather used to tell me that he named the original homestead 'Sanctuary,' but when my grandmother came out from the East she made him change it."

"Did you know her?"

McCall shook her head. "She died before they finished the new house. She was a gentle lady who hated this life as much as my grandfather and young father loved it. My grandfather used to say that if she hadn't gone to Heaven that spring, she would have gone back to Boston with or without her husband and son."

Sloan looked at the map more closely, wondering what the crazy old woman was trying to tell them.

"What's for supper?" McCall asked as she spread the map on the table. "I'm starting to get hungry."

"Can't you cook?"

"Can't you?" she countered.

Sloan smiled. "How about we work together on this, General, before we both starve?"

"All right." McCall stood. "After we eat we'll try and decide what Miss Alyce is attempting to tell us with this map."

Twenty-five

❧

"HOW MUCH TIME did you say Miss Alyce spent at this place?" Sloan asked as he moved between the trees. McCall carried the map. He held a shovel and lantern.

McCall took the lantern as she folded the map. "Not much. She and her father used to come by during my grandfather's early days. She was always around when I was small. Holden didn't like her much. He never said anything to her, but I don't remember her visiting us once during my marriage. She was here when we buried him, though. She helped me pack to move to the station that night. I guess you could say she's been around all my life, but never stayed as a houseguest. It wouldn't have been proper with only grandfather and father around."

"You think she buried something of value here?" Sloan stepped off the paces Alyce had written on the map.

"I don't think so," McCall answered as she followed like a shadow behind him.

They were a hundred yards from the back of the barn where a break of trees had been planted years ago. The wooded area was shady and cold in the late afternoon breeze. When he stopped, she bumped into him.

Sloan took her by the arms and moved her out of the

way before he began to dig. He felt a chill suddenly pass through him like some people say they get when they step on a grave.

The shovel struck metal after only a few inches. "Well, whatever she wants us to find, she didn't bother burying it very deep." Sloan raked the shovel along the metal.

In a few minutes, he'd cleared the dirt from what looked like a small door. McCall lit the lantern as he continued. Between the clouds and the shade, the light was so dim she was unable to see their find without the lantern.

"This isn't logical," McCall said as Sloan used the shovel as a wedge to pry open the old door.

As the metal fell back against the layers of leaves beneath a tree, McCall held the lantern down. It lit a narrow stairway.

"I'll go down first," Sloan volunteered. "From the rust on that door, I'd guess no one's opened this in ten or fifteen years."

McCall nodded and stood back, looking like she wasn't sure she wanted to follow.

Slowly, Sloan tested his weight on each step. The wood held. Whoever built this place had built it to last. The door had been almost airtight, keeping out leaves and rain.

As he moved further down, heavy cellar air filled his lungs and spiderwebs barred his path. Dusting the few webs aside, he shone the light lower into a room.

"Oh, my!" McCall whispered in awe from a few steps behind him. "This is the original dugout Grandfather built. This is 'Sanctuary.'"

Sloan touched the ceiling of the room that was too short for him to stand in. "He must have reinforced the roof, then closed it off with the door years ago."

"But why?" McCall searched the room. "We have a cellar closer to the house. I remember when I was a child he was always planting trees near this spot. When he died, I was about twelve. I remember Father thinking of burying him near here. He said after they built the new house Grandfather used to walk out here and sit among the trees until dawn."

Sloan glanced at the only piece of furniture, a bed. "Maybe he used this as his guest room?"

McCall touched a dusty but neatly stacked pile of bedding. It looked as if years ago it had been laundered and put at the foot of the bed. "Maybe. But it makes no sense. Why didn't I know about this place? I don't think my father knew it was still here." She wrinkled her forehead. "Why would Alyce know about this place and never tell me?"

Sloan checked the corners. "I have no idea, but I know why she told us now. This is the only safe place for us to stay. Your house is an open target. Anyone could get a shot in from any direction. But here, no one would ever find us. Maybe your grandfather left it in case of Indian attack. Or maybe he thought he'd store guns in it during the war. Who knows?"

McCall looked around. "You're right. If I didn't know of this, neither will anyone else. It's warm and dry. I'll be able to sleep the night here and you can sleep in the barn."

Sloan wasn't sure he heard any of the words she said beyond the "I." She was making it plain he wasn't invited to share the bed. He wasn't about to ask, after what they'd said to one another today, but it hurt his pride that she felt the need to say no anyway. "I'll carry over a good mattress," he mumbled, hiding his feelings.

"I'll get the bedding before it gets too dark outside to find the opening among the trees." McCall walked past him, lifting the lantern from his head and carrying it up the steps.

For a long while Sloan stood in the darkness, telling himself he hadn't really planned to sleep with her again. He'd told her the only reason he was here was to see her safe, then he'd be gone. But part of him had been fool enough to believe that they might stay together one more night. If she wanted that, she wouldn't have run out on him the morning after they made love.

How could the greatest night of his life have been so easily forgettable to her? All afternoon, he'd thought of the way her skin felt to his touch. The way her body moved against him. The way she smelled of dampness and roses after they'd made love. But he hadn't touched her. It never seemed like the right time. He didn't want her to think he was some kind of animal who attacked her at every opportunity. Even if the thought was in his mind most of the time.

This morning seemed a million miles away. Had he really kissed her only this morning? And felt her legs wrapped around his waist? Had it only been hours since he'd tasted passion?

For a short time, they'd been so right together. Nothing else in the world mattered. But the time passed and he had no idea how to get back to that magic loving place. He couldn't just say that he wanted to make love to her again. The woman he'd slept with had disappeared and been replaced by someone he couldn't get close to.

Any other woman would be frightened and want someone nearby. McCall was doing what she did best . . . organizing.

Sloan forced the thoughts to the corners of his mind. He needed to have all his wits about him. Trouble was riding toward him at full speed. She could sleep here and be safe. He'd bunk in the loft of the barn where he could watch the road, at least.

He climbed the stairs and walked to the barn.

An hour later he was too lost in the task of cleaning some of the equipment to notice McCall until she was almost close enough to touch him.

"What are you doing?" she asked casually.

He wanted to yell, "Keeping my hands busy so I don't make a fool of myself by attacking you," but instead he said, "I thought I'd oil some of these harnesses before sundown."

"Will we be safe after dark?"

"Since those searching for us have never been here, and this place is hard enough to find in the light, I'd say we're safe once the sun sets. Bull Willis won't know what he's riding into at night, so he'll wait for daylight."

McCall nodded and began saddling one of the horses.

"Where do you think you're going?" Sloan snapped.

"I'm going for a ride. Don't worry, I'll be back soon. I know how to travel without being seen."

"You can't—"

"There you go again, telling me what I can and can't do." McCall pulled the cinch tight.

"How about I stop talking to you at all!"

"That would be a great blessing, I think, for the one thing I don't need is a man telling me what to do."

Before he could answer, she swung up onto the saddle and moved through the door. Sloan was only seconds behind, but she'd almost disappeared out of sight before he cleared the barn.

He followed, but as always she knew no speed but fast. She was familiar with the land and he had to guess his way. But he managed to keep her in sight as the sun set. Within a mile he realized she wasn't just out riding, but was heading to a certain point.

She rode north, closer to town, but didn't follow the

road. At the far corner of her land, she turned onto a small lane that led up to a cottage sitting just far enough off the road to go unnoticed by travelers.

"Lacy?" she called as she neared. "Lacy, are you home?"

Sloan slowed and watched from the shadows as a stout woman came to the door of the cottage. "Who's out there?"

"It's McCall Harrison. May I come to call?"

"Mrs. Harrison. Well, bless my soul. Do come in, child. I haven't seen you in a month of Sundays. You know you're always welcome."

McCall lowered herself from the horse and tied the reins to a post. She'd known Lacy since she'd married. Lacy had moved in about that time to this small house and began making desserts for the station. Everyone in the county knew her by her fine cooking.

The shorter woman held her door open wide. "I was thinking of you only today when I heard about the trouble over at Howard's station. I was sure glad you was gone and didn't see what someone did to Mr. Howard. He ain't an overly kind man, but he don't deserve a beating."

Sloan moved a little closer to the house. He could smell fresh bread and see loaves lined up on a table inside. Lacy was a woman in her forties, maybe old enough to be Mc-Call's mother. She was short and well-rounded, with white hair only lightly peppered. Her bustline seemed a solid roll from her double chin to her thick waist.

"The men who hurt Mr. Howard were looking for me," McCall said as she pulled off her gloves.

"I heard that, but I can't imagine why." Lacy moved inside. "Anyone who'd want to hurt you must be crazy. I've known you for years, and you never done a soul a bit of harm. Would you come in, child, and rest a spell? You look tired and I got some hot tea ready."

"Thanks." McCall moved past the woman. "I'd like that."

Once inside, Lacy seemed a little nervous. The older woman often visited with McCall when delivering pies to the station. A few times they'd shared a meal there, but McCall had never made a social call.

"Do you like sugar in your tea?" Lacy dusted an already spotless side table.

"No." McCall watched her closely. "I like my tea just the way Holden did."

Lacy rattled the cup and saucer, almost dropping it. "And how is that?"

Suddenly, McCall didn't want to hurt Lacy. She truly liked the woman. "Just plain," she said softly.

Lacy set the cup down before her and lowered herself into the rocker across from McCall without pouring herself any tea. "If you're in some kind of trouble, I'll do anything I can to help."

"Thank you," McCall said. "I think I'll be fine. I've come about something else. Something that has nothing to do with the men who are following me."

"Yes." Lacy stared at her hands. "What is it?"

McCall looked at the little woman, thinking that she should hate her. This woman had been Holden's lover for years. What had Starkie said . . . even *before* Holden married? McCall knew Holden, though from a good family, had little money. Most of the time they'd lived on her inheritance. Even the cottage and land his mistress called home belonged to her. She should throw the woman out on the streets. It would be the proper thing to do.

But she couldn't hate Lacy. She was a kind woman. McCall could understand why Holden would come to her.

Maybe he'd loved her. Maybe Lacy had loved him. For her peace of mind, McCall had to know.

Blinking away the tears, she thought back over the years of her marriage and her husband's death. If Lacy had loved him, she had never gotten to say good-bye. McCall had held him when he died and received all the sympathy as his widow. She'd been the one who'd mourned and buried Holden. Lacy must have only been allowed to cry in silence.

"Lacy," McCall said softly. "I have to know the truth, though it never will go beyond this room. Did you love Holden?"

The older woman didn't answer for a moment, and McCall held the hope that she might have been mistaken about Lacy. Maybe Starkie got the name wrong, or the story wrong. If so McCall would apologize and ask Lacy to forgive her for the late call and the question.

But when Lacy glanced up, she looked like she might cry, and McCall knew the truth before she said a word.

Lacy straightened slightly and mumbled, "I guess you found out. We never meant for you to know. I told Holden after I met you that I never wanted to hurt you, and he was never, ever, to tell you about me."

McCall placed her hand on Lacy's tightly balled fingers, realizing the older woman could have lied. "I don't want to hurt you, either. I just need to know a few things. I tried to love Holden, but I never felt like he let me. It would help me to know that someone did love him enough to make him happy."

Lacy was silent. Her hands trembled beneath McCall's touch.

"He loved you, didn't he, Lacy? You did make him happy." McCall faced the truth.

"I tried." Tears bubbled over the now wrinkled face. "We had some times."

"He should have married you." McCall almost hated him for the first time in her life. If he'd have married Lacy, they might have all been happier.

"I wouldn't let him," Lacy answered with pride. "I weren't nothing but trash when he met me. I weren't no officer's wife. You was that, Mrs. Harrison. You was all the best that could be. There weren't a day back during the war, or since, that I ain't been proud of who my Holden married."

McCall was shocked. She sat back in her chair and closed her eyes, remembering all the nights that Holden would go for a ride and not return until after midnight. She'd thought he'd gone into the night to think, or to the station to talk with someone. He must have been here with Lacy. All those nights she'd slept in her room alone, he could have been here and she'd never have known.

"I'd think you'd hate me for marrying the man you loved." McCall couldn't understand. They should be throwing rocks at one another, not sitting drinking tea.

"Oh, no!" Lacy answered. "I always felt sorry for you."

"Sorry for me?"

Lacy looked embarrassed.

"Please," McCall needed to hear it all, "I have to hear the truth."

"Holden told me about how you was. Cold and all . . . even in bed. It's nothing to be ashamed of. I think lots of ladies like yourself don't feel that more animal feeling some of us get. It's probably a blessing in the long run of life."

McCall was too shocked to speak.

Lacy patted her arm. "He told me you didn't like to be touched. That you was all proper, all the time. But don't you worry. I know you got deep feelings. You proved that by doing what you did to bring him home. There weren't many women who'd drive a wagon across Indian country to bring a man home to bury."

Tears streamed down Lacy's chubby cheeks. "It meant a lot to me these past three years to be able to visit the grave. I'm always real careful, never going when anyone is around. I hope you'll still allow me to, now that you know how it was between Holden and me."

McCall slid from her chair to the floor in front of Lacy, watching the woman cry. "Of course you can," she whispered, wishing she could also cry. The woman had taken her husband's love. But all she could see was how much greater Lacy's loss was. "You're welcome anytime," McCall whispered as she wrapped her arms around the woman.

Lacy's tears were rivers now as she clung to McCall. "I miss him every day, and I ain't never been able to tell anyone. I've lived in fear that someday you'd find out and have me kicked off this land like the trash I am."

McCall thought of all the heartache she'd caused this woman without ever knowing it. "I'm so sorry you were afraid. Holden should have deeded this square of land to you. I'll see it's done."

"You don't have to do that." Lacy wiped her cheek with her sleeve. "Holden was right not to give me any of your land. It wouldn't have been right. You was just a child when he married you. When I found out, I was madder than a wet hen. I told him he better never hurt you or be mean to you or he'd answer to me."

The knowledge of how close Lacy and Holden must have been for her to threaten him so sank into McCall. She never would have dreamed of saying such a thing to him.

"He weren't, was he?" Lacy asked. "Mean to you?"

"No. He never beat me or was mean to me," McCall answered. Unless indifference could count as cruelty. "He treated me much as my father had before."

McCall had to ask. "Was he good to you, Lacy?"

Lacy smiled. "He was always good to me. From the first time I was with him, he never would let me be with anyone else. Paid me most of his money so I could live without taking in laundry. He was always giving me things and telling me how I was in his heart when he was away fighting."

McCall couldn't imagine the Holden she knew ever using those words.

"Sometimes I still miss his arms holding me all night long." She looked down at McCall. "I've heard tell some men are one-woman men. I guess for Holden there was two women. Course I wasn't near as important as you. He gave you his name."

"No." McCall's training of always telling the truth wouldn't allow her to lie now. "He was a one-woman man. He was your man, Lacy. I may have had his name, but you had his heart."

"Oh, no, child!"

"Yes," McCall argued. "In all the years we were married he never hurt me, but he never held me in his arms through the night. You were the woman he slept beside in his thoughts and dreams, when he couldn't be with you all the time."

"I thank you for telling me that." Lacy wiped her nose. "It means a great deal to me. I'll hold them words in my heart till I die. I promise I won't ever tell nobody about being with him. You do him proud as his widow. If folks knew about me and him it'd only muddy his name."

Reaching in her pocket for her handkerchief, McCall touched Holden's watch, which she'd meant to give to

Annie. "Would you like this?" she asked as she handed Lacy the watch.

"Oh, yes," Lacy cried, turning the gold over and over in her hand. "I'll treasure it. He always put it on the night-stand so he wouldn't stay too long and have to ride home after sunup."

As Lacy opened the watch, she cried in surprise.

McCall looked at the inside of the watch case. The letters M and L had been scratched there. "What is it?" McCall asked.

"He always put them letters on his notes to me. I can't read, but he said they meant 'My Love.' He said whenever I looked at them I was to think of him, for he was thinking of me."

Tears streamed down Lacy's face as she held the watch to her. "Oh, thank you."

McCall smiled and leaned to kiss the woman on the cheek. "You're welcome."

Lacy looked up in question. "And thank you for not hating me and telling ever'one so's I'd be run out of town. What I did, I did because of the way I felt for him. It never had nothin' to do with you. I felt bad that if you ever found out you'd be hurt and hate me. But you brought me this instead. Now I can look at this watch and know he was thinking of me ever'time he looked at it, no matter where he was."

"I'd never hate you," McCall answered. "And I'm glad I could give you the watch." Something that had meant nothing to her, Lacy would cherish. "I have to go now, but will you promise to come see me in the spring? We'll visit the grave, and maybe we could plant some flowers in the cemetery."

"I'd be honored. Your visit has lifted a weight off my soul that's been mighty heavy."

"And your honesty has let me see the truth, Lacy. I can understand how Holden could love you so dearly."

"Thank you, Mrs. Harrison. You is the finest lady I ever met. There ain't nobody who'd have done what you just did. Giving me the watch and all. I won't never forget it."

McCall hugged Lacy and walked out, not noticing Sloan slip away from the window only a moment before.

Twenty-six

❦

SLOAN RELEASED HIS horse into the corral and climbed the ladder to the loft just in time to see McCall break through the line of trees to the north and ride in. The moonlight danced in her long hair as she galloped. He couldn't help but smile, thinking she was her most beautiful when she rode.

He felt a strange kind of pride about what she'd done at Lacy's home. She could have caused a scene the entire town would have heard. But she hadn't. His proper little general had been kind. Kinder maybe than any other woman would have been.

Gripping the sides of the loft opening, Sloan fought the desire to go down and be with her. He could almost feel McCall's pain, knowing that her husband gave his love to another over her. The watch had been proof. Lacy was his lifelong love, not McCall. She was only his widow.

Sloan watched her take care of her horse in the moonlight. If she were his wife, he'd never go to another. How could Holden have been so blind?

But McCall didn't want him any more than Holden wanted her. Sloan might stay near her a day, maybe two, but then he'd have to leave. They'd never said a word about the future, and Sloan didn't know where to start.

He moved to the center of the loft and gripped the beams, fighting himself to keep from going down. She'd be in the little dugout by now. With only the light of the lantern, she'd probably be undressing. He could see her every curve in his mind's eyes. The perfection of her would haunt him the rest of his days.

Why hadn't he touched her all afternoon while they'd been alone? If he'd told her how deeply he wanted her, maybe . . .

Sloan slammed his fist against the beam. She'd left him! How much more did she have to do to tell him she didn't want him? What did it matter? A few weeks ago he hadn't known she existed; now the loss of her was ripping him apart. Why couldn't she have been a woman like Lacy? A woman with little in this world who welcomed men into her bed easily. Why'd he have to care about the great Widow Harrison, whose heart was as big as her legend, it seemed, but who had no room for him? She deserved more than he'd ever be able to give. He was only marking himself an idiot for trying.

"Sloan?" Her call broke into his thoughts. "Are you up there?"

He didn't answer as he heard her climb the ladder.

"There you are," she said as she stepped onto the loft floor. "I looked for you in the house. Still not speaking to me, I see. I guessed you'd sleep up here by the opening. It's the most strategic spot on the place."

Sloan wasn't sure he could talk to her without making a fool of himself. He stared out at the stars from the loft door.

"I wanted to say good night and see if you needed anything." She dropped a blanket. "I thought you could use another quilt."

He could hear her moving closer, but he didn't let go of the wood.

"I'd like to thank you for staying to protect me. It's kind, but not necessary. If there is one thing I'm fairly good at, it's taking care of myself. You're free to leave if you like tomorrow."

He could feel her standing just behind him, close enough to touch.

She took a deep breath, as if determined to say what must be said. "You asked me this morning why I left you at the station. I didn't answer. I'm not sure. I think I was hating you as well as myself."

He raised his head, wishing he knew the right words to say. But how does a man beg a woman not to regret loving him? He could never do such a thing.

The ranch house and the land stretched before him in the moonlight. Until today he'd never realized the difference between them. She was leaving to ruin more than he'd ever own. This was the kind of place he used to dream of having to raise horses. But that was before the war, when he allowed himself to dream.

"Do you have everything you need?" She took a step away.

Sloan nodded once, biting his lip to keep from telling her how much he needed her.

"Well, good night, then." She moved another step away. "I'll see you in the morning."

Closing his eyes, he didn't want to see her walk away. He didn't want to hear her leaving him. He felt like he'd lived a lifetime since he'd met her, and if he heard her leave, he'd be dying. He hadn't the energy to fight anymore. She didn't want his loving, and he was too proud to ask again.

Sloan let out a low groan and gripped the wood until it splintered. He wouldn't watch her leave. He couldn't say good-bye to the only person he'd cared about.

McCall stood in the blackness of the loft, watching him. She should go, she told herself. He didn't want to talk to her. But she couldn't leave. The power of this silent man fascinated her.

His shirt was stretched so tightly across the muscles of his shoulders, he looked like a man made of granite. She guessed he was still angry. She couldn't blame him. Though she'd said it would be a blessing if he didn't talk to her, she wished he'd at least say good night. He was the most frustrating human she'd ever met. For a man others said was without honor, he had his share of pride.

He didn't seem to live by the same rules she always thought men lived by. He thought talking to Winter was as important as talking to an adult. He'd saved a horse no one else would have bothered with. This afternoon he'd helped her toss out expensive things that he saw as worthless if they made her unhappy.

She moved a step closer. Now, alone with her, he seemed his most interesting. She could almost smell the wild passion within him, but when he touched her it had been hesitantly. McCall couldn't help but wonder how he'd touch her if he were secure in her response. She couldn't ask him to stay longer, not after he'd made it so plain that coming here was a mistake. He was a drifter who wanted no ties.

Suddenly, he broke and ran to the ladder. Before she could call him back he was to the ground and running out the door toward the room they'd found. McCall watched from the window as he slowed when almost to the trees.

He walked a few steps closer to the opening, then turned around and walked slowly back, his head down, his shoulders defeated.

He climbed back up the ladder and spread the blanket she'd brought out on the hay. Then he moved to the loft door again and looked out once more, as though staring at the dugout. She could see his back clearly in the moonlight, but his face was in shadow. She could feel the tension in the air, like the kind of energy that sparks before a lightning storm.

Silently moving closer as he ran his fingers through his hair, she watched him grab the frame once more above his head. He looked so young. His movements were quick, almost jerky, showing indecision and youth. His lean body was not yet to midtwenty, though his eyes seemed years older.

A board creaked beneath her foot and she felt him tense, but he didn't go for his gun. His senses were too keen to panic.

She advanced, watching him closely.

His eyes were closed but she guessed he knew she was there. He reminded her of a wild animal, feeling someone near. Not needing sight.

She moved behind him, knowing he was probably still angry with her for leaving. Anger had driven him to follow the stage and anger had flavored his kiss this morning. But she needed to be close to him. When she'd watched him run half the distance to the dugout, she saw he needed her also. If he wouldn't take the last few steps, she would.

Very lightly she touched his back and felt him tighten, as though her fingers burned. Slowly, she moved her hand down his back.

He didn't turn, but she knew he felt her. She touched his

back again, more boldly, almost expecting him to pull away.

He remained stone.

Pulling his shirt out at his waist, she placed her hands on the bare flesh of his back and moved gently upward.

He arched slightly, but didn't turn around or say a word. From his stance, she couldn't tell if her touch brought him pleasure or pain.

McCall's fingers moved around his waist and unbuckled his gun belt. The weight of it surprised her. She lowered the weapon to the floor carefully, wanting to disarm him of more than the Colt.

She leaned against his back as she unbuttoned his shirt. His body warmed her and the smell of soap and leather blended with the passion that always surrounded him. Her fingers fumbled with the buttons. Each time her hands moved against his chest, she felt him stiffen more.

There was so much that needed to be said between them. But she didn't know where to start. All she knew was that she needed to touch him. She needed to make a lie of what Lacy and Holden had believed about her. And more important, she needed to feel him holding her so tightly she thought he might never let go. He was the only one who'd ever held her like that, and she craved the touch once more.

When his shirt was unbuttoned, she pulled it open so that her hands could move across the hardness of his chest. She wanted to feel him, really feel every part of him. She spread her palm over his heart as she rubbed her cheek against his shoulder. She could hear the pounding with her ear against him and feel it with her hand.

If he didn't like her touch, all he had to do was say one word to stop her. But he remained still, accepting her caress as silently as he'd accepted the beating the night they'd met.

She pressed her body against his back as her hands moved below his belt and over his pants. He jerked slightly as her fingers slid over the center of his need. He didn't have to speak; she could feel his desire.

Pulling his shirt off his shoulder, she tasted his skin. From the look of him, she couldn't tell if she were bringing him joy or sorrow. But touching him was bringing her pure pleasure.

The taste of him sparked a hunger deep within her. She suddenly wanted the taste of his mouth as well. She pressed her hands around his chest and raked gently across his skin before suddenly stepping away, leaving him gulping for breath.

Sloan stood in place for a long time, then turned slowly. He took a deep breath and plowed his fingers through his hair as though trying to control himself. Moonlight shone in his hair and reflected off the long line of tan skin beneath his open shirt.

He took a step toward her. "What are you doing, McCall?"

She had pulled off her boots and was unbuttoning her short riding coat. "I'm getting ready for bed," she answered, as if she'd said those words to him every night for years.

"McCall!" He tried to talk but his mouth felt like it no longer knew how to form words.

She turned then and met his gaze. Her beauty almost stopped his heart.

"I need to sleep in your arms," she whispered in a voice that was almost childlike.

But the look she gave him was all woman.

"Just any man's arms?" He couldn't be just the "any man" she ran to after learning her husband was unfaithful.

What happened between them tonight couldn't be about another.

"No," she answered and dropped her jacket on the hay. "I want to sleep in *your* arms."

Sloan moved slowly, still not sure. "But you ran from my arms two days ago."

"I know, and I may run again." She unbuckled her belt. "But I'm not running now."

She slid her riding skirt to the floor, leaving only a thin layer of cotton to cover her legs.

Sloan could do nothing but watch. She was doing it again. Changing from one person into another. An hour ago she'd yelled at him and told him to mind his own business. Now she was undressing in front of him as if she'd done it all her life. Half the time he didn't know who she'd be when he next looked at her. But right now, as she opened her blouse to reveal the lace of her camisole, none of the general remained. The person before him was all woman, from the lift of her breasts above the lace to the long length of her black stockings. She was more woman than he'd known or ever hoped to hold.

Grabbing her arm, Sloan pulled her roughly to him and kissed her soundly. He'd half expected her to pull away, but she moved her fingers into his hair. His boldness hadn't frightened her.

He kissed her again, and his kiss was hard and demanding, as if he were daring her to step away. But she moved her body into his and twisted her fingers into fists with his hair intertwined.

He molded his hands down her body. Pressing into her softness, he never hesitated. If she wanted to be in his arms, she'd be there by his rules tonight. He felt like he was on fire with longing for her. He wanted no games between them.

Shoving her blouse aside, he pulled her camisole open with a tug.

He looked down at her closed eyes and slightly opened mouth as he widened his stance and pulled her against him. With his hands covering her hips, he kissed her passionately. Sloan slid his hands up her body, pulling her arms over his shoulders so that he could move his hands along the sides of her breasts. He paused along her rib cage and pressed slightly, swallowing her cry of pleasure without letting her mouth free. Her soft breasts moved slightly against the bareness of his chest, making him deepen the kiss.

When he finally pulled away, her breath was coming in short gasps, lifting and lowering her full breasts to his view.

But he didn't touch her there. He gripped her shoulders and pushed her onto the red blanket she'd brought to him. A moment later, he was next to her. Spreading his hand over the flesh of her stomach, he pressed slightly. She drew in a breath, flattening her abdomen even more and lifting her breasts.

"I want you to have my children," he said, without thought that she'd hear the words. "I want my seed to grow inside here, so that every time I look at you I'll see you as you are now."

He moved his hand lower atop the undergarment. She arched slightly as his fingers spread between her legs, feeling her boldly. "I want all of you, McCall. If you stay here tonight, there'll be no holding back. Come to me whole or not at all. I can't just love a part of you."

He lowered his mouth over hers and kissed her as his hand slid across her warm flesh, tugging the cotton of her undergarment lower. "Let go," he whispered as he moved to her throat. "Let me love all of you. Give all your passion to me . . . or none."

McCall raised her arms above her head and moved to his touch. His hands were warm and strong over her skin as he cupped her breasts, then traced a line down to where cotton still covered her. When his mouth claimed her breast, she cried out in surprise, but he didn't stop. His hand on her leg tightened. The weight of his side held her still as he pulled the softness of her mound into his mouth.

She struggled for a minute as the warmth of his advance flowed over her. When she began to move with him, he lifted his mouth and returned to her ear. "That's the way, darlin', relax and let me have all of you. You're beautiful and you taste of a passion deep. Give yourself to me, McCall. I want all of you tonight."

Part of her wanted to cover herself and run. She was sure respectable people never did what he was doing to her. But it was too late. The need for him was too great. Lacy was wrong; there was a part of her, a need basic and raw, that demanded satisfaction. The kind of satisfaction only Sloan could give.

He turned to her other breast, pulling it into his mouth and tasting until she stopped trying to move away and accepted the pleasure. He was doing it again, giving her the feeling that he'd swallow her whole and consume all of her if she'd allow it. Tonight she not only planned to take all he offered, but demand it.

When she was rocking slowly back and forth beneath his strokes and responding to his kisses, he rose above her suddenly and rolled her over. His hands moved her hair away from her back. Slowly his fingers traveled from her shoulders down. Feeling. Molding. Branding.

"Relax, darling," he whispered as his hands worked across her flesh. "Relax and let me touch you, all of you."

She shivered and he added, "I'll warm you when I'm finished."

The need to feel her warmed his palms as he stroked her with long, hungry hands. When she would have rolled toward him, he stopped her, longing to touch her fully. He moved above her, caressing her until she relaxed and allowed him the freedom he craved. His touch grew bolder, his mouth hungrier for the taste of her as she whispered his name in a voice thick with need.

Finally, he lowered his body over hers, pushing her deep into the soft hay. His hand moved between the blanket and her until it closed around her breast. While those fingers tightened around her fullness, his other hand twisted into her hair and pulled gently, exposing her neck. His open mouth found her throat as he moved against her hips in need.

Mindless with the feel of him over her, McCall whispered his name over and over. The smell of him blanketed her, drugging her with desire. The feel of him covered her back while his hand circled her breast. His mouth feeling the pulse in her throat was maddening. Pure need for him throbbed through her body, stronger than a drum. She was lost in his passion, captured completely in his desire. When she cried in pleasure, he pressed harder against her and closed his grip in total ownership over her breast. All her senses were of him. All her thoughts were of him.

"Say it!" he whispered in her ear as he tugged at her hair, forcing her face closer. "Ask me to love you!"

"Love me," she whispered as he stroked her boldly. "Please, love me."

"Say you need me, McCall." He combed his fingers over her hair gently and released her breast.

"I need you," she whispered as he moved to his side.

Moving his hands lovingly along her back and over her hip, he added, "Again . . . say it again."

"I need you."

Suddenly he was gone, and she cried out for his touch. "Love me, Sloan, please love me." For a moment she thought he'd gone, leaving her.

Gentle hands rolled her over to her back and tugged at her legs. "I do, darlin'," he whispered as he kissed her mouth softly. "And I will."

McCall wrapped her arms around him as he entered her and cried out in joy as he moved above her.

Like riding wild, she held tight and rode the storm of passion. Her body was damp and hot, her heart pounding. She held tighter, demanding more. Faster and faster she rode, until suddenly the world shattered and for a moment she left the ground and rode among the clouds in paradise.

Sloan held her tightly as she lowered back to earth. He stroked her hair and whispered words she couldn't grasp in her ear. McCall smiled and closed her eyes, loving the feel of his arms, loving the nearness of him. Loving the way he touched her as if he'd always touched her, as though they belonged to one another.

"Don't let go," she whispered, already near sleep.

"I won't, darling," he whispered as he gently stroked her damp skin. "I won't."

Deep into the night, Sloan wrapped her in the red blanket and carried her down from the loft and across the clearing to the dugout. She acted as if she were asleep as he slowly moved down the dark steps and into the little room her grandfather had called "Sanctuary." Gently, he laid her on the bed.

When he stood, she gripped his arm. "You said you wouldn't go," she whispered.

"I thought you were asleep." He pulled away and closed the door to the dugout. "I was only locking us in."

"I am asleep," she laughed. "Come closer, it's cold."

"I'll warm you." He lifted the blanket and slid in next to her. "Are you naked?"

"I think so," she whispered as she rolled against him. "Want to check?"

And he did.

Twenty-seven

❧

SLOAN AWOKE SLOWLY from a deep sleep. The dugout was almost completely black, with only a tiny sliver of light coming from above the door. The air was thick and earthy. He could never remember sleeping so soundly, or being awakened so often . . . and always with one purpose—loving. He lost track of the number of times McCall had awakened him by touching him knowingly, or rolling over to press against him in sleep, unaware of how her nearness aroused him. When he'd told her he wanted all of her, with nothing held back, he remembered thinking he could handle her. Now he wasn't so sure. Unless he'd been dreaming, she made love to him once while he was asleep.

Her bare leg lay across him now. Her breast pressed against his side. Her hair covered his shoulder. He could feel her slow breathing against his neck and still taste her on his lips.

"I'd die for you," he whispered as he kissed her cheek.

She moved against him, pressing closer, begging in her sleep to be caressed.

Moving his fingers along her side, he whispered, "Loving you is the only Heaven I've found on this earth. The only Heaven I'll ever need."

He kissed her sleeping mouth. She still tasted of passion. Even in sleep her lips parted in welcome. Her body moved slightly as he stroked her. She was craving his touch and the knowledge made him hunger for her once more. He'd given her his love all night and she was still wanting more. The thought made him smile and silently promise to satisfy her.

Sloan wanted to stay at her side forever, but with dawn, he realized he'd left their clothes in the barn. He thought he'd get them and start the fire in the kitchen before coming back to awaken her.

As he slipped from the bed, he thought of how he'd wake her. The fire would have the kitchen well-warmed by the time he carried her back to the house.

He wrapped a blanket around himself and silently climbed the stairs.

The sun was much brighter than he'd expected as he opened the door. He swore, realizing he'd slept far longer than was wise. But he wouldn't have changed the night if it meant this day would be his last. Making love to McCall left him satisfied and hungry for more at the same time.

He stepped from the dugout and carefully closed the door. Something among the leaves caught his attention. His clothes, gun belt and all, were piled a few feet from the opening.

Something crushed leaves only a few feet behind him.

He was not alone.

As he reached for his gun, Alyce Wren's voice made him freeze in midstride. "You know, for a man who has only one pair of pants, you sure do go leaving them in the strangest places."

Squaring his shoulders, he turned to face the old woman.

"Good morning, Miss Alyce," he said as he pulled on his pants and dropped the blanket with far less modesty than he should have shown. "Nice to see you, too."

"I see you found Sanctuary. It's a great love nest, isn't it?" She moved closer and leaned on her cane.

Sloan couldn't help but laugh. "I guessed that's how you knew about it, but I didn't say anything to McCall. She might not be shocked by anything you did, but I'm not too sure about how she'd react to knowing about her grandfather."

"Well, if you didn't say anything, she'll never catch on. That child is as dumb as a stump when it comes to matters of loving."

Sloan fought down a comment. McCall had gone to school for several hours last night. If he'd have had the chance to awaken her as he'd planned, she might have graduated.

Alyce swatted him with her cane. "Wipe that smile off your face, soldier. You haven't done anything I didn't know you were capable of doing the night I saw you. I knew you were the man I needed when I saw McCall touch your heart."

"I'm only following your advice. You've been throwing her at me since the night I met you. You shouldn't be surprised I finally became wise enough to listen."

Giggling, Alyce asked, "I take it you gave her a toss on the blanket?"

He refused to answer the obvious.

Alyce raised an eyebrow and straightened like a judge. "Do you love her, Sloan? I mean, the kind of love it's going to take for a woman like McCall? Do you love her enough?"

Before he could answer, the door flew open and Mc-Call stormed out. She'd wrapped the red blanket around her bustline, but her shoulders were bare. Her hair was wild from the loving, flying around her like a beautiful cape. Fiery blue eyes stared hot enough to set the woods aflame.

"I'll thank you two to stop discussing me like I'm some dumb horse you're thinking of breeding." She held the blanket with one hand and pointed with the other.

Sloan and Alyce laughed.

McCall took a swing at Sloan and almost tripped over the tail of the blanket.

"Morning, darling," he said without anger as he stepped out of the way. "Remind me to remember the mood you wake up in so I can always plan to be gone by dawn."

"You won't have to worry about being gone because you'll be dead if you ever stand around discussing our private life again in public."

"Public?" Sloan ducked another blow. "It's only Miss Alyce."

"And me," a deep voice said from the shadow of the trees.

All the valley seemed to pause. No birds. No sounds. Not ever the air moved for a moment.

Sloan dove for his gun. McCall pulled up her blanket. Alyce screamed and raised her cane like a weapon.

"Wait!" the voice yelled again from the safety of the trees. "Don't everybody panic." Starkie stepped into the morning light. "I just came to check on ye. I didn't have any idea where you'd be, so I stopped by and asked Lacy, just hoping she'd know. When I saw the old woman heading this direction a while ago, I followed in hopes of finding ye."

To McCall's horror, Lacy stepped from the shadow of the big man.

"And I decided to come along." The chubby little woman was redder than McCall's blanket. "I thought maybe I could help. I didn't want my Mrs. Harrison to be in any trouble." She smiled shyly and bowed slightly to McCall. "Glad to see you're doing fine."

Years of dignity took over. McCall squared her shoulders. "Welcome," she managed to say to them both. "If you'll excuse me, I'll dress for breakfast. I hope you all plan to stay."

She turned with all the proper pride she'd always worn and walked toward the house. Not a single person dared to crack a smile.

Alyce glanced at Lacy. "Morning, Lacy. Wanta help me mix up some breakfast? It may take McCall a while to get herself in order."

"At that house?" Lacy looked frightened.

"I don't see any other, and McCall says you're welcome, so welcome you are."

Lacy stood a little taller. "That she did. I'd be glad to help you cook a meal."

Alyce Wren looked at Sloan. "If you're not too tired, would you and this big stranger unload my wagon? And be careful of my rocker. I worried about McCall all night and decided I was coming out to stay awhile. I had no idea she was in such good hands."

Sloan shook his head. "Sure, come right in. We're probably going to be attacked any moment by bloodthirsty wild men who want to cut my heart out, but don't let that ruin your appetite. Join us for breakfast."

Starkie laughed and slapped Sloan on the back. "That's why I came, mister. I aim to see that you and Mrs. Harrison stay alive, should those five men show up again. I

think one may be too badly wounded to come after you, so
that only leaves four. After all the fun I had yesterday, I figured I could get in on some more action if I headed this
way. I haven't felt so alive since the war." He grinned.
"Besides, fighting double our number seems about right
for making it interesting."

He lifted his rifle from the saddle and led his horse as he
moved with Sloan toward the house. "Oh, and one other
thing while I've got a minute alone with you . . ." His
voice lowered so only Sloan could hear. "If you don't treat
that little lady right, you'll be praying the bloodthirsty wild
men kill you first."

Sloan gave the big man what he hoped was an angry
stare and swore. He'd had one night in Heaven and now it
looked like the day would be spent in hell.

Within the next hour, before they all sat down to breakfast, Lacy and Alyce Wren had taken time to issue him the
same death threat. No one commented on McCall also
being in the dugout. He thought of telling them that it was
she who seduced him last night, but he knew no one would
believe him. The memory of her standing behind him,
touching him as he fought not to turn and hold her, was
branded in his mind. When she'd unbuckled his gunbelt,
he'd known he could no longer hide his feelings for her.
But these people would never believe such an act of their
beloved widow.

McCall entered the kitchen, looking as if she'd never
done anything wild or improper in her life . . . reinforcing
his belief. Her blouse was starched and white, her choco-
late skirt clean and pressed, her hair in a knot at the nape
of her neck.

Sloan felt like he'd been dragged through the streets
after an all-night drunk and she looked like she'd been to

church. Her form of worshiping under the covers would make an old man of him within days.

He held out her chair and she sat down with a proper thank-you as all watched as if expecting him to do something wrong. What did they think, that he didn't know how to treat a lady? He'd show them that he knew how to treat the lady in her, and tonight he'd show her he knew how to love the woman in her.

Sloan took the only empty chair at the other end of the table and watched her. She was like a queen holding court. She complimented Lacy on the rolls until the woman shone with pride. She asked Alyce's advice about transferring over the deed to Lacy's land. She shot question after question at Starkie about the outcome of the gunfight. He told her exactly what Sloan had predicted. As soon as the men saw them ride off, they fought to leave. Only it took some time to get around Starkie's and Bryant's guns, then pry the gate open. By the time they reached the back gate, Sloan and McCall were long gone. The only casualty was the reverend's box of Bibles. They took a direct hit and began to bleed pure whiskey. At which time Mrs. Rogers beat him into sincere repentance with her parasol.

While the women began to clear the table, Sloan and Starkie went outside.

Starkie leaned against the porch railing and pulled out his pipe. "They're coming," he said simply. "Ye do know that. I had a look at them. They're the kind of varmint who'll not let go. They're like a hound who's tasted the kill."

Sloan watched the horizon. He could feel it also. "I know. I guess I figure this is as good a place to make a stand as any. I wish McCall was away to safety, though. This is not her fight."

Starkie shook his head. "She's where she wants to be—beside her man in trouble. It's as much her fight as yers now. And if she fights, I stand beside her."

Glancing at him, Sloan wondered if he had any idea of what he said. "I'm not her man," Sloan said, more to himself than anyone.

"Did ye come to the station yesterday morning to get her out of trouble?"

"You already know I did. If I hadn't made the stage, I'd have followed it all the way to Fort Worth."

The big man lit his pipe. "Do ye love her with every drop of life in ye?"

"And more," Sloan answered, realizing loving her was bone and blood in his makeup. It wasn't something that suddenly happened, it was simply something that was. "She's the only thing in this life I've found worth dying for."

"Then I reckon ye're her man."

"But I'm not good enough for a woman like her." Sloan hated saying the words out loud, but they were the truth.

"No man is ever good enough for a good woman." Starkie laughed. "Just ask their mothers." He took a long draw on his pipe. "But my guess is she'll whittle off the edges and you'll do."

When Sloan didn't answer, he added, "Far better than Major Harrison ever could have."

Sloan shot him a quick glance. "How can you say that, Starkie?"

The big man laughed. "I can say that because I was with the major for four years. He was a great leader, a good officer, and probably my best friend, but he weren't much of a husband. He never cared much more for her than he did his horses. She might never have admitted it, but she knew it in her heart. And she showed him over and over how valuable she was. Even in the end she showed him. But her cheeks were never so rosy, her eyes so alive, as they were this morning when she climbed from that cellar. Even fighting mad at you, a blind man could see she was a woman in love."

He laughed again to himself, silently shaking his big frame. "It was worth the trip just to see that. I never would have guessed it, but ye got yourself one fiery woman there." He pointed his pipe. "She's a lady all through and through, but from the looks of ye, she's a handful to handle in bed. Ye look like something the cat drug up and left on the porch."

Sloan rubbed his hairy chin. Here he was waiting for trouble he knew would eventually find him, and he was thinking about shaving and cleaning up. His world had gone completely mad.

"You think you could keep an eye out while I shave?" Sloan couldn't believe he was asking. "I won't be long."

"Sure." Starkie folded his arms. "I'll stand guard awhile. Ye take yer time. All I ask is that ye get Lacy to bring me one of them rolls left over from breakfast. The four I ate melted in my mouth before I got a chance to enjoy them properly."

Sloan went inside and delivered the message to Lacy, then asked her if she'd boil him some water so he could clean up. McCall was nowhere to be found, but Alyce Wren told him the first room upstairs had been the grandfather's and it probably still had all the shaving equipment.

He had no trouble finding the room and everything was there as Alyce had said it would be. Within a few minutes, he'd stripped off his shirt and Lacy had delivered the hot water. Before he finished washing, Lacy walked in again without knocking.

When Sloan grabbed a towel, she giggled. "You ain't the first man I've seen and you won't be the last, so no use getting embarrassed." She set a stack of clothes on the bed. "Miss Alyce said she found these in the attic. They belonged to Mrs. Harrison's father. You're welcome to them until you can get to town to buy you a change. Miss Alyce says to try and remember where you take them off."

Sloan glanced at his dirty clothes and then at the ones she'd brought. "Thanks."

As he slipped on the pants, the door opened for the third time. "Didn't you ever learn to knock?" he asked, expecting Lacy again.

"Not in my own house," McCall answered.

"Oh." Embarrassment climbed up Sloan's throat. "I'm sorry. I thought you were Lacy."

"Women come in and out of your dressing quarters often, then?"

"It seems that way." He watched her moving toward him as he buttoned his pants. "I didn't get to say good morning to you."

He raised his arms, half expecting her to refuse now that she was all dressed and proper. But she moved easily into his gentle embrace.

Lightly touching the starched lace and wool of her dress, he whispered, "I'd like to hold you as I did last night right now."

She touched his bottom lip with her finger. "There are too many people and problems now. But no matter what happens today, I'll be waiting for you tonight."

"Promise," he kissed her finger, "you'll sleep in my arms tonight?"

"Promise," she answered.

Sloan watched her move away, hating the way her

clothes hid her softness, but loving the thought of undressing her later. He'd never known a woman could so completely consume a man, driving all else from his thoughts.

As the day passed, Sloan had to force himself to concentrate. Starkie rode the perimeters of the property, finding all quiet. Lacy helped McCall pack away Holden's things that hadn't been given away. Miss Alyce sat on the porch in her rocker, napping when she wasn't busy telling Sloan what he should do. The old woman acted calm, but he noticed a six-shooter beneath her lap quilt and a rifle beside the rocker.

The house was not as much a target as he'd thought. McCall showed him a room that was lined with rifles and weapons like he'd never seen. Most were too old to be of any use, but a few were loaded and placed beside each window.

Sloan felt they were as ready as they'd ever be about midafternoon when he heard riders coming. He lifted the field glasses to his eyes and frowned. Five men rode fast, directly toward the house, as though they expected little trouble in killing Sloan and McCall. "Take cover," he ordered quietly.

McCall met his gaze. As he'd seen before, there was no panic in her eyes, only understanding of what had to be done.

Starkie moved to the corner of the house where he had good cover. The women stepped inside.

"Are you coming?" McCall glanced back at Sloan from the doorway.

"No," he said as he checked his Colts for the tenth time.

McCall lifted the rifle from just inside the door and held it against her shirt. "Then neither am I." She took a step toward him.

He looked at her with his mouth already open to argue. This was no game. If he had the time he'd drag her into the house and demand she stay safely out of sight. But they were coming, and she was standing beside him with that "I'm going to do it my way" look about her.

Suddenly all the anger left him. He realized what her action was telling him and the world. She would stand at his side even till death.

"Go," he said softly, wishing he could hold her. "I don't want you hurt."

"But . . ." His gentleness left her speechless. She'd prepared for a battle and he offered none.

"You've nothing you have to prove to me by getting killed." His words were just above the sound of riders nearing. "I could love you no more."

McCall stared at him. He'd never said he loved her, only that he wanted and needed her.

"Go inside, darling."

McCall turned toward the door just as the men on horseback raised their guns.

In one twinkling of light off the rifle's barrel, the entire world seemed to splinter.

Bull Willis fired.

Sloan and Starkie returned the volley with reflex actions finely polished by war.

And McCall cried out and crumpled at Sloan's side, blood splattering across her blouse.

The other riders pulled up as if unprepared for the fire they encountered. Only Bull kept firing. Sloan's bullet wounded the rider on Bull's left. Starkie's rifle dropped another man to the ground. Lacy and Miss Alyce's rapid fire from the upstairs windows hit nothing but provided a cover for Sloan as the riders fired shots in retreat. Bull was forced to follow or stand alone.

Sloan holstered his empty Colt and dropped to his knee. "McCall!"

She didn't move.

With no concern for the battle, he lifted her in his arms. Cuddling her close against his heart, he hurried into the house. He held her tightly, screaming her name if only in his mind.

She didn't move or make a sound as crimson spread across white starched cotton.

Twenty-eight

❧

"CLEAR THE TABLE!" Alyce ordered. "Lacy, get water on to boil! Sloan, press your palm over that wound."

For an aging woman, Alyce Wren moved faster than a child. They'd left Starkie on watch in case the men made another attack, and now all that mattered was McCall.

"She's so white," Sloan said as her blood seeped through his fingers. "Do something, Alyce!"

"I am." Alyce pulled on an apron and scrubbed her hands. "I helped bring that child into this world, and she's not going out while I'm still alive. I promised her grandfather I'd keep an eye on her, and I plan to until she has to bury me."

Lacy was crying as she followed Alyce's orders. She brought towels, built up the fire, covered the kitchen table with a clean sheet, all the while mumbling about how this never should have happened to Mrs. Harrison.

"Hush, woman!" Alyce yelled louder than Lacy cried. "You're starting to bother me."

Alyce worked, adding crane's bill root to a mixture as she instructed Lacy to get the scissors and cut the blouse away from the bloody shoulder.

"It looks too high to have hit her heart," Alyce said as

she mixed first one bag then another into her boiling pot. "If we're lucky, the bullet will have missed her lung as well."

"I can't," Lacy shook as she held the scissors a few inches from McCall. "I'm afraid I'll cut her."

Sloan lifted his bloody hand only a moment as he ripped the blouse away with one jerk. Blood covered her shoulder and soaked into the lace of her camisole. He shoved the strap of her undergarment aside as he'd done hours before in loving, only now his thoughts were of keeping her alive.

"Put her on the table and sit at her head. If she comes to while I'm working, you'll have to hold her down." Alyce looked straight at Sloan. "Can you do that, no matter what?"

"I can," he answered. He'd seen enough wounds to know what Alyce was asking. He'd seen grown men beg to be left to die before a surgeon was through with them.

Lacy stood in the corner with her eyes covered as Alyce Wren worked. Sloan buried his head against McCall's hair while his hands bruised her arms with his hold.

She struggled in pain but his hold never loosened. Mumbling, crying out, she fought to free herself from the point of the blade. Alyce never hesitated. She did what she had to do, cutting flesh away enough to pull the bullet out clean. McCall stiffened in pain and fainted, escaping into darkness.

Blood covered McCall's torn blouse, Sloan's hands, Alyce's apron. When she came to, he held her tightly as he whispered into her ear. His voice reached her and she stopped struggling, accepting the agony stiffly without moving.

Finally, the old woman raised her head and nodded slightly, indicating it was over. "Bring me the boiled water now."

Lacy moved to follow orders, her hands shaking as she splashed water toward the table.

Alyce dipped a cloth into the water and cleaned the wound, then packed it closed with the mixture of herbs and powdered roots to prevent an infection. McCall relaxed against Sloan's arm as the pain seemed to ease.

As she wrapped the shoulder, Alyce ordered Lacy to mix crushed violet into her strong tea to hold back the fever. Sloan cradled McCall on his lap as Alyce forced the liquid down her throat.

When the cup was empty, Alyce took a deep breath and relaxed slightly. "I've done all I can do. Take her upstairs. She'll rest for a while and then we'll see." A wrinkled hand tenderly pushed a strand of McCall's hair from her face.

Sloan lifted her gently. Her blouse was little more than a bloody rag. Her shoulder was now wrapped in the white bandage. McCall's arms were bruised by his hold. Her hair was stained with blood.

As he carried her to her room, one thought drummed in his mind, drowning all else. All of this was his fault. She'd wanted to stand with him and he'd told her to leave. He'd watched her move to safety, but she'd turned toward him a moment before the bullet struck. If she hadn't been on the porch? If she hadn't turned? She might not have taken the bullet meant for him.

She'd made it all through the war without a scratch and now she'd be forever scarred. All because of him.

Lacy met him at the door to McCall's room. "I turned down her bed," she said as she stepped aside and wiped her wet face with one of the kitchen towels.

"Stay with her." Sloan laid her down on the covers. "I'll be back as soon as I can." His fingers lightly brushed the bandage. "No scar can ever shatter the perfection of her."

He leaned and kissed her forehead. "I'll be back. I promise."

Sloan took the stairs two at a time as he reloaded his guns without slowing. He found Starkie still on the porch, watching, but the day was quiet, as though nothing had happened in this place for a hundred years.

"I'm going after them," Sloan said with the coldness of a killer. "Can you watch the house?"

"That I can," Starkie answered. "But you've no reason to move. They'll find you soon enough."

"I'll stay within the sound of a rifle. Fire once should they return, and I'll be riding fast for home. But I can't just wait for them to come."

"Your best chance is here, not in the open."

"I don't need any chance. All I need is one clear shot at Bull. I'm through with running and waiting."

Sloan hurried across the yard to the barn, and a minute later he rode out at a speed not even McCall could have matched.

Hours passed, but Sloan never slowed. He crossed the land searching. He found the trail of two of the four riders who'd escaped. He knew he was headed right because one rider left a trail of blood.

When he crossed a stream an hour later, he finally saw the two men. One was leaning over the other, trying to wash the wound. They didn't hear Sloan until his Colt had cleared leather.

"Stand back!" Sloan ordered so he could see both men's hands. "Where's Bull?"

The man on his knees raised his hands. "Don't shoot, mister. It's over for me."

Sloan moved closer without lowering his weapon. "I asked where Bull was."

"We didn't know he was going to shoot the woman. If

we'd known that we never would have gone with him. Bull told us he was just going to talk to her." The stranger looked frightened and sorry as only men do who face the barrel end of a gun.

Without moving his aim, Sloan studied the area for any sign of someone watching.

"Bull said we was going to get us a yellow-belly. But you ain't that for sure, mister, the way you stood on that porch facing us head-on." The man was almost crying. "I'm real sorry, and my partner's dead for our foolishness. We shouldn't have listened to Bull. He's half crazy. But he's a big talker."

"Where is he?" Sloan asked, his first finger a fraction of a pull away from killing the man.

"He turned back a few hours ago. He said he wasn't in the habit of leaving a job unfinished."

Sloan fired an inch away from the strangers' horses. They bolted and ran. "Don't let me ever see you in this county again."

"Don't worry," the man mumbled as he stood. "I'm leaving the state."

Sloan didn't look back as he ran for his horse among the trees and rode toward home.

It was almost midnight when he reached the house. He could see Starkie lighting his pipe as he rode in. All must still be peaceful. Sloan took a long breath and felt his body relax for the first time since the shooting began.

"All's quiet. McCall's been sleeping most of the day away." Starkie helped him with the mount. "Have any luck fishing?"

"Some," Sloan answered, "but one got away."

Starkie nodded in understanding. "Lacy's kept supper for you. Lordie, can that woman cook. I'm thinking of courting her after this is over. If I can't die fighting, I might as well find a woman who can cook and die in bed of old age."

Sloan smiled at the big man. He and Lacy made sense. "I'll check on McCall, then relieve you for a watch."

Starkie patted him on the back. "Your lady's going to be all right."

Sloan didn't answer as he entered the house and took the stairs with no regard for anyone sleeping. He had to see McCall. The need to be with her had pulsed through him all day.

The door to her room was slightly open and the lamp was turned low. He pushed the door gently with his boot as he tried to dust some of the dirt off himself. She'd be all clean in a white lace nightgown and he looked like he'd been rolling in mud.

Miss Alyce sat in the rocker with her back to him. McCall lay in bed, the covers almost completely covering her.

He moved as silently as he could to her side and knelt between the rocker and the bed. Slowly, he lifted the covers off her face.

Terrified eyes met his.

Sloan pulled the covers down. She was tied and gagged! He glanced at Alyce Wren. The old woman's hands were tied to the rocker. Her face was stone as she stared into the darkest corner of the room.

A panic like he'd never known climbed up Sloan's spine.

"Welcome," Bull's voice sounded from the shadows. "We've been waiting for you."

Moving slightly, Sloan watched the man materialize. His worst nightmare was flesh.

"Don't try it!" Bull stepped into the circle of light. "If you reach for your guns, I might not get but one shot. I promise you it'll be at this pretty little woman of yours."

Sloan eased his hands to the covers, laying them in plain sight as he stood.

Pure evil seemed to poison the air as Bull moved closer. "I couldn't keep her quiet so I had to gag her. The old woman had a little more sense. It seems all I have to do around here is threaten to shoot your lady and you both co-operate."

"How'd you get in?" Sloan didn't want to think that he may have already killed Lacy.

"I just waited for the big man to get interested in his supper. While he and the cook were on the porch, it was easy to come up the back stairs."

Bull waved toward the door with his gun. "I've no wish to kill them unless they get in my way. Or the old woman, for that matter. But I would like your lady to see you die and know that she'll be joining you. There's nothing like the terror in a woman's eyes when she watches her man fall in his own blood. After meeting you two on the prairie, I figure you belong together."

Sloan stood slowly. "Kill me," he said without hesitation. "Cut my heart out just like you said you would." He opened his hands, brushing Alyce's rocker. "But let the women alone. They're not part of what's between us."

Bull laughed. "It's not what's between us anymore. I've forgotten all about threats I made in the prison. So have the others, if they're still alive. But during the war I discovered something about myself. It's fascinating to watch a man die. It's a game I can't seem to deal myself out of playing. I convinced the fools with me that it was for a nobler cause, but just between you and me, I've grown to like the sight of death's eyes looking back at me. I love the power of sending a man to his Maker.

"During the war I was a hero for what I did. Killing gets me excited." He smiled at McCall. A smile of lust excited by promised pain. "That's why I'll kill your wife second. After I'm finished with her. I haven't had a woman in a long while and she looks like she'll be fighting all the way to the end. Too bad I won't be able to ungag her and listen to her scream."

Sloan glanced down at Alyce by his side. The old woman looked at her lap.

"Don't hurt her because of me." Sloan moved an inch closer to the rocker. "I'll let you kill me slowly. We can leave here so you can stake me out like you did the others in prison."

Bull almost giggled, enjoying the panic he heard in Sloan's voice.

"She's just a woman. Don't tempt me. I remember having fun in prison those nights. After dark the men would scream and scream before they died and no one would help them."

"I don't care if I die." Sloan pushed his leg against the rocker, testing the ease of movement. "But I can't let you hurt her."

Bull took another look at McCall, trying to judge what made her so valuable to Sloan.

It was the break Sloan had been waiting for. He grabbed the seat of the rocker and shoved hard toward the door as he pulled the revolver from beneath Alyce's lap quilt.

Alyce screamed as she rolled backward in a circle, tied to the chair. The rocker slammed against the door frame and she screamed louder.

Bull turned his gun and fired wildly just as Sloan's bullet exploded into his chest. Before he realized what had happened, another hit his middle. He crumpled like a huge paper doll.

Running to McCall's side, Sloan pulled her gently into his arms. He heard Starkie thundering up the steps and

Lacy screaming just behind him. But all that mattered to Sloan was holding McCall close.

Alyce's chair blocked the door. For a moment it was a rush as Starkie tried to step over Miss Alyce and Lacy fought to untie the poor woman. Alyce screamed a stream of swear words in several languages, all directed at Sloan. But he wasn't listening.

He pulled the gag from McCall's mouth and smiled down at her.

"You almost got me killed!" Alyce Wren stormed at Sloan as she jerked ropes from her arms. "What kind of fool plan was that, using me as the diversion?"

When she reached the bed, she stopped. Sloan paid no attention to her. He kissed McCall as if no one were in the room.

"I've a few things to tell you later." Miss Alyce pointed her finger and lowered her voice. "But if you ever do that to me again, I swear I'll never tell you about any more of your babies coming until my McCall is well-rounded with child."

Sloan broke the kiss. "Babies? Old woman, you fell too hard on your head."

"McCall is going to have a child. I can feel it in my bones. And don't think I won't have plenty of advice for you then. You may be good enough for her now, but you've got a long way to go in the future. You need so much advice I may have to move in here to be able to give it all to you in time before the baby comes."

Starkie lifted the old woman as if she were an aging music box they couldn't shut off. "Come along, Miss Alyce, we need to leave them alone for a while." He set her out in the hall and rolled Bull's body in a rug. "We'll keep supper warm," he said as he picked up the rug and left the room. "If ye get around to thinking about food."

Sloan looked down at McCall. "I'm sorry."

"For what? For loving me? For being willing to die for me? For getting me with child?"

"No." Sloan laughed. "For not being back like I promised to let you fall asleep in my arms."

He kissed her lightly. "I should have told you before the trouble started how much you mean to me and that I loved you."

"I already knew. That's why I turned back on the porch," she whispered, "to tell you I love you also."

He closed his fingers over her hand. "Do you want me to hold you all night, darling?"

"No," she answered. "I want you to hold me every night for the rest of my life."

"And if I say no?" He lightly touched her cheek.

"Then you'd better run fast, because I'll have to track you down."

He spread his hand over her abdomen. "My running days are over. It's time I made a stand."

Epilogue

"EASY NOW, SLOAN," McCall ordered. "You're pulling too hard."

"Maybe it's not time yet? Maybe we should wait a few hours?" Alyce Wren added from behind McCall. "There's no hurrying nature."

Sloan glanced at his wife, then the old woman he'd given up hope on ever being quiet. He pulled the bandanna from his neck and began wrapping it around the unborn's legs. "I've delivered a few before, you know," he mumbled.

"You're right," McCall agreed proudly. "Ten last year and maybe as many as twenty this year." She stroked the mare's nose. "But this one's special."

"This one's special," he agreed as he moved his hands inside the womb and began gently guiding the colt out. "This one will be my son's first horse."

"We'll see." Alyce folded her arms over her chest and paced just outside the stall. "He's not climbing on any animal that's wild-eyed. I don't care what you two promised one another you'd give Scott for his fourth birthday."

"By the time the colt's ready for riding, he'll be able to handle it." Sloan winked at McCall. "If the horse is wild-eyed, we'll give it to Scott's little sister, Taylor Ann. She'll be like her mother in a few years, able to tame anything."

"Stop that teasing," Alyce Wren grumbled. "I'm going to have to live to be a hundred as it is to help raise your children."

Sloan didn't answer as he pulled a beautiful long-legged foal from its mother. With sure, gentle hands, he moved from its nose and across the wet coat, cleaning the animal.

McCall couldn't stop the tears. "She's a beauty."

"That she is," Sloan agreed, wondering if he'd ever grow tired of raising horses.

McCall worked beside him as Alyce Wren backed away. "Well, now I know the horse is all right, I need to go check on the babies. I swear Lacy gets so busy cooking sometimes, she forgets to watch Scott properly. Or she'll let him go off riding in the wagon with Starkie like the man had the sense given a groundhog. She told me they planned to take the children to town this afternoon. I'd better go along."

Sloan opened his mouth to argue that both Lacy and Starkie loved his children and that he couldn't have gotten the ranch off the ground in just four years if it hadn't been for them. He'd started off hiring the couple, but they'd soon become as much family as Alyce Wren.

Winter had quickly decided he was overmothered and headed north where the country was wilder and more to his liking. McCall had been packed every morning for a week, planning to find him and bring him home, but Sloan finally convinced her that the boy had to find his own way. He'd settled on the plains on a huge ranch, and from his letters seemed happy.

Shaking his head, Sloan remained silent and Alyce continued. He knew it would do no good to argue. The only two people in this world who were perfect, according to

Miss Alyce, were his children. She often reminded both
McCall and Sloan of what a wonder that was, considering
their lineage.

An hour later, Sloan and McCall were washing up at the
pump when they heard the wagon pull away from the
house.

"Want to go?" he asked, knowing they could easily saddle up and catch the wagon before it even got off their
land.

"No." McCall lifted her hair and rubbed a cool cloth behind her neck. "I'm kind of tired. I thought I'd take a nap."

The wagon was only a jingle as Sloan curled his fingers
around her throat and leaned to gently kiss her. "I love
kissing you in the open with the sun warming your face."
He couldn't resist sliding his fingers along her open collar.
"I'm not tired, but I might join you in bed for a while."

McCall tried to look shocked. "In broad daylight?"

"It's dark in the dugout."

McCall smiled. "I love kissing you in the cool shadows."

Sloan lifted her in his arms and walked slowly to the
trees and the dugout. The day was warm. She was soft and
yielding in his arms, her kiss already hungry. All around
him the smell of spring filled his lungs. He could hear his
own heart pounding in his ears as though it might explode
from the pure joy of living. The taste of her was passion's
drug he grew more addicted to each day.

As he laid her on the cool sheets in the shadowy dugout,
he slowed, wanting to enjoy every moment of undressing
her. McCall seemed to understand, for she made no move
as his fingers unbuttoned her dress and pushed it aside.

His hand moved the length of her, caressing. As always
when he touched her, he paused over the tiny scar on her

shoulder. The mark always reminded him of how cherished her love was to him.

When he lowered himself beside her, his hand spread across her abdomen, pressing gently. "I want to see my child growing inside you once more," he whispered. "I want to feel a new life moving here every night when I hold you."

"I want it too," she whispered, tired of the precautions they'd had to take since her last pregnancy.

"But I won't risk losing you," he hesitated.

"My deliveries were easy. I want to have another. We'll take precautions after the next time."

"You promise," he whispered as he brushed the hair from her forehead and wondered how she could grow more beautiful every day.

"Or the next." She laughed. "Alyce Wren may have to live to be a hundred and twenty to keep an eye on them all."

Sloan pulled her closer. "I'll do my best to keep her busy."